BUR   Burke, Declan.

The big O

THE BIG O

THE BIG O

DECLAN BURKE

HARCOURT, INC. • Orlando Austin New York San Diego London

Requests for permission to make copies of any part of the work should be
submitted online at www.harcourt.com/contact or mailed to the following address:
Permissions Department, Houghton Mifflin Harcourt Publishing Company,
6277 Sea Harbor Drive, Orlando, Florida 32887-6777.

www.HarcourtBooks.com

First published 2007 by Hag's Head Press, Ireland.

Library of Congress Cataloging-in-Publication Data
Burke, Declan.
The big O/Declan Burke.—1st U.S. ed.
p.   cm.
1. Criminals—Fiction.   I. Title.
PR6102.U74B54   2008
823'.92—dc22   2008011545
ISBN 978-0-15-101408-8

Text set in Adobe Jenson

Printed in the United States of America
First U.S. edition
A C E G I K J H F D B

For Aileen, always

'I asked him one time what type of writing brought the most money and the agent says, "Ransom notes." '
Elmore Leonard, *Get Shorty*

KAREN

In the bar, Karen drinking vodka-tonic, Ray on brandy to calm his nerves, she told him how people react to death and a stick-up in pretty much the same way: shock, disbelief, anger, acceptance.

'The trick being,' Karen said, 'to skip them past the anger straight into acceptance.'

'So you just walk up the aisle—'

'A side aisle. Never the main one.'

'That's why I didn't see you coming,' Ray said. 'So you came up the side aisle, wearing a bike helmet.'

'Always. Visor down. Tinted.'

'Naturally. And carrying, it looked like to me, a Mag .44.'

'Correct.'

'But you still say "Excuse me?" at the counter?'

'That's so no one gets excited. Least of all me.'

'So you've got their attention. Now what?'

'I ask if they have kids. Usually they do. Most nights I don't even have to rack the slide.'

'Lucky me,' Ray said. He sipped some brandy, watching Karen over the rim of the glass. 'Should I feel privileged you just couldn't help shooting at me?'

'I was aiming wide,' she said.

'You still fired.'

'See it my way. You came out of nowhere. Snuck up.'

'I was trying to get a strawberry Cornetto from the bottom of the freezer.' He lit a cigarette. 'Then, I stand up, I nearly get my head blown off.'

Karen had seen him late, in her peripheral vision, Ray coming up fast as if he were lunging. So she'd half-turned and squeezed, dry-firing. It was over before he even knew it was on.

Except what Karen remembered best was his eyes in the split-second when he realised what had just happened. How they got clearer but stayed perfectly still. Tigery eyes, gold flecks in hazel. Karen, knowing he couldn't see her face behind the helmet's visor, had been tempted to wink.

Then the Chinese guy behind the counter had said: 'I just locked up. The money's in the safe. All I got is bags of change.'

'Gimme your wallet,' she'd said, and checked the driver's licence for his address. 'I know where you live,' she'd told the Chinese guy, tossing the wallet back onto the counter. The Chinese guy shrugged, glanced at his watch.

Outside on the forecourt, Ray standing there with his shoulders loose, a strawberry Cornetto in his hand, Karen'd said: 'Fancy a drink?'

And Ray'd said: 'Okay by me.'

RAY

Karen had a place where she dumped the bike after a job. Ray had said he'd follow on, catch her up at the bar. Now they were sitting at the corner of the L-shaped counter, Ray on the short leg of the L with his back to the wall so he could watch the door. Karen bolted down the first vodka-tonic, ordered another and a coffee for Ray. 'So what do you do, Ray?' she said.

'I'm retired.'

'Okay for you. What're you retired from?'

'Baby-sitting.'

'You're a baby-sitter?'

'Not anymore. I quit. What about you, you're a full-time blagger?'

'Nope. Tell me more about the baby-sitting.'

Ray caught a gleam in her eye, and they were nice eyes to start with.

'The guy I work for,' he said, 'that I *worked* for, sometimes he needs people held a while. I'm the one does the holding.'

'Held?'

'Sometimes people owe money and they're in no hurry to pay up. Or you'll have a job where an inside is needed, the guy who can access the security code. So you snatch someone he knows. Wives, mainly. Kids can get messy.'

'And you take good care of these wives.'

'No one's ever complained.'

'Nice job.'

'You're the one brings a Mag .44 to work.'

'You don't use a gun?'

'Not always. Depends on the circumstances. Some people adapt better than others.'

'I thought no one ever complained.'

'Mostly they're gagged.'

Karen sipped some vodka-tonic. 'So how come you're retired?'

'It was jump or be shoved. The Fridge checked out. A new shylock took over.'

'The Fridge?'

'The guy liked to eat.'

'What happened to him?'

'What happens every fridge,' Ray said. 'Bottom of a canal, punctured.'

FRANK

To work with human flesh, Frank would tell his patients, to work *in* human flesh, is a privilege that allows a humble surgeon to aspire to the status of an artist. Moreover, the trust that existed between the artist and his living clay was unique. Michelangelo, Frank would say with a self-deprecating nod to the bust of the Renaissance master in the corner of his consultation suite, never had to worry about whether or not the marble trusted *him*.

At which point the nervous patient—already dizzy with premonitions of needles, scalpels and the strong probability of public ridicule—would rush to assure Frank of her complete faith in Frank's abilities, and Frank would reluctantly slide the release forms across his mahogany desk.

Those were the times when Frank felt most alive. In control of his destiny, a man who was making that elusive difference.

This was not one of those times.

'You're actually serious,' he said, keeping his voice low with some difficulty as he leaned across the table.

'It's foolproof,' Bryan said airily, tapping imaginary ash from his unlit Ritmeester. 'Cast-iron. Lockdown of the year, I'd call it.'

'Okay. That much I'm not disputing. What I'm asking is, are you serious? Or are you, y'know, back dropping acid again?'

'Jesus, Frank. Keep it down.' Bryan glanced over his shoulder as he tightened the marble-sized knot in his tie. He hunched closer and put his elbows on the table, which caused his slender glass of Czech import to wobble precariously. 'It's all there in the small print, Frank. It's not like we're doing anything illegal.'

'The whole fucking *point* is it's illegal,' Frank whispered hoarsely.

Like, if it wasn't illegal, why were they whispering in a remote booth of the Members' Bar? Frank tried to remember if he'd ever strayed this far from the bar before but he couldn't come up with a single reason why he might have wanted to.

He watched, fuming, as Bryan clipped the cigar. 'I ask you to, y'know, stop the bitch from crippling me, swiping everyfuckingthing. And this is the best you can do?'

Bryan pinched a crease in his pants. 'Relax, Frank. They were bound to find a loophole or two.'

'A loophole? The pre-nup's a *fishing* net, Bry. The guy's pouring through *every* which fucking way.'

Frank still couldn't get his head around how Margaret's lawyer was on his case, working overtime the last six months, a labour of love, the guy coming on like red ants. Not for the first time, Frank was haunted by the spectre of Margaret screwing her lawyer so she could screw Frank by proxy.

Meanwhile, Frank was stuck with Bry the ex-hippy burnout, this on the basis of Oakwood's code of etiquette, which stated—as firmly as it was possible for any unwritten rule to state—that it's bad form to cut any of your regular four-ball partners out of the loop.

'I've told you already, Frank,' Bryan said. 'My hands are tied. Maybe if you'd told me about the pre-nup before I went into conference …' He winced. 'Cigar?'

Frank shook his head and began shredding a beer mat. Bryan lit up, exhaled an acrid cloud. 'The best bit about this deal,' he went on, 'is that these guys are pros. I mean, they do this shit all the time. It's what they *do*. So if you're worried about Madge—'

Frank snorted so hard he burnt sinus.

'Okay,' Bryan said. 'So what's to stop you? You've paid up on all your insurance premiums, right? And it's all there in the small print. They're the ones put the clause in, expecting you to pay for it.' He puffed on the Ritmeester. 'So you're entitled,' Bryan continued. 'All you need to do is get Doug to sign off for Trust Direct, extending the insurance until Friday week.' He shrugged. 'You don't want to get Doug involved, you don't want to go down the road of having Madge snatched, then fine. Just remortgage the house and nab the money from the bank instead.'

Frank gritted his teeth. 'We did that already, Bry. So Margaret could move out and live up in Larkhill Mews, have a swimming pool out back. At the time, if memory serves, you justified it by saying maybe she'd fall in and drown.'

Bryan, remembering now, nodded. 'So you go with Doug.'

'Bryan,' Frank said, as patiently as any recently reformed smoker might while trying to dissuade his lawyer from proposing a major felony, 'we could go to prison.'

Bryan sniffed. 'I'd hoped it wouldn't come to this, Frank, but I'm professionally bound to tell you: you're fucked. Screwed. Cornholed. The divorce'll leave you with socks and jocks, and that malpractice suit isn't going away either. I mean, even if you had it in writing, how that poor woman explicitly asked to look like Bob Mitchum, the jury'd take one look at those eyelids and—'

Frank waved for silence, put two beermats back to back, began shredding. 'Convince me,' he muttered.

'It's simple. Grab what you can now. Like I say, it's all there in the insurance contract anyway. What's to stop you?'

'The cops?'

'The big house or the poorhouse, Frank, who gives a fuck? I was you, I'd think long and hard about passing up half a million in cash.'

Frank boggled.

'I didn't mention,' Bryan said innocently, 'that the indemnity's for a half-mill?'

Frank swallowed hard.

'Of course,' Bryan said, tapping more ash, 'I'll be needing a finder's fee. Ten grand, say. And the boys, the pros, they charge a flat fee of fifty large. But four-forty isn't to be sneezed at. Tax-free, too.'

'Half a fucking *million*?' Frank croaked.

'To my way of thinking—and this is just me, mind—five hundred gees is a lowball shot when you're dealing with, y'know, someone's life. But I checked it out and that seems to be the standard rate. And with the contract running void this week, it'd smell if we went fucking around now looking for more than the half-mill.'

Bryan fished a scrap of paper from his breast pocket and laid it on the table, ironing its wrinkles with the heel of his hand. 'All you have to do is ring that number and ask for Terry. He'll look after the rest. You just sit back and watch the green roll in.'

Frank polished off his highball in one gulp.

'Oh,' Bryan said. 'Just one more thing. The boys'll need twenty grand up front, a good-faith gesture. You can stretch to twenty grand, right? In cash?'

Frank stared, owlish.

'Not to worry,' Bryan said. 'In cases like this, and apparently it happens more often than you'd think, the boys'll put up their own good-faith twenty. And don't sweat the vig.'

'Vig?'

'I hear what you're saying. But for twenty large they won't charge more than ten, maybe twelve points. Fifteen, tops.'

'Points?'

'Think positive, Frank. See the big picture. Half a mill.' Bryan got up. 'That's a Scotch, right?'

As Bryan headed for the bar, the spectre loomed large in Frank's imagination again: the lawyer humping Madge, his pinky finger digging into her belly button, Madge lying back on the pillows laughing and smoking a Marlboro red.

Frank gritted his teeth, tossed away the flittered remnants of the beer-mats, put three more back to back.

KAREN

'If you're out of a job,' Karen said, 'how'd you fancy you and me hooking up?'

'I don't know. You always bring a gun on these jobs?'

'Sometimes I bring a tickle-stick. It matches my eyes.'

Ray pursed his lips. 'Guns are bad juju. With armed robbery, you're just asking for trouble.'

'As opposed to, like, just kidnapping people.'

'I told you. I quit.'

'Lucky you. Some of us still have to earn a living. You want another coffee?'

'No thanks, it's crap.'

'I've got some Blue Mountain back home.' Ray just stared, not exactly the reaction Karen'd been hoping for. 'It's Jamaican,' she said. 'Pound for pound, the most expensive beans in the world.'

'And this'd be what, like a date?'

'It'd be a lot like a cup of coffee. Maybe, you behave yourself, some conversation.'

'Conversation's good.'

'Not lately it's not. So are you coming or what?'

'Okay, yeah.'

'Want to grab some beers?'

'No, I'm good.'

'You driving?'

Ray nodded. Karen, slipping down off the high stool, said: 'Impress me. What do you drive?'

'An Audi. German import.'

'Sweet.'

'Although I should warn you, it's twelve years old.'

'Audi's Audi. Listen, I have to use the toilet. You want to wait here or in the car?'

'I like the way you think I'll wait.'

Karen grinned. 'I like the way you think you won't.'

ROSSI

Rossi Francis Assisi Callaghan saw the light, got religion eight months short of the end of a five-year stretch for armed robbery, DUI and resisting arrest. The only break he had caught was when the judge directed that the three sentences should run concurrently, on the basis that all the offences occurred within a twenty-minute period that included Rossi's collision with a motorway median strip, which happened roughly seven seconds after Rossi fell asleep on the back of his Ducati while doing 104 kph.

But that was the only break.

The Big O

'My third jolt,' Rossi said. 'No remission. So here's me, five strokes of the cane later.'

'That's rough,' said the new guy, Ferret, sprawled on the lower bunk.

'Nothing worse than justice,' Rossi said. 'Anyway, I get out in the morning.' He handed Ferret the joint.

Ferret had a toke. 'So you're saying you got religion from this Pat O'Brien guy. Who's he, the padre in here?'

'*Angels with Dirty Faces*,' Rossi said. 'Pat O'Brien plays a priest, Cagney's this gangster. Bogart's in there too. Anyway, at the end, going to the chair, Cagney pretends he's yellow, starts screaming, all this. So the kids won't think he's such a hero type.'

'And this is where you got religion.' Ferret had another toke. 'Stoned, right?'

'On, I should mention, some serious fucking grass. Mostly the shit in here wouldn't keep a nun in giggles.' Ferret took the hint; Rossi accepted the proffered joint. 'I wouldn't mind,' he said, 'but I only got the movie out thinking it was, y'know, a blue someone'd smuggled in. I mean, angels with dirty faces, you're expecting money shots, the works.' He shook his head, disgusted. 'I packed in the sex right there and then.'

'I'm thinking, in here, that wasn't as big a decision as it might have been.'

'Yeah, maybe. Anyway, what O'Brien's saying in the movie, to Cagney? That's me from now on.'

Ferret cocked his head. 'You're going to be a priest?'

'I thought about it,' Rossi admitted. 'God's truth, I thought about it.'

'Yeah?'

'Spend enough time in a cell, you'll think every fucking thought was ever fucking thought. One time I thought maybe God fucked up and was sitting in a cell somewhere, y'know, daydreaming. Us, like.'

Ferret didn't spend too long mulling that one over. 'So what's the plan now? On the out, like. You have a hook-up?'

'It's more in the way of a vocation,' Rossi said.

'Except not as a priest.'

'I've been reading up.'

'Taking courses and shit.' Ferret nodded appreciatively. 'Gets you time off, right? Early parole.'

'Fucked if I know. That's all you'll be needing, it's all in there.' Rossi reached a newspaper off the wooden table, tossed it onto Ferret's bunk. It landed with a solid thump. 'Although,' he conceded, as Ferret hefted the broadsheet dubiously, 'you'll be wanting a dictionary starting off.'

'That and two cranes. Just keep it short and tell it slow.'

Rossi beckoned for the paper, opened it wide and folded it back. 'Okay,' he said, scanning. 'First off, here's an accountant, right? Mows down this six-year-old, he's four beers over the limit. The bagman, like, not the kid. How long?'

'Two years.'

'Seven fucking months. Alright. Next up is some housing authority manager, he's on the take. Yeah? Backhanders and shit. How long?'

'Six months.'

'Suspended sentence. Here's a doctor, malpractice. We're looking at nineteen, it says here, unauthorised mastectomies. How long?'

'A medal, a pension and a gold watch.'

'Disbarment,' Rossi said, not to be denied. 'Plus they're looking into his tax affairs. You tell me, what's that to do with justice?'

'Who said it was about justice? You get caught or you don't, end of story.'

'Fair point. But this accountant, he's doing open prison, conjugal rights, all this. Jammy fucking doughnuts all fucking week. Yeah? He's out hoeing the broccoli, we're banged up in this fucking hole. Am I right?'

Ferret, sprawled on a bunk in D Wing, could hardly demur.

'Know who ends up in here, Ferret? Losers. Fuckwits knocking off bookies and chemists. And for what, a couple of grand a throw?' Rossi sucked hard on the jay. 'Know who *doesn't* end up in here? The bastards wearing ties, the ones with the offshore accounts. The kind, they're not actually stealing from people, they're just investing the cash for them.'

'Without, say, telling them first.'

'Perxactly. See, I have sixty large sitting out there right now waiting for me.'

Ferret whistled low. 'Sweet.'

'Except it's cash. Not so sweet when you're looking for a loan. I mean, I'm wearing the wrong suit, no tie. So there's forms to fill in. Questions asked. Where's the sixty large come from, whose did it used to be, what's the fucking serial number on every fucking note. All this.'

Ferret made a sympathetic clucking sound. Rossi waved it off.

'They won't stop me,' he said. 'The sixty grand'll cover me for the first year. And once I'm up and running, I'll be applying for all sorts.'

'Cover you for what?'

'Overheads. Rent and shit on the office.'

'You're going into business?'

Rossi nodded solemnly. 'An advice centre. The Francis Assisi Rehabilitation Concern. For ex-cons, like. Although, with the name, I might need permission from the pope first.'

Ferret squinted. 'Advising cons on what? Where's best to fence their shit, that kind of thing?'

'See,' Rossi said, stabbing the air with the jay for emphasis, 'there's the problem right there. Everyone expects when a man gets out that it's only a matter of time before he goes back in. Am I right?'

'Most of us do.'

'Okay. But say you're a booze hound, right? Hitting it hard. What do you do?'

'Al-Anon.'

'You're a junkie, where do you go?'

'Methadone programme.'

'But if you're an ex-con wanting to break the cycle, who can you talk to?'

Ferret scratched an ear.

'The Francis Assisi Rehabilitation Concern,' Rossi said. He bounced a thumb off his chest. 'Me.'

Ferret thought that one over. 'You'd be like a counsellor? Some shit like that?'

'Perfuckingxactly.'

'And you've trained for this? Done courses and shit?'

'Believe it. At the university of hard fucking knocks.'

'So you're not actually, y'know, qualified.'

'I've done the crime, Ferret, *and* I've done the time. Three fucking jolts' worth. So you tell me, am I qualified to tell cons what's what? Or would you rather talk to some poncy tart in a white coat waving a clipboard with a face on her like a robber's dog?'

'I hear you,' Ferret said. 'I'm only saying, if you don't have the certificate framed on the wall ...'

'See, this is the beauty of it,' Rossi said. 'Know what kind of qualifications you need to start a charity?'

'A charity?'

'Fuck yeah, a charity. You kidding? Charities get all the tax breaks going. Then, every time you pick up a paper there's some charity in there getting press. Or they're on TV. And all for free, like. It's cancer this, AIDS that, fucking Africa the other. Then there's your basic fund-raising activities. You see what I'm saying.'

Ferret lay back on the bunk, head pillowed on his arms. 'Sounds to me,' he said slowly, 'it could be the basic blueprint for a con's co-op. What d'you think, would a union be a step too far?'

'I don't know,' Rossi admitted. 'I mean, if you want to fleece the system all the way down to the bone, politics is the only way to go.'

After a while, without opening his eyes, Ferret said: 'My brother-in-law's brother, he's into me for two grand in snow.'

'Yeah?'

'Yeah. I could give you his address, get you to call around. Then you cut me in on the ground floor for two large.'

'I'll do you five points.'

'That's more than generous, Rossi.'

'"A helping hand," Rossi recited loftily, '"not a boot in the balls."'

'The Francis Assisi Rehabilitation Concern, right?'

'FARC for short.'

'I like it. Neat and tidy.'

Rossi nodded, pleased. Then a frown clouded his face. 'All I'm hoping,' he said, 'is the pope doesn't fuck me around on the name. What d'you think, will he want points?'

KAREN

Karen had a crooked jaw from the time she repeatedly smashed her chin on the rim of the bathroom's porcelain sink, her father downstairs on the kitchen floor, flat on his back with a fork lodged just above his heart.

The jaw gave her mouth an ironic twist, pushing out the lower lip, so people who didn't know Karen thought she was all the time sneering, or laughing at some private joke. The upside with that was, when Karen took a stool at a bar she generally managed to get quietly drunk without too many interruptions. The worst she had to deal with was some skinny-assed pimple-factory telling her cleavage to cheer up, it might never happen. To which Karen'd reply: 'I carry a knife.'

What she liked about Ray was he didn't crowd her. Sitting near enough so she caught a whiff of minty breath but not so close she needed to back off to breathe. He held himself well, careless but angular, and he was tall enough to carry it off. Wearing a pale blue rumpled shirt, navy denims that looked new. Had all his hair too, even if it was brushed up in a dopey quiff.

Then there was the way he talked to her eyes. Okay, it was a pose: the only complaint men had about Karen's cleavage was the lack of a mirror wedged in there too. But what Karen liked about that was his self-control, the way he kept his eyes on hers.

She touched up her lip gloss, giving herself the once-over in the bathroom mirror. Then smiled, remembering Ray's line, how he was a tough-guy kidnapper. At least it was original. Karen had heard all the lines so often she was starting to feel like her own understudy. If Karen stuck around until the end of the night, any night, some guy was bound to take an interest.

Lately though, Karen hadn't been sticking around too long. Once in a while, maybe, when she felt the need. But even that wasn't happening so much anymore. Karen'd said to Madge, only the Friday just gone: *Like, when even the skinny-assed pimply guys are married, you get to thinking, how much do I really need that need?*

What mattered about all this was, by the time she met Ray, Karen hadn't been laid in over six months. How much over Karen didn't know, and she didn't want to know. Once it went more than six months, Karen stopped counting.

Plus, she was still buzzing from pulling the job. From experience, Karen knew she wouldn't be getting much sleep that night anyway.

RAY

Ray lit a cigarette and cranked the window, humming along with the stereo. Wondering how it was Bruce always got himself hooked up on these women called Mary. 'Thunder Road', 'The River', 'Mary's Place' ... Christ, the man was obsessed.

Ray, if he was Springsteen, he'd have shot through for Mexico long ago, nabbed himself a Juanita, some shit like that. Ray'd only ever met one Karen before, this Kiwi blonde in Hamburg with an oral fixation. Ray getting blow jobs on buses, trains, even one time in the linen closet of a motel on the outskirts of Saarbrucken, near the French border. Ray on his back in a pile of dirty sheets coming up with a whole new language all his own.

Ray figured her reaction to the Transit van, Karen expecting an Audi, would tell him as much as he needed to know for the time being.

The Big O

Then he was waiting so long he started wondering what the hold-up was, if maybe she wasn't running some kind of gag, keep the dumb guy hanging around the car park all night. He checked the clock, decided to give her another five minutes, and then the coffee hit. By the time Karen finally appeared, backlit in the bar's doorway, Ray was seriously considering a sneaky pee around the back of the Transit.

She caught his headlight flash, strolled across, climbed up into the cab.

'So what happened?' she said, looking around. 'The clock strike twelve or something?'

'Maybe you shouldn't believe everything strange men tell you in bars.'

'Don't flatter yourself. You're not that strange.'

'That might well be the tragedy of my life.'

'Next you'll be telling me you're not this hotshot kidnap artist.'

Ray, sheepish, jerked a thumb over his shoulder. Karen glanced into the back of the van, where the floor was littered with empty paint pots, roller-brushes, multicoloured splash-sheets. 'You're a decorator?' she said.

'I paint murals.'

'Murals?'

'Wall art. In kids' bedrooms. Y'know, Winnie the Pooh, the Lion King, Lord of the Rings. That kind of thing.'

'Which is why you're a babysitter.'

'Sure, yeah. Listen, you live far from here?'

'Near enough. Why?'

'That coffee's run right through me. Mind if I scoot back inside?'

'Prostate trouble?'

'Harsh,' Ray said, opening the door. 'Unnecessarily harsh.'

KAREN

He was more articulate than she was used to meeting, Karen thought, watching Ray stiff-leg it across the car park. Not that he used big words, complicating things. More that he spoke clearly, sounding cautious, alert to the consequences of what he was saying. In Karen's experience most people said the first thing they thought of and stuck with that. Or, like Rossi, they were foul-mouthed mumblers, so everything sounded the same.

Karen, it was instinctive by now, compared everyone with Rossi. Favourably, as it happened.

She shook a cigarette from the deck on the dashboard and ran through her checklist. She hadn't been expecting any hook-ups, not on a Wednesday night, and definitely not on any night she was pulling a job. But the bra and pants were okay, nothing fancy but nothing too granny either, and she'd shaved her legs and pits after a long, luxurious bath the day before. The towels were probably still on the bathroom floor.

She tried to remember what kind of mess she'd left the apartment in, if she'd made the bed. Karen wasn't exactly house-proud to start with, and dusting wasn't all that high on her list of priorities when she had a job coming on.

Then again, Ray didn't seem the kind to object to a little clutter. The rear of the Transit was a mess and the cab was strewn with sweet-wrappers, empty cigarette boxes, used parking stubs. Karen, curious, reached down and slid the neat pile of large white cards out from under the driver's seat. She turned them around, exhaling at the windscreen, then frowned.

The first card read, in blue crayon: *You have no reason to be afraid.*

Karen flicked through the rest, eight in total, glancing across at the door of the bar. Then she shoved the cards back beneath the driver's seat. Breathing fast and shallow.

This would be a good time, she acknowledged, to just walk away. Hail a cab, get herself home, forget all about Ray.

But Karen had never met a tough-guy kidnapper before. And she had prickles at the nape of her neck, tingles trickling up the back of her thighs.

Plus, if things got out of hand, it was in her bag: Karen was still packing the .44.

DOYLE

'Hey-up,' Sparks said. 'He's back.'

Doyle brushed her hair off her shoulder, glancing around at the tall guy with the quiff crossing the bar towards the toilets. Definitely not bad, she thought. Doyle liked them tall. And no ring. Doyle, she couldn't help herself—she liked them better when they weren't married.

'You going to, y'know, *do* anything?' Sparks said.

'Like what?'

'Ask him for a birthday kiss.' Sparks snorted a drunken giggle. 'Thirty-four of 'em.'

'And then, you're the only one came out for my party drinks, we just send you home. Is that it?'

'You wouldn't share?'

'I know where you've been, Sparks.'

'Me-fucking-ow. Hold on, here he comes again.'

But he didn't even look in their direction. Just crossed the bar, pushed out through the door.

'Guess he scored with the tart in the leathers,' Sparks observed gloomily.

'With an ass like that in leathers? You're surprised?'

'Fucking bitch.' Sparks brightened up. 'Anyway, he didn't take half long enough in the toilet. A real man, he'd need about five minutes just to unfold his dick to take a piss. Maybe you're just saving yourself another disappointing night.'

'Want to know,' Doyle said with feeling, 'what's disappointing? If we come in here together one more time, we're officially a couple.'

Sparks winked and blew a sloppy kiss. Doyle went to the bar.

RAY

Ray knew from experience to keep his mouth shut once a woman has made up her mind. Ray, thinking he was negotiating his way between the sheets, had talked himself out the front door more than once.

So the plan, as he climbed into the Transit, was to let Karen do most of the talking. This until they turned out of the car park and Karen said: 'Tell me more about how you quit babysitting.'

'I was kidding. I told you, I paint murals.'

'You have no reason to be afraid,' Karen recited. 'You are in no danger. I mean you no harm. You will be well treated.' She paused. 'Want me to go on?'

Ray looked across. Karen raised a quizzical eyebrow.

'What do you want to know?' Ray said.

'Why you quit.'

'I told you. A new guy got involved, I didn't like him. So I quit.'

'Try me on details. I like details.'

'Details get people fucked, Karen. And when the people I know get fucked, everyone gets fucked. I'm making this clear, right?'

'To me.'

'To you, yeah. Who else?'

'I mean, you're saying it to me. Who you interrupted in the middle of a stick-up.'

Ray considered that. 'How much detail?' he said.

'You get going.' Karen lit two cigarettes, handed one across. 'If I think you're leaving anything out, I'll say.'

Ray shrugged as he exhaled. 'This new shylock,' he said slowly, 'I just didn't like his style. Take today, I'm on my way home from work. So when the guy asks if I'm carrying I think he means drugs. Except the guy's asking about mobile phones. Has this thing where he doesn't want anyone around him with a phone turned on in case anyone takes a call that could incriminate him. I'm thinking, okay by me, the guy's a thinker. So I turn off my phone, I tell him, "That's genius, man." And he goes, "Only the cautious survive." I mean,' Ray said, glancing across at Karen, 'he's saying this with a straight face.'

'The shylock,' Karen said. 'He's a guy who loans money, right?'

Ray nodded. 'He's new in for the Fridge. To bankroll Terry's ops.'

'What kind of ops?'

'Say Terry wants to blag a payroll run. He'll need hardware, transport, manpower. Maybe he needs to drop a wedge for an inside touch. All that takes money, and any decent businessman wants to spread his risk around. So the shylock fronts up and Terry cuts him in for points.'

'Points being a percentage.'

'Right. Twenty percent of the take, that's twenty points. Usually off the gross.'

'Okay.'

'But this guy's fucking me around. See, I work off a flat twenty for any job up to two hundred grand. After that it's twelve points on the gross. The higher the gross, the more risk I'm taking.'

'Makes sense.'

'Except the shylock, being new, he's saying, "How come it's a flat twenty?" I say, "Terry knows all this already. It's set, it's been set since the start. You didn't ask Terry?" And the shylock says, "I'm asking you."'

'So you'll know,' Karen said, 'who's in charge.'

'I'm sitting there, I don't answer straight away. The last guy, the Fridge, I liked him. Y'know? A serious guy. Could be philosophical. This is a guy who's known and respected for being cautious. Gets called in to resolve disputes. This is why the cops only ever raided him for show. He's what they call a calming influence.'

'What happened to him?'

'What I'm hearing is it's some Balkan crew, new in town and looking to shake things up, bunker in. I'm guessing the shylock's fronting for them, that he's fingered the Fridge for points on the Fridge's book. This is why I'm around at Terry Swipes' place earlier on.'

'Terry *Swipes*?'

Ray nodded. 'I'm looking for the inside line from Terry. See if he doesn't want to dissolve our arrangement now the Fridge is gone. But the shylock's already there in the office when I arrive. Sitting on the corner of Terry's desk.'

'So Terry knows who's boss too.'

'Absolutely.'

'What's he look like?'

Ray shrugged. 'Blocky, hard. Shaved head. He's wearing this suit, baggy in the crotch and too long in the cuffs. The kind that always need a good ironing but still look like they'd stand up by themselves propped against a wall. Y'know?'

Karen nodded.

'Anyway, this guy's keen to give the impression he's ruthless, brutal. Looks to me like he's suffering from squinty-eye syndrome, but you don't want to jump to conclusions. The Slavs are hardcore. Sociopaths. Incapable of grasping the concept of something for everyone.'

'Not the kind you just walk away from.'

'This is the point,' Ray said. 'I don't know if I can afford *not* to walk away. With the Fridge gone and a Balkan crew moving in, it's only a matter of time before the cops come down heavy on everyone.' He glanced across. 'You might want to think about that.'

'Some of us don't have a choice, Ray. Go on—the guy's giving you grief about twelve points.'

'I'm playing it straight,' he said. 'No edge. All I say is, "I charge a flat twenty on anything up to two hundred." The shylock thinks this is hilarious. "And after two hundred," he says, "what then?" "Then it goes to twelve points," I tell him. "Really?" he says. "A whole twelve?"'

'Taking the piss,' Karen said.

'I can see it from his perspective,' Ray conceded. 'He's looking at some guy in overalls covered in paint spatters. I mean, who the fuck am I to him? But then he starts getting personal.'

'Oh yeah?'

'"You're talking to me about points?" he says. Laughing it up, trying to get Terry in on the joke. Terry sitting there staring at me, y'know, wanting me to play along. Except the shylock goes, "You should be talking to your barber, man. With that fucking fringe? The King is dead, get out the fucking shears."'

'He's disrespecting the quiff?'

'I couldn't believe it. The guy thinking I'd want to duke it out over a haircut. I just went, "That's twelve on the gross, by the way." Terry nearly shit.'

'What'd he say to that?'

'"You're on a giraffe."'

'A giraffe?'

'Having a laugh. I say no. He says, "Say we tell you it's two hundred. How do you find out it's more?" "Maybe I don't," I say. "But what if you do?" he says. "Don't worry about it," I say, "I probably won't find out." "Anyone ever gipped you before?" he says. By now I've had enough. I tell him he should be in the movies and get up, head for the door. The shylock's going, "Where the fuck do you think you're off to?" I tell him, if he wants someone snatched, I'll keep them out of sight until he gets his hook-up. That to me is worth twelve on the gross. But if he doesn't go that high, no harm done.'

'What'd he say to that?'

'Nothing. I jumped across it, asked Terry, "Hey, Terry—where'd you get those blinds?"'

'Blinds?' Karen said.

'Sure. These double-rolled bamboo on the window behind the desk.'

'Window blinds?'

'This is what the shylock is saying. By the time he gets his head around the switch, I'm gone.'

KAREN

'Okay,' Karen said. 'But window blinds?'

'See, it starts out with murals. Then, you're halfway through, they start wondering about backdrops. Contrasts on the covings, the skirting boards, that kind of thing. Before you know it, they're talking about window blinds.'

'Take the next left,' Karen said. Ray indicated, turned off.

'Go on,' she said.

'I swear, there's someone out there who spends their whole life coming up with new blinds. Soon as you get a handle on one, another'll pop up. Some sort of pleated Venetian or sheer horizontal. Double-rolled bamboo. Won't be long,' he warned, 'before you'll need a degree in origami just to let the sun in.'

'Take the second left off the next roundabout.'

'I wouldn't have put Terry Swipes down for dabbling in the black arts. But there it was behind his desk, a chunky lateral bamboo, except it's rolled vertically to one side of the window. I'm wondering, is it something new for autumn or is it a retro thing. Y'know?'

Ray came off the roundabout and pulled in when Karen pointed to wrought-iron gates set into a dry-stone arch. Beyond the gates, under orange lights, was a half-empty car park, a neatly manicured lawn, four squat three-storey apartment blocks.

'That's me,' she said, unclipping her safety belt and opening her door. Then she realised Ray wasn't moving. 'You're not coming in?'

'You want me to?'

'That was the idea. So you could taste some decent coffee.'

'Even after all the, y'know.'

'You're not so tough. Besides, who'd want to snatch me?'

'That's not the point.'

'If it'll make you happier,' Karen said, digging out her mobile, hitting a button. While she waited she stared boldly at Ray. Then, when the answering machine kicked in: 'Madge? Hi. It's about one-ish, I've pulled, and the guy's worried that I'm not worried about making him coffee. So—he's called Ray and he drives a white Transit van, registration number nine-six-dee-one-nine-nine-five-three. Buzz me tomorrow.'

She hung up. 'Happy now?'

Ray turned off the engine.

On the way up the apartment-block steps, he said: 'So this coffee is the best, right?'

'Now you're a connoisseur?'

'Just fussy. And all the time, not just with coffee.'

'I'm supposed to be flattered now, right?'

'Only if my opinion counts for anything. Why, would that be a problem for you?'

Karen, buzzing on three vodka-tonics, one of them a double, had to think that one through while she put the key in the lock. 'Not right now,' she said. 'Tomorrow, though, yeah. Probably.'

Ray shrugged. 'So let's just drink some coffee.'

MADGE

When Karen rang, Madge had other things on her mind. For the past hour or so, ever since a passionate Doug had moaned 'Honey-mums' just before he shot his wad onto her hip—he'd been aiming for her breasts, but Madge, for one, wasn't disappointed his ambition exceeded his ability— Madge had been awed by the number of names she answered to. So she let the phone ring out and click through to the answering service.

Madge? Hi. It's about one-ish, I've pulled, and the guy's worried that I'm not worried …

Madge, she thought. Was that even a name? It sounded, if you said it a certain way, like some kind of stain, strawberry jam squished into the carpet. She took a pull on the loose joint she'd managed to roll, sluiced down another gulp of iced brandy-ginger, and tuned back into the message.

… nine-six-dee-one-nine-nine-five-three. Buzz me tomorrow.

The phone clicked dead.

'Who was that?' Doug wanted to know.

Madge looked down, surprised. She'd forgotten Doug was still there, sprawled across her pillows, sweat glistening through his comb-over. 'Just someone I know,' she said.

'Sounds like she's about to get lucky.'

Madge thought about that. 'She could get pregnant tonight,' she said. 'Or pick up a dose she can't put down. Or the guy could be a fruitcake, turning nasty once she lets him in.'

'Possible, I suppose,' Doug said, scratching one-fingered at the inside of his thigh.

'Or say he doesn't. Say he's just hopeless in bed, can't kiss, getting sloppy, slimy. Then, tomorrow morning, she can't get rid of him. He's like a dog, sticking around with his tongue hanging out.'

'When you put it like that …'

'Or he could be married. Like you.'

'I take your point. Do you want me to go?'

'Doug,' Madge said, admiring her new belly-button ring, 'I didn't want you here in the first place. Remember? The bit before you started crying on my doorstep?'

Doug sounded a lot like damp wallpaper as he peeled away from the sheet. He really did sweat a lot, Madge observed, noticing how Doug's hairy back stained through his shirt. She wondered if all men sweated as much. Frank had been a pumper too.

'Will I see you this weekend?' he said, hauling on his jockey shorts.

Madge took another hit off the joint. 'I wouldn't have thought so.'

'What about—'

'I'll be busy.'

'But you don't even know when—'

'I'm going away, Doug. To work in the slums of Calcutta. I'll send you a postcard.'

'Not to the house,' he said, alarmed. 'Christ, Audra'd be asking all sorts.'

'To the office, then.'

Doug nodded, struggling with his left sock. Madge didn't have the heart to tell him that Audra was too busy fucking half of Oakwood to notice a blue whale coming through her letterbox, let alone any Calcutta postcards. Not that Madge was passing judgment. At least Audra had standards, refused to screw anyone who played off more than a twelve handicap. Madge, on the other hand, was fucking one of the few men Audra wouldn't touch with a ten-foot pole, even if her allowance depended on it.

'Doug?'

'What?'

'When you see Frank, at the golf? Tell him I need that five grand fast.'

Doug stared, aghast. 'You think that's wise?'

'If I was any way wise, Doug, I wouldn't be humping you.'

Madge waited until she heard the front door slam, then got the joint lit and went back to wondering about all her names. Her parents had been generous, christening her Margaret Dolores Assumpta Bernadette— Margaret after her maternal grandmother, Dolores for some reason Madge never discovered, Assumpta because her father had pushed the boat out when he heard christening names came free, and Bernadette because her mother said you had to have at least one properly martyred saint.

Somewhere along the line Margaret had been shortened to Mags, although once she hit puberty it had lengthened again, to Madge. By then Madge had taken Frances for her confirmation name. Later on, when she got married, Madge had accrued yet another title: Margaret Dolan. This along with all sorts of dopey cute names from Frank, most of them baby-talk slush he thought was sexy. And soon after that, Madge had had to get used to being called Moms.

She'd always believed Jeanie and Liz used the plural because they were twins, but whatever the reason, Moms was the name that irritated Madge the most. Although she had to admit, even Moms wasn't as bad as the names her father had used when speaking to her— bellowing, actually—for what proved to be the last time. Slut, whore, tart and round-heels were only some of the variations on what had quickly become, for Madge if not for her father, a boringly repetitive theme.

Now, she thought, sucking on the loose joint and brushing the hot-spots off the quilt, she was going to have to get used to yet another title. As a divorcée Madge would be expected to revert back to her maiden name. The thing about that was, Madge wasn't sure she would respond to anyone who called her by that name. It was so long since she'd used it that Madge felt the name belonged to someone she had sat beside in school but hadn't seen, or wanted to see, in half a lifetime.

Which was why, at the age of fifty-one, sitting up in bed with the quilt tucked around her thighs, halfway through the first joint she'd ever rolled, her hip still sticky, Madge heard herself whisper: 'Okay. But who the fuck am I, really?'

KAREN

Karen went straight through to the kitchen, waving Ray into the living room. 'The stereo's in the corner,' she called.

But when she came through with the tray, having changed out of the leathers into denims and a top with just enough V-neck to make it worth his while sneaking a peek, he was still leaning over the side of the couch looking at the CD rack. 'What do you want to hear?' he said, without looking up.

Karen sat on the couch too, at a discreet but not insurmountable distance, and placed the tray on the low table. 'I don't mind. Whatever.'

'It's your place.'

'You're the guest.'

He held up a CD. 'How about these guys, The Smiths?'

'Works for me.'

He fiddled with the stereo while she plunged the coffee, Ray sniffing the air with a cheeky glee. Karen nodded along with the intro, 'Bigmouth Strikes Again'. Then it hit her.

'I get it now,' she said. 'With the fringe? You remind me of Morrissey.'

'I get that a lot.'

'Liar.'

'I get that a lot too.'

'And you're not half as good-looking as you think you are.'

'That's still pretty good-looking.'

'Says you.'

'Says my agent.'

'You have an agent now?'

'I have an agent in every time-zone. It's the only way to keep up.'

She liked the sound of his voice, a mellow timbre that made Karen want to tuck it up under her chin, roll over on her side. Although the quiff, she decided, would have to go.

'You okay?' he said.

'Sure, yeah. Fine.' She toasted him with the coffee mug. He smiled and toasted her back.

And then Karen heard herself tell the fork story, up to and including the conversation with the female warder.

Karen couldn't believe it. Okay, she was drunk, and Ray looked entirely passable—she could understand how people might tell Ray things they shouldn't just to see his eyes glow like that, turn tigery. But Karen usually waited until after she got her jollies to tell the fork story, this to get rid of the guy. And if that didn't work, Karen'd introduce him to Anna.

Right around then was when they'd start having trouble with their mobile phones.

'The day my mother died,' she said, 'was the day I realised you can beat someone to death without doing it all in one go.'

Ray winced.

'This is when,' she said, 'I've just turned fourteen. At the time I wasn't sure who I hated most. Him for dishing it out or her for—'

'Hey, Karen?'

She waved him off. 'That only lasted until he started in on me. He racked up one snapped tibia, three concussions, two broken ribs and a perforated eardrum. This in about four years. Anyway, the last time, one of the concussions, I come to in the kitchen. He's spark out on the floor, but he's breathing. There's a fork stuck in him, here, just above the heart,' she said, patting the fleshy part of her shoulder.

'The fork was you?'

She nodded. 'After, they said it only caused superficial damage. The stroke he got from the shock of being attacked back.'

'Karen, you don't have to tell—'

'Bear with me. Okay—I leave him there, go to the bathroom. There's a bruise swelling up over this eye but that's not enough, not nearly. So I spend about twenty minutes bouncing this,' pointing to her crooked jaw, 'off the round corners of the sink. Y'know, the porcelain ones?'

Ray swallowed dry.

'Anyway, I collect the teeth, clean up, go downstairs and ring the cops. He gets four years, eighteen months suspended. I gave it two weeks and went to visit. I wait until everyone's into their conversations, it's all whispers. This is when I start screaming about how he's been fucking me up the ass since I was eight years old. So they hustle me out and call in this warder from the female block, put me in a quiet office, bring us tea. I told the warder it was all lies, he never touched me that way. But I told her he'd killed my mother, taking fourteen years to do it. She says, "So this kiddie-rape stuff—you want me to spread it around?"'

Ray nodding along. After a while he said: 'Forked anyone since?'

'Nope.'

'Ever wanted to?'

'Yep.'

'But you didn't.'

'Nope.'

He sipped his coffee. 'Okay by me.'

But in the bathroom, brushing her teeth, she caught herself staring at her misaligned jaw, the twist in the corner of her mouth, the faint discoloration of the false plate behind her lower lip. She spat and rinsed, leaned in over the sink close to the mirror, thinking, *He can't see what you see.*

He was sitting on the near side of the bed when she got in from the bathroom. As she turned sideways, edging between the wicker laundry hamper and the bottom of the bed, she said: 'There's condoms in the top drawer.'

'Uh, no thanks. That's fine.'

From his tone Karen understood he wasn't turning down the condom, thanks all the same. Which Karen had been expecting, Karen a lucky girl, always meeting these guys who'd had vasectomies.

No, Ray was turning down a jump. Turning Karen down, and in her own bedroom too. She stood on the other side of the bed staring at the back of his head, feeling foolish. Then, because it was her bedroom, she got mad. Like, what had he been expecting, a Tupperware party?

He twisted around to look up at her across his shoulder. 'If it's okay with you, I'd like to see how we fit together in the morning first.'

'Yeah, okay. If that's alright with you.'

All of which was so much bullshit. Karen didn't have a stopwatch handy, but she guessed he went about six minutes that night.

Which wasn't bad going, because halfway through Karen decided there'd be a second night. Even though she'd also decided the fit-together routine was probably Ray's best line.

KAREN

In the kitchen, Karen showing Ray how she liked her coffee in the morning, she said: 'What're you thinking?'

'How come women always want to know what you're thinking?'

'Don't get excited. We just want to be sure you're actually thinking.'

Karen leaning against the fridge, Ray smoking, tapping ash into the sink. She said: 'So do I get your number?'

Karen, maybe she was a sadist, but she loved to watch that one land. Some guys were flattered that Karen wasn't taking any chances on them not ringing, but most backed off fast, giving Karen the talk of shame.

Like Karen gave a rat's ass. One of her favourite lines from the movies was Dietrich in *Touch of Evil*, Orson facedown in the mud and Dietrich drawling, *Vot does it matter vot you say about a person?*

'Sorry,' Ray said. 'I don't give out my number.'

'Crap. Neither do I.'

Ray was cute, no doubt about that, but Karen wasn't changing her game-plan for just cute. Give out your number and you spend three weeks half-expecting some asshole to ring. Or the guy rings alright, two in the fucking morning, wanting to know what colour pants you're wearing.

'Look, Karen—no games.' He drank off his coffee, rinsed the mug, swished away the cigarette ash. 'I'm guaranteeing you now, I'll ring. You have my word.'

His word? Karen wouldn't budge. In the end Ray proposed a date for later that evening.

'Nothing too hectic. Just a few drinks. If you've nothing else on.'

Karen said okay, mainly because the sun streaming through the kitchen window picked up on those glints in his eyes. Plus, he'd rinsed his mug.

She put the front door on the snib and walked him down the hallway to the glassed-in porch of the main entrance. He turned on the top step and kissed her lightly on the lips, his breath still tasting faintly of mint.

'Maybe we can grab some sushi,' he murmured. 'I mean, we won't need any forks for sushi.'

Karen closed the apartment door and leaned against it, arms folded, thinking, hmmmmm, okay, maybe. Then saw the clock, shit, twenty past eight. Late again, third time in a week, Frank'd be having square pumpkins …

ROSSI

When anyone called Rossi 'Ross', either for short or because they thought he mispronounced his own name, for Chrissakes, or were taking the piss, like the screw was now, Rossi'd say: 'It's Rossi. Like Ross with an e, except it's an i.'

The screw, a square-head redneck wearing his hat-brim low, glanced down at the release form. 'Shame, that. It says Ross Callaghan here.' He looked up at Rossi again. 'You want I should stick this in the bin?'

Rossi squinted, trying for Pacino in *Scarface*, the way Al freaked the spics with his dead-eyed stare. Rossi liked Al, the guy was a role model, someone a man could look up to—although, Rossi had to admit, you couldn't actually look up to Pacino, the guy was a dwarf. Even Rossi clocked in at five-six.

Still, the way Rossi saw it, all the great Italians had been small men. Mussolini, De Niro, the popes, Napoleon … midgets to a man.

'That right there,' Rossi said, 'the Ross crap, that's disrespect for my cultural heritage.'

'You don't say.'

'I could have you done for racial hatred.'

'Fine by me, Ross. Want to go back to the cell, fill out a complaint form?'

Rossi, deflated, fell back on Plan B. 'Okay, it's Ross. Ross E. Callaghan.'

While the turnkey considered that option, Rossi thought about how he'd like to meet the guy some night, somewhere dark, Rossi packing a chib up his sleeve. How he'd get the fucker down and slice his ankle tendons low, where they'd never stitch them right again. Not because he was a screw, a burglar, but because the bastard actually enjoyed locking people away.

Eventually the screw signed off on the release form and nodded at the other turnkey. The gate clanked once, slid open. Rossi stepped through, a free man.

The redneck followed him all the way to the main gate, just so he could say, as the gate swung closed, 'See you soon, Ross.'

Rossi, walking away, decided he liked that. Still pissing them off, even after he was gone.

FRANK

Frank turned to the property section, wondering if everyone winds up not wanting to look across the breakfast table first thing in the morning. Or if it was just him.

Lately, Frank'd been turning up a lot of things that seemed to be just him.

He laid the paper back against the fruit bowl. 'Any more coffee, hon?'

Genevieve put down her emery board, picked up her cigarette and inhaled. 'Loads,' she said. 'Try Brazil.'

Then exhaled, placed the cigarette back on the ashtray, picked up the emery board again. At no point did she lift her eyes from her magazine.

The smoke billowed across the table to curl in around both sides of Frank's *Times*. Frank closed his eyes, trying to sniff at the blue haze without letting Genevieve know. Wondering if it was all something to do with turning fifty. Like, who makes it to a hundred these days?

He sighed and stood up, crossed to the marble-edged worktop and put the kettle on to boil, then strolled to the patio doors and stepped out into the garden to bask in the crisp chill, sipping the muted sparkle of an early autumn morning.

'Jesus fucking Christ, Frank! Were you born in a stable? Close the fucking door!'

Yeah, and maybe it wasn't just Frank.

He stepped back inside, glancing at Gen as he moved towards the worktop. Sap rising, the way it had the first time he'd met her, Frank at a conference, Gen a junior sales rep for a pharmaceutical company. Frank could still remember the stomach-sucking moment when he first heard Gen's coarse rasp, the delicate little Cupid's-bow mouth saying: 'So who's a girl have to blow to get a fucking name tag around here?'

Frank had done his best. A nip here, a tuck there, elocution lessons all over. No joy. The girl was tramp to the core. Now she lounged back in her chair, the silk kimono riding up her tanned thighs and falling open to reveal the merest hint of the pert breasts she called Pinky 'n' Perky. Frank noted the strawberry lip gloss, perfectly applied even at eight-thirty in the morning, the gloss the precise shade of the nail polish. The ashtray a mess of glistening butts.

Frank shuddered, plunged the coffee and carried it back to the table. There he retreated behind the *Times* and morosely scanned the Take 5 section, a comparative study of property prices from around the world, and was briefly excited by the news that he could, if he sold up and shipped out, afford to buy a small Maldive complete with pool and fully furnished five-bed villa.

Then a fresh seeping of smoke curled in around the paper and Frank remembered he couldn't even scrape together the twenty grand good-faith down payment that would get Madge snatched and solve all his problems.

Frank didn't want to get too paranoid about it but it was virtually impossible not to come to the conclusion that, when he looked around at his life, the whole fetid mess wasn't the result of every woman he'd ever met, everywhere, all the time, breaking his balls.

Gen for one, back smoking again even though she knew how that would torture him, especially first thing in the morning over coffee. His twin daughters, Jeanie and Liz, rapacious as those wolves Frank had read about, the ones who founded Rome, Remus and Rufus, some Latin crap like that.

Then there was Margaret, on the chisel for more and more alimony even after screwing him for the new house up in Larkhill Mews. Karen at work with her knowing smirk, sneering with Frank's patients behind his back because they all knew better than Frank, knew their bodies better. Frank, he could see it in their eyes, was just some grey-haired sap who helped the world see the way they really looked under all that flab, the orange-peel asses, the laughter lines. Frank never could work it out, how women spent all their lives laughing and wound up so depressed they came to him to make it right.

He cleared his throat, folding the paper. 'Anything planned for today, hon?'

Gen took her time lighting a new cigarette from the butt of the old.

'Right now,' she said, wreathed in a pungent haze that caused Frank to dribble slightly, 'I'm thinking of invading Cuba. Want me to bring you back a stick of rock?'

'Y'know, Gen? With the sun streaming in and all, you look about ten years older than you think you do.'

'Which still leaves me about twenty years younger than you. And Frank?' She reached the little blue plastic container off the table and rattled it, still without lifting her eyes from her magazine. 'Think you can remember today to bring the sweetener with you? I mean, you're still on that diet, right?'

Frank left the kitchen pretty sure it wasn't just him.

ROSSI

The bell tinkled sweetly as the door swung closed behind him, but Rossi wasn't fooled. Sweet or not, tinkling or otherwise, the bell was an alarm. A white-haired woman, sixty-ish with a tight blue-rinse perm, bustled forth from a door behind the shop's counter. She had the curves, Rossi thought, of an old ship in a storm, her rigging at full billow.

'Yes?' she said through a warm smile. 'Can I help you?'

'I need a suit. Something classy.'

'Hmmm. We're low on suits at the moment.' She set sail for the rear of the shop, Rossi rolling along in her wake. 'Do you know your size?'

'I'm expecting to be filling out a bit soon,' Rossi said, trying to ignore the aroma of stale cat-piss. 'So size doesn't matter so much.'

'Super.' They arrived at a rack of three or four limp-looking suits that gave Rossi the impression their previous owners had been sucked out of them. 'That's all we have right now,' she said. 'If there's nothing that, ahem, *suits* you,' she simpered, 'you could always come back on Monday. That's our big day for donations.'

'That's okay. I'll try the grey one.'

'Really?'

'Yeah. Why?'

'Oh, no reason.'

Rossi tried on the suit, stepped out of the changing room. She stood beside him as he checked it out in the mirror. 'It's a little on the big side,' she said dubiously.

'Roomy,' Rossi agreed, liking it, a double-breasted grey with chalk-line pinstripes. Okay, someone had fucked up and dyed the pinstripes a faint pink, and not yesterday, but Rossi thought the detail gave the suit an Italian edge, stylish but not too flashy. And the way it was about three sizes too big put Rossi in mind of Cagney, *Kiss Tomorrow Goodbye*. 'I'm thinking,' he said, turning sideways and squinting at the mirror, 'a shirt and tie might help.'

'They might,' Sally murmured, scuttling away. Rossi settled on a red shirt and a bottle-green kipper tie.

'I'm not entirely sure that that's the fashion these days,' Sally said.

'Never in fashion,' Rossi said, walking past the mirror to glance sideways at his profile, 'always in style. Know what'd set this off nicely?'

'Some shoes?' Sally said hopefully.

Rossi looked down at his battered trainers.

'Maybe,' he said. 'You do shoes?'

Sally shook her head.

'Actually,' Rossi said, 'I was thinking more in the way of suspenders.'

'You mean braces.'

'Fat as you can get 'em.'

The suspenders were also pinstriped, black on white. Rossi strolled around wriggling his shoulders, feeling his way into the cut. Sally watched, chin in hand, a forefinger flattening her lips.

'How about hats?' Rossi said. 'You do hats? A fedora, maybe.'

'I think,' Sally gurgled, 'there's some in the back.'

She was gone ten minutes, coming back red-eyed and empty-handed.

'No worries,' Rossi said. 'A hat might be a bit much anyway.'

'So that'll be,' Sally said, closing her eyes to tot up, 'twenty-seven in total.' She opened her eyes again, smiling. 'We'll call it twenty-five even.'

'Come again?'

'Twenty-five. For the suit, shirt and tie. I'm not charging you for the, um, suspenders.'

'Let me get this straight,' Rossi said. 'You're *charging* me for the gear?'

Sally blinked. 'Of course.'

'But you're a charity.'

'Well, yes, but—'

'That's me,' Rossi said, bouncing a thumb off his chest. 'I'm a charity case.'

'That's as may be, but—'

'You're selling this stuff and sending the money to Africa, right? They're homeless, starving, have AIDS, all this. Yeah?'

Sally nodded cautiously.

'Okay,' Rossi said. 'Meanwhile, *I'm* homeless. Haven't a bean to my name. I can't get a job without an address and I can't get a kip-down without a job. You see what I'm saying.'

'I understand that. I *do*. But—'

'No buts, Sally. Charity starts at home. And me, I been away, but now I'm home again.'

'I have a responsibility to Oxfam,' Sally said, her voice shaking by now, 'to take payment for any goods sold in this shop.'

'I hear you. But *I* have a responsibility, right now, to me. All I'm doing is cutting out the middle-man.' Rossi held up both hands, palms out, in the universal gesture of non-confrontation. 'It's nothing personal, Sally. You want me to sign an IOU or some form so you can write the gear off as tax-deductible or some shit like that, no worries, I'll do it. But I'm walking out of here right now wearing this suit and that's flat.' He considered. 'Actually, if you wouldn't mind, I'll take a handkerchief before I go.'

Strolling down the street, catching his reflection in shop windows, Rossi couldn't help but notice the stir he was causing. One woman, staring, pushed her pram into a lamppost. Rossi pulled his shoulders back, stuck out his chest. Maybe, he thought, he should look up a decent hat after all.

FRANK

Frank tried to catch Karen's eye as he crossed the reception area, but Karen was poring over the file lying open on her desk.

'Morning, Karen,' he said going by.

'Hi, Frank,' she said without looking up. 'Coffee?'

'Please. Is it fresh?'

'Can be in about twenty minutes.'

'That'll do.' Frank jiggled the key in the lock of his consultation suite, pushed the door open. 'I hope you don't mind me saying, but have you done something new with your hair?'

'Nope.'

'Well, it looks smashing this morning.'

'Thanks, Frank.'

He closed the door, hung up his overcoat and sat in behind the broad desk, waiting for the buzzer to sound. When it did he picked up, noticing the red light flashing. 'Yes, Karen?'

'Couple of messages, Frank.'

It irritated Frank how Karen always let him get inside his office before she told him he had messages. Ever since she'd blown him that time, Karen had been reluctant to meet Frank's eye. Which, to Frank, seemed childish and petty. Except whenever she did look him in the eye, Karen seemed on the verge of a gut-busting belly-laugh, and that wasn't good either.

Worse, the hummer had cost Frank fourteen hundred to date. The only consolation there was that the extortion would remain at two hundred smackers per month for the foreseeable future, or at least until Karen offered a reprise on the finest goddamn blow job of Frank's life—which, Frank had to admit, wasn't much of a consolation. If Frank was offered a trip to Mars or a proper go at Karen, maybe even on a bed this time, Frank wouldn't be needing any zero-grav boots.

'Karen, when you're addressing me regarding appointments, I'd prefer it if you called me "Doctor".'

'Great, yeah. Okay—Mrs McDonald cancelled her eleven o'clock. I've given it to Mrs Lennon, she's keen to get her new nose returned to, and I quote, the diseased fucking elephant you swiped it off. And that's your wife on line five.'

Margaret always asked to be put on hold no matter how long she'd be waiting, so she'd be steaming mad when Frank finally picked up. She made her calls collect, too. Karen always accepted the charges.

'For the last time, Karen, Margaret is my *ex*-wife.'

'Should I tell her to call back?'

'Christ, no. How long has she been waiting?'

'Oh, about twenty minutes or so.'

Frank cut Karen off and braced himself for the calm, reasonable tone that always made him feel claustrophobic. He cleared his throat, punched button five. 'What can I do for you, Margaret?'

'You got the brochures, right?'

Frank groaned. There'd been a manila envelope sitting on the desk in his study for a few days now; Frank had taken one look at the handwriting and Fosbury-flopped in behind the wet bar. A letter from Margaret generally cost Frank somewhere in the region of a quart of Scotch before he screwed up the nerve to bite the bullet and open it.

'Brochures?'

'The travel mags, Frank. The girls' itinerary.'

'Shit. How much?'

'Don't you even want to know where they're going?'

'Give me the bad news first. *Then* break my heart.'

'Jesus, Frank—chill the fuck out.'

Chill the fuck out being, Frank presumed morosely, the latest buzz phrase Margaret had picked up from the globe-trotting duo, Jeanie and Liz. Ever since the divorce had been finalised, Margaret had, in Frank's considered opinion, regressed to adolescence. Hence the pierced belly button, the smoking of hashish, the unsuitable young men.

'How much?' he said.

'They'll be needing five thousand, Frank.'

Frank felt his chest constrict. 'Christ. Where're they going, into orbit?'

Margaret exhaled with a hiss. Frank reckoned the whole world was smoking except him.

'You just don't get it, Frank. They're off to university. They may never see their friends again.'

'The campus,' Frank said as evenly as his gritting teeth would allow, 'is only two miles away. That was one of the reasons you wanted a house in Larkhill Mews. Also, you said they could practise at home if they made the college swim team.'

'Uh-huh. But Frank, their whole class is off to Colorado on a ski trip, to say their last good-byes.' What Frank was at a loss to understand was how Margaret could say such outrageous things in so reasonable a voice. 'Are you going to be the only father who doesn't love his girls enough to allow them say their last good-byes?'

Frank, despairing, shook his head. It was almost like old times. The emotional blackmail, the deadly calm, the *apercu* of contempt.

'No way are they going to Aspen,' Frank said. 'I've seen documentaries.'

'Where they go isn't your problem, Frank. How they *get* there is your problem.'

Five whole fucking grand. Frank could have cried. 'Can you hold a minute, Margaret?'

'Don't you dare put me on—'

Frank punched button five, then buzzed Karen.

'Yeah?'

'Ten Marlboro, Karen. The reds. And make it quick.'

'But what about the coff—'

Frank punched five again. 'Margaret?'

'So I'll need that five thousand by Friday, or sooner if possible. Now, about the pool—Frank, that pool hasn't been cleaned in weeks. And the guy who came around the last time, I think he's blind with glaucoma or something. And if he's missing half the leaves, Frank, what other crap is he leaving behind? You want your daughters to pick up some disease that could leave them infertile just because you're too cheap to …'

The voice was so monotonous it bordered on hypnotic. On and on she droned, lulling Frank into a soporific state where all he could do was chew a hangnail and wonder what the hell was taking Karen so long with the cigarettes.

Five fucking grand. Where was he going to get five *grand*?

When Karen finally dropped the smokes on his desk—no matches, naturally—Frank was startled to realise he'd been daydreaming about Margaret. Seeing her gagged, cuffed and blindfolded. And not in a sexy way, either.

RAY

Ray sat down on the hard-backed chair and gave his name to the over-weight woman with straggly hair on the other side of the hatch. She riffled through the box on the counter, found Ray's card, and slipped it through the narrow gap beneath the pane of bulletproof glass. Ray signed his name, passed the card back and smiled.

'Thanks,' he said.

She returned the smile with a wan one of her own. Then she winked. 'If you're going to take the trouble to change your clothes,' she whispered conspiratorially, 'you really should go all the way.'

Ray looked down at his paint-spattered boots. 'I'll bear that in mind,' he said, grinning.

And that was all it was, a quick one-two. But even that was too much for the asshole in line behind Ray.

'Whyn't you just get her number, chief?' The voice was a hoarse bray. 'Get a *room*.'

Ray heard some snickers, a guffaw. Saw the woman blush up with a purplish tinge, the tentative smile dying fast, the eyes draining out. Then he stood up and turned around.

There were nine or ten men waiting in line in the high-ceilinged hall but Ray caught the comedian straight away. A small guy, midthirties, with a thin pale face and teeth like a mouthful of half-chewed cashew nuts. Wearing this baggy suit with pink pinstripes, so the guy looked to Ray like Charlie Chaplin gone anorexic.

Ray stared.

The small guy caught the challenge, bristled up, stepped out of the line working his neck and shoulders. 'Something I can do for you?' he said.

Ray just stared.

The small guy looked around, then swaggered a little closer. 'Maybe there's a problem,' he said, 'I'm the only one can fix it.'

Ray just stared. At some point, he knew, the guy would have to move towards the hatch counter, and then he'd either go through Ray or go around. If he went around, Ray was planning on walking out through the snickering crowd. And if he went to go through Ray, well, Ray'd just have to deal with that one if it came up.

But there was no way Ray was walking around *this* miserable midget.

The guy, coming on slow, said: 'What are you, deaf and dumb? Or just plain fucking stupid?'

Ray just stared.

By now the guy was so close Ray could smell stale sweat, a hint of garlic, cold grease. Ray had to credit the guy's balls, shorter than Ray by a good five inches and giving away maybe two stone.

'Get out of my fucking way,' the guy growled, 'or I'll have you planted.'

Saying it just as the security guard came through the glass doors at the end of the hall. Ray, watching the security guard over the guy's shoulder, leaned in close and said: 'What do you do, fuck dwarves or pay extra for the tall ones?'

A farmer-looking kid whooped. That got the small guy whirling around, tight-lipped, which brought the advancing security guard into his line of vision. He looked back at Ray, smiled a cold one, then tapped a finger against his eye.

'I'll see you later,' he hissed. Then he moved to one side.

Ray strolled out, shrugging his shoulders at the security guard as he passed. The last thing he heard, before the glass doors swung to, was the ratty guy whining: 'How the fuck would I know my RSI? I've been infuckingside the last five years. You see what I'm saying?'

Ray grinned all the way to the Transit, enjoying the warm sun on his face, the pleasant ache in his groin. It'd been a while since Ray last scored, a couple of months at least. And Karen, she was upfront in more ways than one. A nice ass too, and lots of it.

He climbed into the cab, cranked the engine and punched the tape-deck, waited for Bruce to kick in. 'Thunder Road', the live version, just Bruce and a piano, some harmonica. Ray rolled out of the car park into heavy traffic, singing along.

Scream those psalms, Mary it's just sweet …

They weren't the right words, Ray knew. But he liked the song better that way.

KAREN

Thinking it over, Karen didn't like the way she was thinking about Ray. Not that she was thinking about him in any particular way; it was more that he was on her mind. Karen had other priorities.

First off she needed to pull a job, the end of the month coming due. Also, her period was coming on early; Karen could always tell, it was when the cramps finally stopped from the last time. When it came to biology, Karen'd drawn one of the shortest straws going.

Plus, Rossi. That skinny prick would be getting out soon, and Karen'd take the cramps over Rossi any day of the week.

So the last thing Karen needed was Frank coming on all Demi Moore over the intercom. Cancelling all appointments, he was feeling unwell and didn't want to offer a degraded level of consultation. The usual hangover crap. But, Karen thought, sounding nervy with it. When Frank had a hangover he sound dull, nasal. Karen had always thought that if seaweed could talk it'd sound a lot like Frank with a hangover.

Today Frank sounded highly strung, as if he were about to start twanging. And Karen could hear, over the intercom, the Lone Ranger crap playing in Frank's office. The last time Frank'd started twanging and playing his opera shit, it'd taken a hummer to loosen out his knots.

Not that Karen was complaining. All Karen'd had to do was jerk Frank off behind her nose, hand low down on his shaft. Frank had been none the wiser. Better still, he caught a dose of the guilties and tried to buy them off with a raise for Karen, two hundred a month.

The thing about that was, next time out the ante would be raised. Karen didn't mind giving out hand jobs, it was even good exercise for the wrists. But Frank'd get in Karen's pants the day the pope proposed, down on one knee with a yellow rose stuck in the crack of his ass.

'Jesus, Frank. It's short notice, don't you think? Most of them are already on their way.'

'Do your best. Some of them have mobile phones. And make sure to apologise profusely to those who arrive.'

Profuse my hole, Karen thought, imagining the reception area full of blue-rinsed harridans squawking like moulting parrots. Then she twigged.

'Hey, Frank—if you're not going to be around, I can take a half-day, right?'

Frank groaned. 'Isn't there any filing you could be doing?'

'Sure, Frank. Filing. On a sunny Thursday.'

'Okay, Jesus. Take the fucking half-day.'

'Thanks, Frank.'

'And Karen?'

'What?'

'It's "Doctor" on the intercom, Karen. Please.'

'Okay by me.' She winced at that, hearing Ray say it. 'And can I say "fucking" over the intercom too?'

The connection clicked dead. Karen thought about bringing him in a coffee and slopping some on the desk so she'd have to lean in low mopping up. Frank just loved it when that happened. Then she caught a flash of Ray, the way he'd woken up and turned around, saying sleepily: *Hey, is it too late to try that fit-together?*

She wrinkled her nose, sloughed the memory off that way, then thought about what she'd do for the afternoon. Go see Anna, maybe. Anna'd need to know, and soon, that Rossi was getting out. Karen didn't want Rossi turning up unannounced to see her.

The last thing Karen needed, with everything else that was going on, was trying to find Anna a new place to stay after she'd ripped Rossi's head clean off his shoulders.

ROSSI

The scene at the brew with the weirdo—that one spiked Rossi's buzz a little. Still, the freak'd keep. Rossi'd stake out the welfare office later on, maybe in a month's time, see how well the fucker stared with just one eye.

It wouldn't be the first time he'd done it, gouging the blunt end of a fork into the socket behind the eyeball, then levering back—ping-fucking-splat. Okay, it'd been a hound that time, but Rossi couldn't see how the procedure would be any different with some Elvis-looking freak.

Mostly it was the injustice of it all that burned. The freak turning around, picking Rossi out in the queue. Rossi'd been minding his own business until the guy made it personal, staring Rossi down.

Rossi didn't even know who said what or why, but one thing he'd learned inside, you don't back down. Don't go looking for it, but never walk away. You do, every asshole with a blade fronts up and you wind up like Bogie, *Dark Passage*, head in a bandage, face flayed to shit.

He took a cab into town, relaxing again, enjoying the ride; even tipped the guy for dropping him right to the front door of the shopping centre. Rode the escalator down to the department store that took up the entire basement floor and wandered through the aisles, keeping an eye out for Karen, watching the hordes of sad-sack retirees comparing prices on spaghetti sauce. Rossi had to laugh. Most of the punters drifting through the aisles in these saggy yellow jogging suits, they'd flip if they had to do time, even a single night inside. But they had no problem spending half their lives stuck between high walls of breakfast cereal, this ghastly plinkity-plonk muzak tinkling down from invisible speakers …

A heavy hand clamped down on his shoulder.

'What the *fuck?*'

The heavy hand turned Rossi around and pushed him back against a display of Rice Krispies.

'Sir,' the security guard said, 'if you're not engaged in the purchasing process, I will have to ask you to leave.'

'The purchasing process?' Rossi squawked, outraged at this latest infringement of his civil liberties. Worse, the infringer was an African-looking motherfucker, all thick lips, flat nose and perfect fucking English.

'Yes sir. The purchasing process.'

Rossi squirmed and wriggled but failed to shake off the heavy hand. 'This is fucking harassment,' he said.

'This isn't harassment.' He grinned, showing straight white teeth. 'Would you like me to show you harassment? Out back?'

Rossi stopped squirming. The security guard increased the pressure on Rossi's shoulder, propelling him down the aisle.

'But I didn't come here to do any shopping,' Rossi protested.

'I can see that, sir.'

'I mean, I'm looking for someone.'

'Sir, I suggest you try a dating agency.'

'Someone who works here,' Rossi clarified.

The security guard, still pushing Rossi forward, said: 'Does this person have an actual name?'

'Yeah. Karen. Karen King. She works on the tills.'

'Very well, sir. Why don't I take you around to Personnel. Perhaps they can help.'

Rossi tried a simultaneous nod and shoulder wriggle, which only caused the guard to clamp down tighter. Thirty seconds later Rossi was outdoors and staring at a high red-brick wall against which had been carelessly parked a number of large grey rubbish skips.

'So this is Personnel,' Rossi said, a sinking sensation in his stomach. 'It could do with some, I dunno, potted plants maybe.'

The security guard released his grip. Rossi turned around, backing away and massaging his shoulder.

'We don't have any Karen Kings working here,' the security guard said. 'Haven't since I started on the job.'

'Maybe she left.'

'Maybe she did.' The guard jerked a thumb in the direction of the skips. 'If you come back,' he said, '*ever*, I'll put you in one of those and leave you overnight. The one we use for fish.'

Rossi, picking his words with care, said: 'But if Karen doesn't work here anymore, I won't need to come back.'

'Good boy,' said the security guard, patting Rossi on the head.

FRANK

It was all very simple to Frank. All he needed was a favour from one of his golf buddies. And Frank, in his time, had done favours for his golf buddies above and beyond the call of four-ball duty—cost-price implants for their wives, mostly. But Doug, for some reason, was playing it coy.

'I don't know, Frank. How come you need to extend the policy for just eight days?'

Frank regripped the phone. 'Because there's no *point* extending it any further. I mean, the divorce goes through on Friday week. Why would I want to insure Margaret for *after* we're divorced?'

'This is what I'm not getting. Why would you want to insure her now? I mean, what's likely to happen in the next eight days?'

'I don't know. Isn't that why we have fucking insurance in the first place?'

'Sure, yeah. But still, I don't know.'

It dawned on Frank that Doug was bitching because his commission on eight days' worth of insurance wouldn't buy him a vegetarian breakfast.

'Look, Doug, just think of it as bridging insurance. And once I get this one out of the way for eight days, I'll be back for the full works again. For me and Gen, like.'

'It's all highly irregular, Frank. I mean, for eight days? I'd have to, y'know, load the policy. Otherwise there'll be questions asked.'

Frank groaned. 'How d'you mean, load the policy?'

Doug had him by the curlies, knowing Frank couldn't afford to shop around. Two years now Frank had been suspended pending an investigation on the eye job that went wrong. Christ, it wasn't a surgeon the woman had needed, it was a *bona fide* miracle from the Bible, a bolt of lightning or some shit.

Still, Frank wasn't one to complain. By virtue of one of those little quirks in the law—Bryan, the acid-fried waster, had managed to winkle it out during a moment of clarity—Frank couldn't practise but could still consult, refer cases on, take a percentage off the top.

After two years of that, though, and with little hope that the Medical Ethics Committee would ever get its act together, deliver a final judgment, Frank was pretty much running on empty.

'Weeeell,' Doug said, 'I couldn't just give you car and house, contents, that kind of basic package. You want something irregular like you're asking for, you'll have to take the comprehensive. I mean, everything.'

Frank swallowed hard, held the receiver away at arm's length, exhaled as quietly as he could. 'You mean,' he said cautiously, hardly able to believe his good fortune, 'the exact same package again. For eight days?'

'Sorry, Frank. It's the whole deal or nothing.'

'Everything, right?'

'Absolutely. It's standard practice, Frank. My hands are tied.'

Frank's left foot was tapping out an involuntary Scottish highland fling. 'That's a pisser, Doug.'

'Oh, and Frank? This being an unusual kind of deal, I was hoping you'd meet me halfway?'

'Halfway? How?'

Doug cleared his throat. 'Audra's been asking about those pills you dropped on her before. The Vervocaine?'

'Nervocaine. What about them?'

'She's wondering if you could see your way to, y'know, sliding her some more without all the hassle of getting a prescription. She's pretty busy these days.'

Audra my skinny white ass, Frank thought. Nervocaine being one part antidepressant, it was the kind of speed-based diet pill that worked wonders for a guy who was having a problem with his putting, ironing out his yips.

'I don't know, Doug. I have to account for every last pill that goes out.'

'The way,' Doug countered, 'I have to keep an eye on every insurance policy that goes across my desk.'

'I hear you. I'll see what I can do.'

'You free this afternoon?'

'I'm booked solid, Doug, but I'll find you a window. I'd hate to think of Audra suffering. Three-thirty at your office?'

'Actually, if it's not too much trouble,' Doug said quickly, 'how about we meet around four-ish, say outside the Canadian Embassy? I have to get to the, um, bank this afternoon anyway.'

'And you'll have that policy with you.'

'I'll do my best, Frank. It's all pretty short notice.'

'I appreciate that, Doug. And I'll see what I can do about the Nervocaine.'

'Four-ish.'

'I'll be there.'

KAREN

Karen waited twenty minutes after Frank had left, then turned off the office lights, set the alarm and sauntered down the wide stone steps to the tree-lined street. She wheeled the bike out from beneath the steps, straddling it while she adjusted her helmet, then stamped the starter and revved the bike raw.

Heads turned, prim lips tutting, but Karen didn't give a damn. She was off to see Anna and she wanted everyone to know. She roared off down the quiet street and cut out into the heavy lunchtime flow. Horns blared. Karen flipped them the bird.

Out at Pheasant Valley she steeled herself for the onslaught. She hadn't been to visit for three days now and Anna would be *full* of the joys, hoo boy, a force of fucking nature, bounding towards Karen with the broken, shambling gait that seared Karen's heart.

She staggered backwards as Anna reared up and clamped on: when Anna wrapped a hug on she was a weird hybrid of limpet and squid. The thing about that was, Karen was the only person Anna liked to hug.

So Karen let it go on until she was about to pop, then gasped: 'I brought chocolate, Anna. *Chocolate.*'

Anna was a fiend for chocolate, especially the new Willy Wonka bars, which were especially thick and chewy. Karen didn't like to watch Anna eat, the way the stuff got all tangled up and stringy in her huge teeth. But then Karen had to admit, etiquette wasn't really Karen's thing: in the past she'd screwed guys who'd damn near gone face-first into the pasta over dinner.

So she stood and watched Anna chewing and snuffling, telling her what a good girl she was, a *good* girl, as she prepared to tell her the worst news the girl could ever hear. Karen feeling faintly ridiculous, knowing Anna wouldn't understand anyway.

And maybe she would, who was Karen to say?

'Uh, Anna?'

Anna barely glanced up, licking now at the silvery paper inside the chocolate wrapper. Karen hunkered down to stroke the crown of Anna's head.

'Anna? Rossi's on his way.'

Anna's yellowy eye widened. She looked up, licking at some brown dribble hanging from her upper lip and growling way back in her throat.

'It's okay, hon,' Karen said, taking Anna's face in her hands, cupping her beneath both ears and kissing her on the forehead. Anna squirmed pleasurably and wriggled free of Karen's grasp, the huge tongue lolling in anticipation of a game.

DOYLE

Sparks stuck her head around the door to Doyle's office.

'Some guy just got mugged in the financial district,' she said.

'Whoa,' Doyle said without looking up. 'Stop the press.'

Doyle was having a tough day trying to decide how to file her latest case-load—alphabetically, chronologically or by stench. All the dying fish wound up flopping around on Doyle's desk.

Sparks popped a gum bubble and said, 'This guy forgot he had a briefcase. I mean, that the mugger took it.'

'Oh yeah?'

'Did I mention he's a doctor?'

Doyle put down her coffee. 'Pretty absentminded for a doctor, wouldn't you say?'

'For a plastic surgeon, yeah, I'd say.'

'He's a plastic surgeon?'

Sparks crossed her eyes and made sucking sounds.

'Who's with him now?' Doyle said.

'Hansberry.'

'Okay. Ring Hansberry's wife, ask her to hold for him. Then give it five minutes and call him out to the phone.'

'Will do.'

'Hansberry say anything about Nervocaine?'

'Hansberry's too busy scoring an invite out to Oakwood for some big boys' marbles.'

Doyle mimed sticking a finger down her throat. 'Cheers, Sparks. That's another one.'

'Fight the power,' Sparks said, bunching a fist and touching it to the side of her head.

Doyle pushed her files to one side and scrabbled around for a pad and pencil, trying to decide if she felt lucky. Like, actually felt it, the tingle. Sometimes Doyle just felt lucky. Sometimes she even got lucky, caught a few breaks when she really needed to, which was how she'd made it all the way to the glass ceiling at the age of thirty-four, a little earlier than she'd planned but nothing she couldn't coast through without breaking a sweat.

Mainly Doyle couldn't be doing with the politics, the boys-together bullshit, the boozy late nights that played havoc with her skin and left her washed-out, bloated. Then, this one time, Doyle'd been sent on an errand, all the way out to Oakwood with an urgent message for the Super, incommunicado during Wednesday's brisk nine with the deputy mayor, a retired judge and a twice-convicted drink-driving barrister out on a shrink-approved afternoon's recreation and rehabilitation.

Doyle diverted home, grabbed her vampiest spikes, then changed out of her flats in a bunker off the sixteenth green and waited until they were all ready to putt before tottering across to the Super, churning tiny divots in the immaculate turf. Doyle didn't have to run any more errands after that. But they gave her the back office, the one near the holding cells with no window, and dropped all the dead fish on her desk.

The upside there was, Doyle wasn't under any pressure to score results. She was running a one-woman show and getting nothing but laughs, so no one expected too many arrests, convictions, records of surveillance, reports in triplicate, bullshit like that. All Doyle had to do was keep her books balanced, expenses down, so she spent most of her time riding around in her car working up the kind of mileage people might expect from a busy detective. Although, usually, she didn't abuse the system any more than the system abused her.

The plastic surgeon was probably nothing, routine. The guy unlucky, wrong place, wrong time. But one of Doyle's dead fish was prescription drugs, black market, Nervocaine being the latest, a diet pill three parts speed to one part antidepressant, one part MDMA. Busies up the body, ran the unofficial sales pitch, loosens out the head. Exactly the kind of thing, Doyle reckoned, a slicer might run as a sideline, super-sizing scripts to *soi*-bored socialites still twenty pounds shy of committing to your actual liposuction.

Besides, it irritated Doyle that a doctor wouldn't remember losing his briefcase in a mugging. Doyle'd lost a few handbags in her time and could remember each and every one, damn near every last thing in them, old lipsticks, cinema stubs, the works. One, a boxy Chanel-a-like, beaded, retro and *very* French, Doyle still wanted to cry when she remembered it.

Maybe, she thought hopefully as she passed Hansberry in the hallway—Hansberry holding the receiver away from his ear, a pained expression on his face—maybe the surgeon was in shock, concussed. It was hard to credit, sometimes, the things people confess to while in shock. Plus, later in court, a guy claiming concussion wouldn't be the most reliable witness as to what he did or didn't say.

Doyle swept into the interview room and checked the tape wasn't running before sitting down, beaming a smile.

'Hi,' she said. 'I'm Detective Doyle. What was in the briefcase?'

FRANK

Frank thought he was doing okay. Tipsy, sure, after his gin-and-tonic lunch, and a little peaky from the mugging. But mostly okay, bearing up.

Apart from the wobbly crown on his front incisor, courtesy of a punch flush on the lips, Frank was pretty much tikkity-boo.

All Frank had to do was remember that the woman detective was only doing her job, that she wasn't prosecuting the vendetta being waged against Frank by every woman everywhere. Just hold that thought, Frank told himself, and we're home free. He breathed through his nose. Keep it simple, he thought, low-key.

'So you're saying,' Doyle said, 'he was an escaped lunatic.'

Frank nodded. 'Completely fucking dingbat.'

'Is that a professional diagnosis?'

'I'm a *surgeon*, miss, not some fucking dream-chaser shrink.'

'Fair enough. But just watch the language, sir. Thanks.'

'Language?' Frank was outraged. 'The bastard called *me* a moolie motherfucker. A jungle-bunny spade-chucker.' Frank tugged his cuff back off the wrist. 'That's a *tan*,' he said. 'I've been in Majorca.'

'Maybe he was just colour-blind,' Doyle suggested.

'You're saying I look black?'

'Would that be a problem for you?'

Frank thought fast. 'Would it be a problem if it wasn't?'

Doyle frowned. 'What?'

'See?' Frank said. 'Not as easy as you think, is it? Not so straight-forward. Next question.'

Some fucking day, Frank thought while Doyle consulted Detective Hansberry's notes. First off Margaret tries to screw him for five grand. Then he gets mugged. Frank, ringing Doug's mobile, wondering what was taking Doug so long, found himself embroiled in a tug-o'-war over the briefcase with some skanger on the plaza outside the Canadian Embassy. Frank getting himself a smack in the puss for his troubles.

The only bright spot Frank could see was that Doug had turned up before the cops arrived and had handed over the insurance forms before he realised Frank's stash of Nervocaine had gone west.

'Any sign of those cigarettes?' Frank said.

'They're coming, yeah.' Doyle flipped a page in her notebook, sucked on the end of her pencil. 'Now, a description. You get a look at this guy?'

Frank considered. 'Tall,' he said. 'About six-four, six-five. Wide as a house. Plug ugly.' He thought some more. 'Had a scar, from his eye to his ear, down the left side.'

'His left or your left?'

Jesus wept. 'His.'

'And you haven't seen him,' Doyle said, gesturing at the mug shots littering the desk, 'in any of those.'

Frank picked some imaginary lint from his tie. 'I don't know. He looked like a ratty skanger. All these scumbags look the same to me.'

'And all he took was the phone and the case.'

'The case?'

'The briefcase. The brown leather satchel.'

Frank felt a gin-heat rush to his cheeks. 'But I didn't have a briefcase.'

'So you've said.' Doyle picked up Hansberry's pad, flipped back a page. 'But here it says a witness saw the guy grab your case. A doctor's bag, he called it.'

Frank cleared his throat. 'He must have been mistaken.'

'An unusual thing to make a mistake about, sir. Wouldn't you say?'

Frank groaned.

'Tell me again,' Doyle said, flipping over a new page of her pad, 'how you came to take the half-day today.'

RAY

Ray, swivelling in the leather chair in front of Terry Swipes' cherrywood desk, said: 'So where'd you get them?'

'Get what?'

Ray nodded at the window behind the desk. 'The double-rolled bamboo.'

'Funny thing, Ray, but the whole curtain frammis slipped my mind. I'll get on it first thing in the morning.'

'Sarcasm's the lowest form of wit.'

'Says the guy who paints cartoons.'

'They're murals, Terry. *The Last Supper*, da Vinci's, was a mural.'

'This is what I keep hearing. So what exactly are you looking for?'

'I'm not sure,' Ray admitted. 'Something remote, maybe even a lighthouse. You have any lighthouses?'

Terry pushed a leather-bound folder across the desk, a portfolio of property, just one of Terry's diverse array of legit cover operations.

'There's a tower in there somewhere,' he said. '*Bona fide*. Parapets, the works. Folks used to shoot arrows and shit off the roof, pour down boiling oil.'

'Yeah?' Ray flipped through the laminated cards. 'Much work needed on it?'

'Plenty. The last owners, I'm guessing, didn't pour down enough oil. Anyway, what's wrong with a normal house?'

Ray shrugged. 'I'm just liking the idea of living outside town. Like, way out. Maybe even an island. You do islands?'

'You want it badly enough, can pay for it, I'll get you Greenland.'

Ray flipped on past the lakeside cottage, run down and a little too crowded by trees for Ray's liking, but—from its picture—basically solid. 'I look like an Eskimo to you?' he said.

'It's a job, killing seals and shit. I mean, you're out of work now, right?'

Ray, still flipping but thinking about the lakeside cottage, nodded. 'Looks like it, yeah.'

'The shylock won't like that.'

'There's a lot of things the shylock doesn't like. Me, for one. I'm just doing him a favour by jumping.'

'You're definitely out?'

Ray slid the folder back onto the desk. 'Definitely.'

'Because the shylock's a prick.'

'Mainly.'

'Mainly?' Terry leaned in, elbows on the desk, hands joined. 'There's a frau involved?'

'Maybe. I don't know.'

Terry chuckled. 'You're going legit for a Jane?'

'Since when is that a crime?'

'Since always, but it's your funeral. Listen—it's short notice, I know, but something's come up.'

'Spare me. One last job?'

'That's up to you. But this one is strictly you-me, no shylock. Terry junior picked it up.'

'Go on.'

'This lawyer got in touch, he has a client wants his wife snatched. His ex-wife, actually. Insurance scam.'

'And Terry junior is vouching for him? The lawyer?'

Terry nodded.

'How much?' Ray said.

'Half a mill.'

'What's the split?'

'Forty a piece, you and me. Except then Terry junior gets five points from both of us, a finder's fee. How's it sound?'

'Fucking terrible. Ex-wives can get messy. What's the guy do?'

'He's a doctor. A surgeon.'

'And he's into kidnap scams? Christ.' Ray shook his head. 'They have kids?'

'Twins. Girls.'

'And we know where they can be found.'

Terry nodded. Ray shrugged. 'Have Terry junior call me,' he said.

'Will do.' Terry waited until Ray had zipped up his jacket, then said: 'You're not going to ask?'

'Ask what?'

'About the cottage on the lake. You're not going to ask how much?'

'What cottage?'

'The one,' Terry said, nodding at the folder, 'you don't want me to think you like.'

'I told you. I'm looking for an island.'

'I should warn you, there's been interest already.'

'In the cottage?'

'Yep.'

'From who, Hansel and Gretel?'

'It being an old Forestry Commission cottage,' Terry said, considering, 'they're more in the way of Little Red Riding Hood and the Big Bad Wolf.'

'Interesting,' Ray said.

MADGE

Madge turned off the main road into the forest, crossed a rickety wooden bridge and found herself on a rutted track with a steep-sided gully on one side, a high bluff on the other. The right front wheel caught a pothole straight away, causing the Crossfire to slide towards the gully, Madge braking hard. Then the car slewed in the thick mud and came around to face the high bluff.

'You want me to drive on *that*?' she demanded.

'It gets better,' Karen said, 'further in.'

Twenty bumpy minutes later Madge said: 'So when does it start getting better?'

'Any second now.'

Five minutes after that they arrived at a barrier, a long white-washed pole slung between two cement-block bollards. Madge switched off the engine. 'From here,' she said, 'I suppose we walk.'

'It's just around the corner. See the tall pine? That's in the back garden.'

'There's a garden?'

'*If* there was a garden, then that pine'd be in it.'

Madge pulled on her bright green Wellington boots. 'And you're saying there's no running water.'

'Or electricity.' Karen lacing up her hiking boots. 'But the view is fantastic.'

'It's only a lake, Karen. Which is a big puddle, basically.'

'And that'd make your swimming pool what, exactly?'

Madge got out of the car and inhaled deeply, smelling wet pine. The quiet bristled. Leaves rustled, the wind a faint soughing high up in the pines. Madge experienced a pang; the sharp, pure ache of unrequited love.

'So it's what,' she said, 'a woodcutter's hut?'

'A Forestry Commission cottage. Now out of commission.' Karen got out, closed the car door. 'No need to lock it,' she said as Madge fumbled for her keys. 'Who's going to find us out here?'

Madge shuddered. 'Don't even *say* that.'

They skirted the barrier, the track narrowing to a muddy path that might have allowed two people to walk abreast if it weren't for the puddles, the mini-landslides and the protruding branches that required a little improv limbo-dancing. The path curved away and down to their left, the lake a grey glimmering through the trees. Karen saying, in a hushed tone, how she wasn't just looking for four walls and a microwave. How she wanted a place to call home, a home that called to her.

'Girl,' Madge grumbled, 'if you heard this place calling from all the way out here, you should insure your ears.'

And then they emerged into a fern-fringed clearing, a grassy incline that ran up to the rear of the cottage. To their right a small orchard of straggly apple trees hugged the bank of a chuckling stream; to their left the forest was dark, a ragged army of elder, poplar and pine stumbling away up the steep cliff.

'Oh wow,' Madge breathed.

'Wait'll you see the view from the porch.'

'There's a porch?'

'Around the front. I see myself,' Karen said, leading the way up the muddy incline, 'knitting in a rocking-chair watching the sun go down.'

'Or smoking a joint.'

'There's a law says you can't do both?'

The cottage had been built into the crown of the tiny hill. Its colours had long faded, the paint fissured by now, but the door had once been painted blue, the window-frames trimmed in green. Even the roof-tiles, Madge thought, were now a somehow shallow pink. But the clearing to the front ran all the way down to high reeds on the lake's shore, in the middle of which was a shingle beach with a short wooden pier. Across the lake the mauve-tinted mountains were streaked with shadows as the sun edged away to the west.

Karen stepped up onto the bare boards of the porch, scraped some mud off her boots. 'So what you do think?' she said.

'It's fantastic, yeah. Once you get here. Now tell me the bad news.'

Karen jerked her chin at the padlocked door. 'Three rooms. Bedroom, living room, kitchen.'

'But no bathroom.'

Karen pointed out a tall wooden outhouse off to the side. Madge grimaced. 'What kind of money are they talking?'

'Well, there's three acres goes with the cottage.'

Madge knew a stall when she heard one. 'How much?'

'And then there's the cost of fixing the place up.'

'With, like, electricity and stuff.'

'Plus the fencing.'

'In case Anna wanders off.'

'I'd be more worried about someone straying in, Anna not expecting them. I mean, Madge—the girl's lethal. You know this.'

Madge nodded. 'So how much?' she said softly.

'You'd be surprised how much it costs to fence in three acres to a height of twelve feet.'

'And maybe I wouldn't. How much?'

Karen gazed out across the lake. 'Three-fifty. All in.'

'Three hundred and fifty thousand,' Madge said slowly. 'This is including the helicopter you'll be needing in winter, just to get home.'

Karen shrugged.

'What are your options?' Madge said.

'I could always blackmail Frank. Let him know I'm thinking of telling you about the time he, y'know, tried it on with me at work.'

'The divorce comes through tomorrow week. Why would he care?'

'So I sue for sexual harassment.'

'First you'd have to prove it in court. With that space cadet Bryan telling the whole world you're a slut.'

'Who told Bryan?'

'Plus you're getting nowhere near three-fifty. Next.'

Karen turned away and walked the length of the porch, scuffed at the rough boards. Madge ached for her. Without turning around Karen said: 'Maybe I'll rob a bank.'

'Fun,' Madge conceded, 'but dangerous. And usually unprofitable. And there's no way I'm taking Anna in if you get caught.'

Karen turned to flash a watery smile, huddling into her jacket, hands jammed in the pockets.

On the way back to the car, Karen still quiet, Madge said: 'So tell me about Ray.'

'What about him?'

'Start at the start. Is he cute?'

'Not bad,' Karen said, considering. 'He has this dopey fringe he could do without, but he'll pass.'

'And he's definitely not married, right? Or divorced.'

'Not everyone gets married, Madge. Or divorced.'

'What about kids?'

'Jesus. What are you, my mother now?'

'I'm only asking.'

'And working up to *only* asking if I think he'll help out buying the cottage.'

'Well?'

Karen ducked under a branch. 'If some guy I'd only met once offered to chip in to buy a house, I'd ring the loony bin and have him dragged in.'

'Or set Anna on him.'

Karen winced at the prospect.

Back at the car, tugging at her Wellingtons, Madge said: 'Y'know, Karen, if I could help ...'

'That's okay. Really. I wasn't even thinking in that direction.'

'It's just that, with the divorce going through, and Jeanie and Liz off to college, I don't know how things are going to work out.'

Karen reached across from the driver's seat and squeezed Madge's knee. 'This is my problem, Madge. And I'll be okay.'

Madge tried to imagine Jeanie or Liz saying those words. 'You could at least,' she said, 'allow me to feel guilty for not helping out.'

Karen grinned. 'How about,' she said, reaching for the stereo, 'I get some decent tunes going instead.'

Madge groaned. Karen's music, to Madge, made about as much sense as opera. German opera.

FRANK

When the woman behind the till at the off-licence checked his change for him, handing it over with the sort of kindly smile meant for an old man, Frank could have slapped her face. And she wasn't the only one. Lately the laundromat had started delivering free of charge to save Frank the trouble of coming down to collect. Then, just last week, this lollipop lady had held the kids back from crossing the road, waving Frank's silver-grey Merc convertible through instead.

He didn't feel so old.

Trust Genevieve to point out how buying a car the same colour as his hair, even a Merc convertible, mightn't be such a good idea. This during a row after Gen had dented the Merc's rear fender. Frank couldn't work out how Gen was the one who'd dinged the car but she was the one who got to do all the sneering, in the kind of voice you'd use for lip-readers.

Now the latest was the woman detective, talking like she was on *Sesame Street*, telling Frank loud and slow that she'd be in touch once they'd checked back with the witness who'd seen the briefcase snatched.

In the end Frank had admitted that, okay, he *might* have been carrying a bag—after all, that wasn't an unusual thing for a doctor to do. But, he'd warned, psychological trauma can play games with the mind, and Frank was in no position to say for certain that he'd been carrying a bag, or what might have been in it had he been doing so.

It was, given the circumstances, a minor triumph. But when Frank got out of the station, back to the Merc, and checked the insurance forms, he realised Doug—the sneaky prick—had rubber-stamped a date but hadn't signed off.

So Frank had stopped at the off-licence for a pick-me-up treat, a bottle of bonded bourbon, four or five belts of which got Frank back in the saddle again, stretched out on the couch in his study, Gen upstairs watching TV. His confidence ebbing back. There was precious little chance, he knew, of the briefcase ever being recovered. Even if the cops somehow managed to turn it up, the Nervocaine would be long gone. And even if by some miracle the Nervocaine was still *in situ*, Bryan could always plead a plant, standard lawyer procedure, Frank had seen it a million times on TV.

He poured another shot of bourbon and started thinking about his future, thrilling to the prospect of half a million in cash, tax-free. Except, just when everything was coming up Frank, the phone rang and the guy on the line started talking about a cool-off period.

'What the *fuck*,' Frank demanded, 'is a cool-off period?'

'The cool-off period,' the guy said, 'is the time I wait to see if you want to change your mind.'

'But I don't. I want it done *already*.'

'Okay. But that's right now. People change their minds. Which is why we wait five days.'

'But I de*cided*.'

Frank had presumed, when you stump up twenty grand good faith, even when it wasn't your own twenty grand, that a little deference came with the service. At the very least, he expected professional courtesy. Like, what the fuck was he paying points for?

'Look,' he said, his palms sweating, one silvery vein trickling down across his wrist. He hurried some bourbon down. 'What would it cost to bring it forward? What do you charge for an early, er, hit?'

'Nothing. There's no such thing. This is the way it happens or else it doesn't happen.'

'Hey, *I'm* the one paying for this. So *I* should be the one to decide—'

'How about I keep the twenty grand and snatch you instead?'

Frank's stomach flipped over. 'That'd be bad, right?'

'Believe it. But if you keep talking, that's what'll happen. Are we clear?'

Frank had two false starts at whimpering a yes.

'Okay. So what happens is, I call back five days from now. I say, "Yes or no?" If it's yes, we do the job. If it's no, okay, but you never contact us again. This is because you have two daughters and the only thing sadder than dead twins is one of them in a wheelchair still able to tell the story. Do I need to repeat anything?'

'No,' Frank croaked.

The phone clicked dead. Frank emptied his glass, then bolted out of the study along the hall to the downstairs bedroom. He hung over the toilet bowl, not actually puking, just feeling his guts churn. When he realised the tears were due to the ammonia tang, the bowl smelling a lot like Margaret sounded when she was drinking gin, Frank cleaned up his dribbling and went back to the study and the bottle of bourbon.

Thinking, five days, okay. That was what, Tuesday?

Frank could wait five days.

ROSSI

Rossi couldn't believe his luck. Only wanting the phone, he'd swiped the briefcase instinctively, without thinking, just because it was there.

Except afterwards, about to throw it away, not expecting to find anything worth keeping, he'd found it was packing a whole bottle of blue-speckled pills.

Times like that Rossi believed he had a gift. Rossi believed everyone had a gift, like Mother Teresa or 50 Cent. Rossi, the pills were proof, his gift was thieving.

He tried out the pills, got a mellow buzz. Swapped some pills for a phone-charger, copped a bag of good grass and then headed for Shirley's place, Shirley half-simple, always smiling, even late at night down on the canal freezing her ass off on the game.

Shirley let him in and cooked up some eggs and bacon, asking where he'd been, she hadn't seen him in, oh, it must be *weeks* now.

Rossi had a soft spot for Shirley, they'd been in the home together for years, no one wanting to adopt Shirley the half-wit or Rossi the skanger. So he told her he'd been away on holidays, the Florida Keys, holed up during a hurricane with Bogie and Eddie G.

He locked himself into her bedroom, the other room occupied by, it looked to Rossi, a half-naked orangutan, Rossi hadn't seen so much red hair since *Little Orphan Annie*. He rolled a fat one while he powered up the phone; then, when he was good and mellow, he rang Karen.

What Rossi kept telling people, and what people didn't want to hear, which was where the problems started, was Rossi was by instinct meaner than a piss-soaked snake. In order to function, be sociable, Rossi needed to be more or less permanently stoned, preferably on grass.

Which was where a whole raft of other problems kicked in. Like, being good and mellow, Rossi was ringing Karen's number for two hours before he realised the strange tone meant the line had been disconnected. Rossi wouldn't have minded so much, but he'd been expecting that.

He rang directory enquiries, eventually, after finding the number—go away for five years, he thought bitterly, they change everything around, just to fuck you up when you get out again.

The woman on the line told him the only Karen King she had registered was ex-directory.

'That's okay,' Rossi said. 'I only need the address.'

'I'm sorry, sir, but I can't divulge that information.'

'Why not?'

'I'm not allowed to, sir.'

'You could if you wanted to.'

'I couldn't, sir. I'd lose my job.'

Rossi thought fast. 'This is an emergency.'

'In that case, sir, I can put you through to your nearest police station.'

'What if it was the cops I needed to warn her about?'

'I'm sorry, sir. But if you have no further—'

'Hold up. Not so fast.' Rossi slowed the thinking down, sucked hard on the doobie. 'Okay—give me the number for Kingswood Kennels. Same code.'

'Please hold.'

There was a clicking sound, then a metallic voice reciting something Rossi didn't hear, Rossi too busy swearing a blue streak and scavenging through the mess on Shirley's dresser, looking for a pencil or some shit, Christ, who didn't own a fucking *pencil*?

KAREN

That morning, Ray leaving, Karen'd said: 'So I'll see you about nine, same place.'

But Ray'd said: 'Why don't I swing by here first, pick you up? We can go in together.'

Again with the together stuff, making Karen wonder if it was a line after all. Which Karen didn't like, she wasn't in the habit of remaking up her mind.

She showered and changed, ate some tuna salad with chopped peppers and tried to remember how long it'd been since she'd eaten dinner and not had to wash up afterwards. The way it felt to Karen, she was always the one who had to clean up afterwards, especially with Anna, like earlier on, Karen with a paper tissue mopping up the stringy brown mess Anna had dribbled onto the floor. Hearing Madge again: *No way I'm taking Anna in if you get caught.*

Karen sighed and pushed away the plate of half-eaten tuna, rolling her head around on her neck, worn out after the hour's play with Anna. Wondering if it wasn't already too late to ring Ray and cancel—and then remembering, lighting a cigarette, shit, she didn't have his number anyway.

Madge had been half-kidding about Anna, okay, but only half-kidding. Anna was a real handful. And the last thing Madge needed, with the menopause in the post, was a nervous breakdown from trying to cope with her.

But even the idea of Anna in Rossi's hands again made Karen want to scratch something. She wondered if he'd track Anna down this time, or if he'd even try. Anna wouldn't exactly be top of Rossi's list of priorities whenever he got out. And maybe, just maybe, with Anna out at Pheasant Valley now, Rossi'd go looking, not find her too easily, and just give up. With a bit of luck, Karen thought, stubbing the cigarette, Rossi might figure he'd done his best, tried to find Anna, and the rest was up to fate.

Wishful thinking. Rossi'd track Anna down for spite, just to find

Karen, knowing Karen wouldn't be too far away. Rossi wanting to know where his Ducati was.

Ray arrived a couple of minutes after nine, Karen's hair still damp, Ray driving the beat-up Transit van. She said she thought he'd have called a cab but he said he had an early call in the morning and thought he'd lay off the sauce for one night.

'Okay by me,' Karen said.

This one time, horny as hell and about to fly, the guy'd collapsed onto Karen's chest, snoring. He'd dribbled too, all down her shoulder, the saliva snaking in cold along the nape of her neck. So Karen was all in favour of Ray staying on the wagon. He even said he reckoned being sober when everyone else was drunk was just a different kind of drunk. Which was peachy with Karen, so long as Ray didn't bug her into trying it out sometime.

On the way into town he told her, paint pots clanking in the back, how he was thinking of taking classes.

'Oh yeah?' she said. 'In, like, interior design?'

He shook his head. 'Architecture.'

'You want to build houses?'

'Design. Architects don't build, they design.'

'How come? I mean, when you were a kid, were you a Lego freak?'

'I just like unusual houses. I'm thinking,' he said, glancing across, 'of specialising in round ones.'

'Round houses.'

'With lots of glass. Glass all the way around.'

'And there's a demand for round glass houses?'

'I don't know. I'm thinking of designing one first, then seeing what the reaction is.'

'The sack, I'd imagine.'

'Except,' he said, 'no one sacks the boss.'

'You're going to run your own company?'

'You think I couldn't?'

'Ray—I didn't ask what you could or couldn't do. I asked what you're *going* to do.'

Ray met her stare, its challenge, then got his eyes back on the road again, flashing a Ford out of side street. Karen'd noticed, Ray was about the politest driver she'd ever met, went out of his way to be generous. Didn't seem to mind, either, when he didn't get a wave in return.

'Yeah,' he said. 'I'm going to run my own company.'

Karen tingling to his quiet authority, the assurance. 'Okay by me,' she said, only realising as she spoke that it was the second time she'd used it, Ray's phrase, in twenty minutes.

If he noticed he didn't let it show. 'So what about you,' he said, 'what're you going to do?'

Karen wasn't so sure she liked him asking that, the way he thought he had the right to presume she wasn't happy with the job she had right now. Although, if she was honest, he presumed fucking right.

'I'm thinking,' she said, 'of taking classes too.'

'No shit. What in?'

'I don't know if I'm ready to tell you yet.'

'Right, mysterious.' He nodded, flipped his smoke out the window. 'Running Scared' came on the radio. 'Alright,' he said, turning up the volume, grinning across, tapping the steering wheel with his thumbs. 'Roy Orbison,' he said. 'You a fan?'

'Not really,' Karen said. Thinking, no one's *this* straight, right?

Then realised she'd just lied to a man, had felt the need to lie, for the first time in twelve years, since the night she'd forked her father.

Karen didn't like that too much. Except that night, later on, Ray went fourteen minutes without coming up for air.

FRIDAY

KAREN

'So what about you?' Karen said, hunched over the laundry hamper sorting her whites. 'Your parents still alive?'

'Yep.'

Ray towelling his hair, another towel around his midriff. Sucking in his stomach, Karen could tell. 'Both of them?' she said.

'Yep.'

'See them often?'

'I get home, yeah, a couple of times a year. Christmas, that kind of thing.'

'You have brothers? Sisters?'

'Yep.'

He towelled on. Karen said: 'You don't give much away, do you?'

'What's your hurry? You'll meet them or you won't.'

Leaving it up to Karen whether she wanted to meet them or not.

'Hey, Ray?' she said. 'You should know, I don't tell everyone the shit I've told you.'

'What're you trying to do?' Ray said, dragging on his faded denims. 'Freak me out?'

'Why, are you freaked?'

Ray struggled into his T-shirt, popped his head through the hole. 'A bit, yeah. All this about your father, Rossi, Anna ...' He tucked in his T-shirt, buckled his belt, started humming the opening bars to 'Running Scared'. 'I wasn't the gorgeous type,' he said, 'I might think you were trying to get rid of me.'

'Maybe I am.' Karen, bagging her whites, found it hard to believe how normal it felt, doing her laundry with a guy she hardly knew lacing his boots in her bedroom. 'Maybe I don't go for the gorgeous types.'

'Pity for you. Want another coffee?'

Karen wrinkled her nose. 'I'm already running late.' She indicated the laundry. 'And I need to get these in this morning.'

'No worries. I'll give you a lift.'

'You're heading for town?'

'Can do.'

'Yeah, okay.'

Ray walked out into the hall, then popped his head back around the door frame. 'So what's happening with that coffee? Yes or no?'

Karen thought about Frank, heard him whining that Karen was late again.

'Sure,' she said. 'Why not?'

Ray grinned, preening. 'The gorgeous type, yeah?'

'Being honest? I'd rather you could make decent coffee.'

'All I can do is my best.'

'A little home truth, Ray. If you're here making coffee for me, then your best hasn't been good enough so far. Am I right?'

'Tetchy.' Ray pretended to scribble on his hand. 'Must try harder, is that it?'

'Or maybe stop trying so hard. Confusing, no?'

'Remind me again: what're the options?'

Karen threw a pair of balled socks.

ROSSI

Rossi woke feeling the whole world tilt, then somersault, Rossi going with it, nothing to hold on to, no way to stop the whirl—then hit something hard, head-first. He collapsed to the floor, stunned. Rossi prone but the world still spinning.

'Out,' he heard.

He opened his eyes, tried to focus. Realising, shit, orangutans were turning cartwheels across the room.

Then, his vision blurring, coming back into line, Rossi realised there was only one orangutan, the guy dressed by now but with his shirt-sleeves rolled up. The thick forearms were matted with what looked to Rossi like damp candy-floss.

'Who the fuck're—' he began and got a boot in the busters for his trouble. Rossi folded up, groaning.

'Pick a window,' the orangutan growled, 'you're leaving. Shirley's with me now.'

'But Shirley's my—'

This time the orangutan hoisted Rossi aloft, turned him around mid-air, then dropped him on the crown of his head.

'One more word,' the orangutan growled, 'and I'll run you a bath. Want me to run you a bath?'

Rossi shook his head fast, no idea of what running a bath meant but guessing it wouldn't mean bubbles, some Radox.

'I'm giving you five minutes,' the orangutan went on, 'to rev up and fuck off. I see you around here again, I'll break both your legs.'

Three minutes later Rossi went tumbling down the steps outside Shirley's flat, sent on his way with a kick in the pants. He sprawled across the pavement, barking his knees and grazing his chin, lying doggo until he heard the door slam, the orangutan bellow, Shirley shriek.

Rossi hauled himself vertical with the aid of a Renault parked at the kerb. Picked up the briefcase, checked the pills were still inside, the grass, then limped away down the street, one thought on his mind.

The .44.

DOYLE

'The Dolan residence, Doctor Dolan speaking.'

'This is Detective Doyle, Doctor. We spoke yesterday, in the police station?'

Doyle heard the groan, had been expecting it. She said, apropos the latest regulations: 'I hope you're feeling better today, sir. A mugging can be a traumatic experience.'

'You know that.' The surgeon's voice contemptuous. 'I mean, you've been through it yourself.'

No, Doyle thought, I haven't. But then I'm not the kind of muppet who'd wander through the financial district drunk and waving an expensive briefcase around.

'Sir,' she said, 'the reason I'm calling is, we have some more mug shots we'd like you to take a look at.'

'You mean now?'

'It doesn't have to be now, sir, no. But the sooner the better, so the details are still fresh in your mind. How would this afternoon suit you?'

'That wouldn't be good for me at all. I've a full diary today. Very important, all of it. Consultations that simply cannot wait.'

'Okay,' Doyle said in a reasonable tone she didn't like the taste of, 'then how about tomorrow morning?'

'*Saturday* morning? You're kidding, right?'

'Assault and robbery isn't exactly a joking matter, sir.' Down at the station they called it the bash-'n'-cash.

'Well, yes, of course it's not. But Saturday?'

'Can I remind you, sir, that we're trying to help you here? By which I mean, the sooner you can look at those mug shots, the quicker we can get out there and start finding the mugger.'

'I'm sure he's long gone by now.'

'Perhaps he is, sir. But your assistance might help to ensure he doesn't strike again.'

The disbelieving snort set her teeth on edge. 'Sir,' she persevered, 'we would greatly appreciate the civic gesture if you came down to the station to look through those mug shots.'

'Saturday's out. No chance.'

'And I'm guessing the same applies to Sunday. How about Monday, sir? Do you think you could see your way clear to helping us out then?'

A pause, then: 'Yeah, okay. I'll give you a buzz on Monday, make an appointment.'

'Feel free to just drop by, sir. There's no need to ring ahead.'

'Alright then, I'll do that. What's your name again?'

'Doyle. Detective Doyle.'

'Okay. Good work, Boyle. Keep it up.'

'That's—'

The line clicked dead. Doyle hung up, wondering why she bothered.

FRANK

'Who was that?' Genevieve said, sweeping into the kitchen like some weird half-bat, half-geisha.

'Who was who?' Frank said, a hangover like a bell-ringers' convention going off in the back of his head.

'On the phone,' Genevieve said. 'Just now. Who was it?'

'Oh,' Frank said, aiming for airy, 'that was just Bryan. Confirming for this afternoon.'

'You're playing golf? Again?'

'It's more of a business meeting.'

'Except on the golf course.'

'Yeah. Listen, Gen? If any cops ring, tell them—'

'Cops?' Genevieve spilt the coffee she was pouring. 'What cops?'

'It's some fund-raising crap,' Frank grumbled. 'For their retirement fund. We're running a scramble out at Oakwood.'

'And they put *you* in charge?'

'Actually, Bryan's looking after it.' Frank ducked in behind the *Times*, making a mental note to bring Bryan up to speed later on. Besides, Bryan would need to know that Doug had agreed to sign off on the insurance forms out at Oakwood, before their four-ball got underway. 'I'm just helping Bryan out. That's what the meeting's about later on. And why,' he said triumphantly, realising how he could tie it all in, 'it's taking place on the golf course.'

'Bullshit. The reason it's taking place on the—'

'I don't fucking believe it.'

'What now?' Genevieve said, buffing her index fingernail.

'Some guy, it says here,' Frank said, rereading the intro paragraph, 'held up an Oxfam shop yesterday.'

'Big timer,' Genevieve sneered.

'But you get it, right? I mean, the guy stuck up a fucking *charity*. Walks in waving his gun around, just takes the stuff.'

'He used a gun? To stick up Oxfam?'

Frank nodded. 'How fucked up is that?'

'Pretty fucked up. A complete waste of resources.'

'Resources?'

'For the same effort, with the same tools, he could've held up a bank.'

Frank sighed. 'The *point*,' he said, 'is the guy held up a charity. I mean, terrorises this old woman, could do with some eye work from her picture, for a second-hand suit.'

'Frank? Listen to yourself. You're telling me you're not ripping off all these old women? Selling them bullshit, how beautiful they'll look after the nip and tuck?'

Frank couldn't believe it. 'You're comparing *me* to some scumbag sticks up a charity?' Frank thinking about the mugging, the way the lowlife just strolled up and swiped his case, the phone. 'You're putting *me* in the same—'

'Christ.' Genevieve looked up from her magazine. 'You're conning them, Frank. And I'm conning you. Oakwood, later on, they'll be charging you actual money to walk around a big field carrying sticks.' She snorted. '*Everyone's* on the take, Frank. Grow the fuck up.'

Frank, sitting there open-mouthed, was pretty sure it was a female bell-ringers' convention going off in his head.

KAREN

Ray carried the laundry out, lobbed it into the back of the van, climbed in. Karen feeling a little giddy, a couple of strong coffees on board earlier than usual. So she wasn't really paying attention when Ray said, turning out of the car park: 'So how's it work?'

'How's what work?'

'The jobs. I'm guessing, if you haven't been caught yet, there's a system involved.'

'I thought I told you.'

Ray shook his head, sparked up the half-joint he'd blocked the night before, when Karen started getting frisky on the couch. 'All I know,' he said, 'is you rob gas stations and the last time was a bust.'

Karen, remembering Ray humming Roy Orbison while she sorted her laundry, said: 'First I pick the day.'

'Just like that.'

'Keeping it random, so there's no pattern. Except, no Fridays or Sundays.'

'You're superstitious?'

'Friday's your main day for lodgments, pickups, deliveries, your heavy cash movements. Everyone's a bit sharper on Fridays.'

'And Sunday everywhere's closed.'

'Sunday's Sunday. Nothing fucks with my Sunday.'

'So when's the best time?'

'Wednesday morning. No one ever expects anything to happen on Wednesday morning.'

'You hit gas stations exclusively?'

Karen shook her head. 'You have your supermarkets in small villages. Post offices. Maybe a bookies once in a while.'

'Keeping it small.'

'Most I ever hit was seven grand. A complete fluke. Usually it's either side of a grand, give or take.'

'Being curious,' Ray said, 'and no offence, but you don't strike me as someone who grew up in the life.'

'Mostly I was trying to piss off my father.'

'Then armed robbery was definitely the way to go. You couldn't just get a tattoo?'

'Back then, Rossi was the one pulling the jobs. When I met him he had the bike, the leathers. Was into all sorts of drugs.'

'And this is what pisses off your father.'

'I was fifteen. Rossi was eighteen, nineteen. Even without the drugs he'd have been pissed off.'

Ray flipped the butt of the joint out the window.

'After he went down,' Karen said, 'I mean my father, and the crap in the prison, me screaming about him fucking me up the ass, they got this counsellor in. According to him, what I was doing with Rossi was what they call transference. Yeah? I can't control my father's actions, so I'm looking to tame Rossi.'

'Neat.'

'Except where they're going wrong is, Rossi's fucked up all the way through.'

'And your father wasn't?'

'This is the problem,' Karen conceded. 'I can still remember going through photo albums with my mother. Y'know, weddings and shit. And she's telling me, one time with her eye all swollen, that he was a nice guy. I mean originally, before she married him. Even after she married him.'

'He's a boozer? Turns mean on the sauce?'

Karen shook her head. 'He just hit her one day. It came out of nowhere, she'd spilled paint in the garage, some shit like that. Then it's done and he's the sorriest man that ever walked, he's crying, all this. So she doesn't report it. Back then, you didn't.'

Ray nodded.

'The weird thing is, *he's* the one telling *her* to report it. Ring the cops. But she doesn't. He couldn't work it out. Next thing she knew, the bastard was like a kid with a new toy. Couldn't figure out how she worked, so he's trying to bust her instead.'

'Shit.'

'Pretty much, yeah.'

The Transit crawled along in the rush-hour traffic, Karen watching the pedestrians, all the normal people going about their normal lives.

Ray said: 'So your father goes away and you move in with Rossi. Is that it?'

'Not fucking likely. Rossi was already in by then, his first tumble.'

Put into care, Karen had been old enough to say screw school, she knew her rights. So they got her a job on a factory floor making rubber mats for weighing scales, some Korean crew.

Karen didn't mind the work: it was monotonous, but at least you got the feeling of a job done at the end of the day. What got her down was the way the other women just accepted their lot, talking on the breaks about what they'd be cooking for dinner after working a full shift. The husbands at home watching videos, maybe picking the kids up from school if they weren't welded to a bar counter.

Karen stuck that for eighteen months, then split. By then Rossi was back inside again, his second jolt, so Karen took a job stacking shelves, eventually graduating to till-jockey.

'And this is where,' Ray said, 'you got the idea for the stickups.'

Karen shook her head. 'Rossi, the silly prick, gets out. We move in together. Then he gets pinched again. Third time, so he gets the full five years. I mean, for taking down a fucking chemist.'

'A chemist?'

'Codeine, anything morphine-based, your basic amphetamines. Rossi wasn't fussed. Except this time the chemist hands over something new, so Rossi gets the bright idea of trying it out there and then, making sure the chemist isn't passing him duds.'

'Only the cautious survive,' Ray reminded her.

'He gets clean away but the cops didn't have too much trouble tracking him down. Like, he's the guy under the Ducati wrapped around the railings on the wrong side of the motorway. At the hospital they told me he only survived because he was already unconscious when the bike hit.'

'Lucky,' Ray commented.

'The *bike* got lucky. Hardly a scratch. Rossi got two broken legs, a punctured lung, a fractured skull.'

Karen'd been so damn mad the night Rossi went down for five with no appeal that she'd gone out and held up a service station just to show the prick it could be done without getting nabbed. Using his own bike to prove her point. The .44 was Rossi's too, pinched from his lockup along with his spare set of leathers. Karen never told him. She didn't think he'd appreciate the irony.

So she'd walked in, wearing the leathers—helmet on, visor down, hair tucked away out of sight. Up through a side aisle to the counter, stomach churning, no idea of what came next but so pumped and mad she had to be doing *something*.

'Afterwards,' she said, 'thinking back? I was blessed. I mean, it was late, I was the only customer. The fat guy behind the counter had his T-shirt rucked up so I'm looking at his hairy back, he's watching TV on this black-and-white portable. None too interested in schlepping his fat ass down off the stool and helping me out. So I tap the .44 on the counter and say, "Excuse me?"'

'I'll bet he shit himself.'

'The fucker just opened the till, dumped the cash out, went back to watching TV. I had to ask him for a plastic bag to put the money in.'

'How'd you do?'

'Twelve hundred and change.'

'Not bad,' Ray said, flashing a bread van out of an intersection. 'And this, I'm betting, is when *you* shit yourself.'

Too right. Karen didn't pull any jobs for six months after. Shivering whenever she thought about it, every night expecting the cops to kick her door in. Once in a while the *size* of it hit her, the enormity of what she'd done, what it might mean for Anna if she got caught and was put away. This one time she saw a movie about Marie Antoinette, the girl on her knees waiting for the blade to fall. Karen'd cried.

But as the months passed and she began to accept that she'd gotten away with it, the buzz seeped back in. The adrenaline thrill. The sheer nipple-stiffening power of it. Karen'd taken stock, liking the way she hadn't panicked and dumped the dough. Which suggested she had what it took.

So she worked it around, how she'd pulled it off, the factors involved, and came up with a quiet time, a lonely place, not being greedy and not getting caught.

'One-off scores,' Ray said, 'at a grand a pop—no cop's busting his hump chasing that. Plus these places are always insured.'

Karen giggled. 'The time I nailed the seven grand? It made the papers. Said how the cops were looking for a small, skinny guy in leathers.'

'I'd have said slim, not skinny.'

'You'd say anything you think'll get you in the sack.'

Ray conceded the point.

'See the next set of lights?' Karen said. 'Drop me off there, I'll walk down to the laundromat.'

At the lights Ray said: 'So what about tonight? You doing anything?'

'Actually, I am. And no offence, Ray, but I think I'd be tired anyway. Three nights in a row is a bit much for me.'

'No worries,' Ray said, although Karen thought she caught a hitch in his voice.

Strolling on to work after dropping off her laundry, Karen decided on Tuesday. It'd have to be soon, with Rossi getting out, all these cops in tow, heat Karen could do without. Karen thinking how, if Rossi did turn up, get in her way, it'd be different this time. Karen felt stronger, had all she needed. And not because of Ray, either. It was just, Rossi'd have to get used to it, Karen was different this time.

It was only then, going up the steps to Frank's surgery, that Karen realised, shit, she didn't have Ray's number. And Ray, as far as she knew, didn't have hers.

ROSSI

Rossi'd never admit it now, chib any fucker said different, but he hadn't always been so proud of his name, his roots.

He'd taken a lot of stick in the home, the other kids calling him greaser, wop, pizza-face. Shouting the odds about how Italians had sixteen reverse gears on their tanks. The nuns hadn't helped his case either, dropping his first name and calling him Francis Assisi. The bigger kids on Rossi's case: who'd he think he was, a saint or some shit? Rossi scrapping hard just to stop the bigger kids stealing his food.

How the nuns dealt with it was, the kid left on the floor cleaned up the mess. So Rossi spent a lot of time on his hands and knees, scrubbing and starving while the other kids scoffed his grub and called him a greaseball. The only consolation there was, the bigger kids weren't long finding out there were no reverse gears on Rossi Francis Assisi Callaghan.

Then, when Rossi was nine years old, a miracle: Italy won the World Cup, Paolo Rossi scoring six goals that included the opener in the final. That night, pumped on adrenaline, half-delirious with joy, Rossi snuck out of bed and began flailing around the dormitory with the old tennis racket he kept under his mattress for emergencies. By the time they got him down, hustled him out, the damage ran to busted arms, cracked ribs and bloody faces, none of them belonging to Rossi.

After that, once they let him out of the hole, Rossi didn't have any more trouble with the bigger kids.

As he got older, Rossi began to realise how much his own life mirrored that of the great Paolo, who had recovered from personal tragedy—some horseshit about fixing matches; Rossi didn't believe a word of it—to become a national hero to the Azzurri. Rossi could see himself on some Sicilian terrace, eating dinner at a big table, everyone jabbering away, Rossi sipping his wine and chewing it up about how he and the great Paolo had beaten the odds to become champions.

That was why, Rossi *felt* it, it was in his genes, why Rossi liked a sunny day so much. Someone'd once told him how, in Sicily, it only rained two days in every year, guaranteed. Rossi could dig that. When the rain came on, the heavy black clouds, Rossi didn't know whether to cry or stab some fucker in the heart.

But even the bright warm morning couldn't lift his spirits, Rossi barrelling down the canal towpath heading for his lock-up, the Ducati and the .44. He turned off the canal down an alleyway, the lock-up three doors in, noting the rusty padlock that meant no one had been inside in years.

He finally got the key turned, sprung the lock, hauled open the double wooden doors. And stared, dumbstruck.

No bike. No love-of-his-life flame-red Ducati 996 under the tarp. Fuck it, they'd even swiped the *tarp*. And even before he went for the wood-wormy wardrobe against the back wall, Rossi knew the leathers would be gone too, the helmet. He dropped to his knees and scrabbled under the wardrobe for the loose flagstone, groping blind. Knowing the stash would be gone too, his sixty grand, the .44 …

Rossi sat on the sagging, mildewed canvas cot and rolled a fat one to sand down the splinters. The red mist descending.

Karen?

Had to be. No one else had a key. And no one else would rip a man off all the way, strip him bare.

Rossi smoked on, feeling a stirring in his groin, getting hard and mean. Thinking, that fucking bitch Karen.

RAY

When it came to women, in Ray's experience, it wasn't who talked loudest or longest or made the most sense. Mainly it was whoever talked to them last.

Like this fortyish-looking tennis type with the coffee tan and head scarf wrapped tight to her skull, the chemo-chic pose. All made up at nine-thirty in the morning, gazing in wonder around her own kitchen, head to one side saying: 'Blue? You really think so? We never thought of *blue*. But now you say it …'

Ray knew he could call at lunchtime and get a whole new Karen, depending on who she'd been talking to last.

'What you have to consider,' he said, 'is the *kind* of light you're getting back here. Around the front, sure, yellow, to soak up all that sun. But back here, if you think about it, you're going blue, to pick up on how thin the light is.'

Ray had been stuck with a heap of blue, aquamarine, and needed to offload.

The tennis type saying: 'Of course, yes. We were thinking mauve.'

'Too absorbent. Mauve's more your bedroom colour.'

'Really?' Still gazing around her kitchen like it was the inside of a genie's bottle. 'Well, you'd be the expert on bedrooms, Mr Bro … Oh!' A hand fluttered to her lips, a blush rising in her cheeks. She met Ray's eye. 'I didn't mean …'

Ray slipped her the bashful smile. 'Don't worry about it. My mother's called me worse.'

Most days Ray was up for a little flirting. It was part of the gig, one of the first things Ray had learned. He was thinking of using it as a slogan for the side of the van—*Brighten her home, gladden her heart.*

Ray even got a kick out of the banter. Using all these cheesy lines, throwing them out there to see which ones got the good ol' girls a-giggle. The funny ones he used again, off duty. As for the bad ones—the way Ray saw it, when you're thickening up, pushing fifty, and have nothing better to do than get your house redecorated, there's no such thing as a bad line.

This one, the tennis type, she wouldn't even be a stretch. Still working it, the legs good from all the hours spent pounding the courts. More bony than slim but pert front and back. The kind, she'd want him to take her rough, like a pig snuffling truffles.

This morning, though, Ray wasn't in the mood. The thought had occurred to him, the night before, just as he was getting his knees set right, his rhythm going, how maybe Karen'd be the last woman he'd ever get to screw. Not that he was dying or anything. A simple matter of choice.

It wasn't the first time Ray'd had that thought: what made it significant was that it had been the first time the notion didn't cause his rhythm to falter, get him coming too soon. So he said, to the tennis type, keeping it brisk: 'So what'd we decide—the blue, right?'

And saw the fall in her eyes. Ray felt sorry for her, he truly did, the woman hoping for kicks from the hired help. But she wasn't his problem. Ray's problem, as of six hours ago, was how to go about making sure Karen never got to feel the same way. When he'd looked at Karen afterwards, both of them still panting, swearing softly and sweating, there'd been an expression in her eyes Ray'd only ever seen but once, this Ethiopian kid from a famine documentary, three years old with eyes as wide as forever too soon.

That was when it finally dawned on him: it's not the way a woman looks, it's the way she looks at you.

Truth be told, Ray was a little disappointed. He'd presumed it'd all be a bit more complicated. But then, Ray'd read somewhere once how for a woman it's the right guy but for a guy it's the right time. So maybe he'd just arrived in his time.

Leaving, Ray tried to cheer up the tennis type. 'I don't usually do this,' he lied, turning on the top step. 'But if you want to pay cash, I'll cut two hundred off the top.'

She nodded. 'Of course,' she said, with just enough acid to make it bite, 'I'll have to talk it over with my husband first.'

'You do that.'

'I don't believe I got your number,' she called as Ray crunched away down the gravelled drive.

'That's okay,' he said over his shoulder. 'I'll call back in a few days.'

Not saying if he'd ring or actually arrive. Maybe gladden her heart a little that way.

MADGE

Watching Tamisha from under her left armpit, tangled up in some half-assed Lotus Flower knot that was supposed to relieve stress and promote flexibility, Madge despaired of ever achieving the tranquil grace that came so easily to Tamisha.

For one, the girl was built like a corn dolly, triple-jointed, with half the ribcage Madge was lugging around. Plus, as far as Madge could make out, you needed to bathe in patchouli oil and grow a moustache. Tamisha took the natural approach, no wax or razors. Behind her back, the class called her Yoga Bear.

'Annnnnnd … release,' Tamisha announced. 'Okay ladies, take five.'

The high-ceilinged room, mirrored down one side, echoed with thuds and grunts. Fiona, red-faced on a padded mat to Madge's right, rolled onto her back whooping down lungfuls of air. 'It's … so … *relaxing*,' she gasped, beads of sweat clotting her pencil-etched brows.

Madge, still on her hands and knees, unable to speak, just nodded. Wondering if Fiona, and Audra to her left, felt as ridiculous as she did, jammed into leotards and the matching leg-warmers. Madge could see herself in the mirror, Tamisha at the barre swinging her leg like she was auditioning for a can-can troupe, Madge blowing hard as a baby whale, sweat stinging her eyes.

Fuck, she thought, *this*. She hauled herself upright and arched her back, hands on hips, then lurched across the hall to the exit, waving away Tamisha's solicitous enquiry.

Towelling off alone in the changing room, she cast a critical eye over her reflection in the fogged-up mirror. Starting with the feet—Madge had always liked her feet, small and neat, delicate. Slim ankles, the calves chunky but in proportion, the thighs starting to balloon, dimpling now with cellulite. Frank had wanted Madge to undergo dermabrasion but Madge wouldn't wear it. Not that she wasn't as vain as the next girl. It was just that Madge had this problem with taking Frank's advice, seeing herself through Frank's eyes …

The Big O

The belly, yeah, thickening up, the love handles running flabby, the stretch marks like trenches from some abandoned war. But what did they expect, she was fifty-fucking-one, had *twins* for Chrissakes. The boobs, of course, were still good, hanging a little heavy now but basically presentable, especially in a halter-neck. One thing Madge had learned, getting older, was how a hint could say nothing but still say it all.

The neck and throat, okay, getting a little turkey'd up, but lines or no lines, the face was still kicking it, as Jeanie and Liz would say. The eyes wide and brown, the lips full, the nose … Okay, so maybe the nose could do with some filing down, particularly the little bump just below the bridge. But Madge had seen Frank's tools—this back when Frank was still practising—the tiny chisels, the bone saws. No *way* was Madge letting anyone stick a chisel up her nose, maybe hammer it all the way into her sinuses.

Outside in the car park, waiting for Fiona and Audra, a woollen hat tugged down over her damp hair, Madge reached to switch on her mobile and then thought, fuck it, all she ever got were calls from Jeanie and Liz, the girls always looking for something. A life, mainly. Madge couldn't stand mobile phones, the way people were always making calls they didn't need to make, sending texts just because they were standing in a queue. Madge didn't even like that they were *called* mobiles, like they had wheels, could be steered by remote control. If anything, Madge thought, they were portables.

So she reached further into the glove compartment, found her cigarettes, then realised she'd packed the stub of a joint, just enough to take the edge off. She fired it up, thinking how, when it came to busting stress, a smoke knocked a Lotus Knot into a cocked hat …

The kick for Madge wasn't so much the mellow buzz, the chilling out. No, what Madge enjoyed best was that she, Margaret Dolan, mother of twins, was smoking grass, weed, pot, call it whatever. All the movies she'd ever seen, the hippies rolling up in a haze of smoke, Madge'd wondered, okay, it looks fun but how's it *feel?*

Pretty good, yeah. But, like, okay—what happens next? Madge was on the prowl for experience, something—anything—new. Once word had got out about the separation, Madge'd been snowed under by Frank's friends, all concerned as to how Madge was making out, *Be sure to call if there's anything you need.* Doug was the second of Frank's golf buddies Madge had screwed: Bryan first, for spite and to compromise him on the divorce settlement, then Doug from sheer boredom. Madge grinned, hearing Karen say it: *Fuck your A-bombs, there's nothing as dangerous as a bored woman.*

Madge had often wondered how it'd play out on the links, the boys in their baggy pants keeping score on their little white cards. Thinking about how, if she was to casually mention to Frank about Bryan and Doug, it might even qualify as some kind of handicap, Frank putting for par and getting those yips he was always crying about, Frank on the fidget thinking about Doug pouring the pork to his ex-wife ...

Amusing, yes, but Madge had bigger fish to fry. She'd been thinking that maybe it was coming time to push the boat out—like, literally, follow up on a few notions she'd always had, one being a Mediterranean cruise with a toy-boy in tow, something young and rough, Madge had always had a thing for car mechanics and plumbers. The kid screwing Madge senseless 24/7. The way she saw it, it'd be the trip of a lifetime or she'd get it all out of her system.

Either way, Madge had an itch it was coming time to scratch.

Because what Madge had finally realised, after screwing Doug, was that she'd been bored for nearly twenty years. Not that she blamed Frank: Frank was just an asshole who actually *liked* the horseshit, the big-breeze small talk down at the Tennis Club, the Rotarians, the Opera Society—so long as it was some kind of *club*, Frank was happy.

Where Madge went wrong was in presuming that being bored was her part of the deal, like out at Oakwood when you ordered a vodka-tonic and got a swizzle stick whether you wanted it or not. Doug was just as boring as Frank, wriggling around on top like he couldn't decide if he was going to fuck her or ask her to guess his weight. Madge's problem, she'd started to realise, was not pointing it out, the problem, and doing it early.

Now she pinched the joint dead, flipped it out the window, as she watched Fiona and Audra totter across the car park towards the Crossfire. Wondering, Christ, who wears heels to a fucking *yoga* class?

There and then she decided, the next time Doug rang, that she'd tell him how she was feeling bad, Audra being such a good friend and all, and that she'd have to spill, couldn't live with the guilt. Hey, she thought, brightening up, maybe she could even tell Doug she was feeling, y'know, depressed, suicidal …

Madge understood spite, for sure. And lately she'd come to appreciate what it meant to be bored. It was where she went after boredom that she wasn't too sure about.

RAY

Ray walked straight up to the counter.

'Listen,' he said, 'this'll sound kind of weird, but there's this girl, we've been out a couple of times but haven't got around to swapping numbers yet. Anyway, she went off to work this morning without making any plans to hook up again. But she dropped off her laundry here first.'

This around noon, the laundromat quiet.

The chubby-cheeked attendant was in her forties, wearing faded dungarees. 'I'm not giving out no one's phone number,' she said, 'for *no* reason.'

Ray nodding along. 'Because I could be a freak, stalking the girl. Plus she already told me she's busy tonight, so it could be she's giving me the easy brush. So what I'm asking is if you'd mind ringing her up and telling her I'm wondering if she'd like to get together for lunch.'

'You're serious.'

'Absolutely. At The Crypt.'

'And you want me to ring and ask her out for you.'

'That way I don't have to find out her number, where she works, anything like that. If she says no, she says no. What're we out?'

The attendant thought it over. 'What's it worth to you?'

Ray patted his pockets, dug out a crumpled twenty and smoothed it flat on the counter. The attendant sighed and pushed the twenty away with the point of her fingernail.

'I'm asking,' she said, 'what's it worth. Like, if she says no, how bad is it?'

Ray considered. 'I'm thirty-seven years old,' he said, 'and I never felt like this about anyone before. Like I actually want to take care of someone. Except, I get the feeling, she could look out for me too.'

'What if she doesn't want to be taken care of?'

'Who doesn't want to be taken care of once in a while?'

'Fair point. But what if she doesn't?'

'Then I'm disappointed.'

'Disappointed?'

'I don't know her well enough to go join the monks, we've only been out twice. But yeah, definitely disappointed.'

The attendant shrugged, reached for the phone. 'What's her name?'

'Karen King.'

'And you're saying,' she said, clicking her mouse, glancing at the computer screen, 'it's The Crypt.'

'Already booked. Hey, if she's not interested, what're you doing for lunch?'

'I bring sandwiches,' the attendant said, dialling up, phone wedged between ear and shoulder. 'Oh, hi—can I speak to Karen King, please?'

KAREN

'I hadn't realised,' Karen said, watching Ray fork some linguini home, 'you were left-handed.'

Ray swallowed before he was ready, sipped some water. 'Just sometimes,' he said, dabbing a napkin to his lips. 'For different kinds of things. Like, if I'm using a TV remote, I'm left-handed. Or for eating. But mostly I'm right-handed.'

Karen took a drag on her smoke while she pushed the vermicelli around her plate. Not hungry, too edgy to eat, and lunch was usually Karen's biggest meal of the day. 'So you're ambidextrous?'

'I think if you're ambidextrous you can use both hands to do everything. I just do different stuff with different hands.'

Karen less interested in what he was doing, with which hand, than where he was doing it. The Crypt had its tables in private booths under pointed arches, gargoyles on the wall, a spooky gothic vibe. Spooky prices too: six-course lunches and a separate menu for champagne.

Maybe that was why she was nervy: Karen had never felt comfortable around unnecessary wealth. Or, she thought, maybe it was her period coming on. And maybe she just felt sorry for Ray, the guy dropping a wad to buy her lunch when Karen was thinking about blowing him off. For the time being, anyway, now she'd decided on Tuesday.

'You want to change that?' Ray said, nodding at the vermicelli. 'If there's something wrong, just get it changed.'

Karen stubbed the cigarette. 'No, it's fine. I just don't eat that much during the day.' She met his gaze, the candlelight picking up on the hazel glints. She wondered if he knew it, if it was why he'd picked the place, candles over lunch. 'Maybe I'll just have a coffee instead.'

'Okay by me.'

He signalled the waitress, and when she arrived he indicated that Karen would be ordering first. And just like that, out of nowhere, Karen felt the butterfly churn, the butterflies getting their signals wrong and coming together in a wild, fluttery midtummy tornado.

She ordered a latte. Ray said he'd have the same, lit a cigarette, smiled across through the flickering candlelight. Karen thinking, okay, yeah, maybe it's just being around Ray ...

'I used to be all right-handed,' he said. 'Back when I was a kid.'

'Yeah?'

'Then this guy, I was fourteen, the last day before school breaks up for summer, he snaps my arm. Like, lays it across two schoolbags, stamps down. Like *that*,' he said, clicking his fingers.

'Fuck. What'd you do?'

'To him? Nothing. The guy was a foot taller than me, twice as wide.'

'But why?'

Ray shrugged. 'He just wanted to do it. Although,' he conceded, remembering, 'he did say he didn't like my name.'

'The fuck was wrong with your *name?*'

'With these guys? Reasons are bullshit. I mean, if I had the same name and was bigger than him, my name wouldn't have been such a problem.'

'Yeah, but … What'd you do?'

'Puked up and bawled my fucking eyes out.'

'You didn't tell anyone?'

'You mean squeal?'

'Christ, Ray. He broke your *arm.*'

Ray tapping ash, smoking left-handed. 'That was the first year. Second year, same thing. That time, okay, he caught me out, I didn't think he'd go two in a row. Third time I was craftier. He had to track me down, grab me in town.'

'And …'

'Yep. In a car park.'

'But … Jesus, Ray. Why?'

'I told you. He wanted to.'

Karen sipped some latte. 'So what happened?'

'I spent three summers in plaster. Three on the fucking bounce.'

'I mean the guy—what'd you do?'

'Nothing. He left school, drifted away.'

'And you didn't …'

'Stand up to him? He's a bully so he's really a coward behind it all?' Ray grinned. 'Like fuck. The guy was six-foot plus at sixteen, built like a brick shit-house. Just one of those guys, he liked to hurt people. The year he got held back—in remedial class—half the fucking school cried, janitors too.'

Karen couldn't help but feel disappointed, expecting a big finale, Ray finally getting around to stomping the bully. Not liking the way Ray deflected her expectations, sending them off on new tangents. Making Karen rethink, a couple of times already, like Sundance, who *is* this guy?

'You could have at least fought back,' she said.

'I did. Caught him some good ones, too, nearly broke my fucking arm for him. You ever punch marble?'

'And that's it? That's the story?'

'What do I look like, Rocky? I'm knocking the guy down in the last round?'

Karen lit a fresh cigarette. 'Don't get me wrong, Ray. I'm not saying it's not an interesting story. But I'm wondering, you take a girl out somewhere flash, then tell her you're this six-stone weakling, how you let some bastard break your arm three years in a row …' She exhaled to one side, keeping her eyes on his. 'I think you're missing the point here.'

'You asked about my being left-handed,' he said. 'And that's how it happened, how I learned to do stuff with my left. Like eat, switch channels, zip my pants. The important stuff.'

Karen shook her head, not getting it.

'The upside?' Ray said. 'I got into this habit, the itching driving me crazy, of just blotting it out. Y'know? Mind over matter.'

'That's some upside alright.'

'Put it this way. If you can blot out pain, you can blot out pleasure.' He winked. 'It's why I can go all night. Just switching it off.'

'And you're not using this technique on me—why?'

'Maybe I don't want to wear you out right away.'

'Take a chance. I mean, if I'm hating it, I'll let you know.'

Ray shrugged. 'It's your funeral.'

'I've always liked the idea,' Karen said, 'of dying happy.'

ROSSI

'Ring this number again,' Rossi snarled into the phone, 'I'll track you down and suck out your fucking eye. What'd I tell you last time? Possession's nine-tenths of the law.'

Then hung up, grinning at Marsha as he tucked the phone into his breast pocket.

'These guys,' he told her, 'don't know when to quit. I mean, the phone's stole already, am I right? So get another one, what's the big fucking deal? Or get the number blocked, fuck me up that way. Only the bastard's too lazy or stupid to do it. Am I right or am I right?'

'I *am* sorry, sir,' Marsha said, getting back into it fast after the interruption, 'but I'm afraid no one is allowed visit without proper authorisation.'

Rossi had never realised before how many people spend their whole lives apologising to strangers. The security guard yesterday. Then, this morning, the tarts on directory enquiries with *I'm sorry, sir, I can't provide that information.* Now Marsha the receptionist in her cute little emerald waistcoat and matching skirt, giving Rossi the fish-eye. Everyone breaking a sweat to keep him out of the loop.

'But she's *mine,*' he protested. 'I'm not authorised to see my own fucking property?'

'Sir, I won't tell you again about the foul language.' Marsha flicking her fringe, the hair straw-blonde and fake as the long nails. Rossi, still hard, maybe from eating decent food again, thought about how he'd like to meet Marsha some night walking home on her own, tottering on high heels and flagging down a cab. 'If you don't refrain,' she said, 'I'm afraid I'll have to call security.'

'You want posh,' Rossi said, wondering how Karen could afford Pheasant Valley, way out in the boonies, a reception area with air-conditioning, leather chairs and can-you-fucking-believe-it *real* palm trees inside. And, naturally, a snooty tart behind the desk. 'Okay,' he said. 'Marsha—may I, begging your gracious pardon, see my one and only Anna I haven't seen in like five whole years?'

'Sir, I'm sorry, but as I've already said—'

'Yeah, yeah, no skangers stinking out the joint. Can I at least ring for a cab to get back to town?'

Marsha frowned, glancing at where Rossi'd tucked the phone into his breast pocket. 'What's wrong, you're out of credit?'

'No, I just thought I'd ask, see how tight you really are.' Rossi winking, letting Marsha know he'd get in there *deep*, turn her dark roots white with fright, maybe match the straw-blonde hair that way. 'That it, Marsha? You tight? I mean, *tight*?'

Marsha flushed and then reached for the cream-coloured phone on the counter; picked up, dialled a two-digit number. Rossi already turning away, heading for the automatic doors, glancing back as they hissed apart. Marsha, watching him go, replaced the receiver.

Marsha thinking he'd be ringing a cab.

Rossi strolled out into the early afternoon, across the car park, soaking up some sun. Patting his pockets, working out if he had enough smokes to last him a couple of hours.

Hoping he didn't.

RAY

When Ray joined the Rangers they told him it was like the SAS and Marines combined. Three months in Ray found himself wondering, Christ, how boring was the Marines?

Hunkered down now over the open suitcase in his lock-up, trying to decide if he should use the Glock or the Sig for the surgeon's wife, the *ex*-wife, Ray was pretty sure he'd used the Sig the last time out. Or, shit, thinking about it now, maybe it'd been the USP, the .40 with the P-load option, the extra-large trigger guard that came in handy if you were wearing gloves. The last gig being seven months back. The wife of an assistant bank manager discovered he was banging some twenty-year-old blonde, a student who came in looking for an overdraft. The wife wanting the girl dead.

'In,' she'd expanded, 'her dirty-sheet whore-rented bed.'

'Whoa,' Ray'd said, 'I don't do executions. You want the money, hurt him that way, then fine, I'll snatch her. Otherwise, no go.'

Ray had heard all the fantasies. Although this one, the wife, maybe she had a point. Her daughter dies of leukaemia and some blonde bimbo turns up at the funeral, draping herself across the coffin wailing about how it was all God's punishment. The wife telling Ray this on the phone, saying: 'I'm asking you as a human being to try to understand the humiliation of that moment.'

'Okay,' Ray'd said, 'I hear you. But we're not making movies here. Understand? No one's dying in anyone's bed.'

Ray hearing the wife breathing hard and shallow on the line. Then: 'Yeah, okay. Take her. While she's *in* her tramp's bed.'

'Fine. Now—one last time, so there's no mistakes after. Yes or no?'

'Yes. *Yes*. God, please, *yes* …'

Ray, knees stiff from hunkering down, said: 'Fuck it.' Eeeney-meeny-miney-moed, picked the Glock, locked the suitcase. Stowed it in the wall-mounted safe, tapped in the alarm code, shut the lock-up. Balled the surgical gloves and lobbed them underhand into the canal, then drove for home.

He hit traffic, rush hour building, wound down a window and fired up a smoke. Turned his head to the side exhaling and saw a Ford Celica, two lanes across, one length up.

Three days after Ray'd dropped the bimbo off in the woods, early morning, still blindfolded, the banker had turned the key in his own Celica and went up, ka-boom, fried alive in his own driveway.

Ray had followed the reports for a while after, the cops with a definite line of enquiry, the wife suing Ford for faulty wiring. Far as Ray knew, nothing had come of either endeavour. Ray wasn't surprised. That Ford Celica was one sweet ride.

But, shit, now he remembered. For the bimbo? He'd used the Glock.

ROSSI

Four hours now Rossi'd been waiting. Sitting on a bench, walking away out of the car park, coming back from a different direction … *all* this fucking shit. When all he wanted was a fucking phone number.

No smokes, either. Even if it was just a straight Rossi could cope, kid himself he was okay. But leaving him without *some* kind of smoke, even for half an hour, was just asking for trouble—Rossi'd get all sorts of edgy, snarled up inside. And by the time Marsha tip-tipped daintily down the steps in her too-high heels, heading off towards Car Park C, it'd been precisely two hours and thirty-seven minutes since Rossi'd stubbed his last smoke.

'Hey, Marsha? Got a cigarette?'

Marsha looking around, car keys poised, eyebrow raised and a smile starting. Expecting someone, Rossi realised. One of the vets maybe, the guys in the fly white coats going in and out past Rossi all afternoon, throwing him the voodoo eye.

Marsha swallowed hard, turned to go.

'Sorry,' she muttered. 'I don't smoke.'

Rossi hustled up, fell into step beside her as she turned into the car park. 'Tell me this, Marsha.' He drew back the lapel of the double-breasted grey to show her the hunting knife stuck in his waistband, the handle covered with a worn rubber grip. 'Is there anything you're *not* sorry about?'

'S-sorry?'

'Think fast or you'll be the sorriest bitch ever walked.'

'I'll s-scream.'

He pulled the blade, grabbing her elbow. 'If you were going to scream you'd have screamed already. Now open the car or I'll hole you where you'll never heal.'

Marsha scraped the paintwork getting the key into the lock. Rossi, glancing around, no one coming their way, heaved from behind when she got the door open wide, caught a flash of blue satin, maybe silk, above sheer black nylon, Marsha's skirt riding up as she tumbled across into the passenger seat. Rossi sat into the driver's seat, tucked the blade under his thigh, beckoned for the keys.

'Okay, you're learning,' he said as she handed them over, hand shaking. He backed the car out, headed for the exit. 'Now Marsha, listen up. Do what I say and you walk away without a scratch. Alright? Otherwise, I swear it, I fuck you and slice your eyes. How would that be?'

That wouldn't be so good, not for Marsha. She started blubbing quietly, her face crumpling like the noisy paper, Rossi thought, you get in a box of chocolates. Which gave Rossi an idea.

'Marsha? Where you live, there's a shop near there, right? Somewhere I can get smokes, some chocolates. You think they do truffles?'

FRANK

'It's like telling a gag,' the club pro once told Frank. 'Get the timing wrong and *you're* the joke.'

Frank feeling lonely in the gathering gloom. Flexing his fingers on the black rubber grip, legs wide apart, shoulders loose. He looked up one last time to fix the position of the flag, squinting into the dull reddish glare, the sun low behind the green. Wondering if he should break it all up to wipe away that one prickly bead of sweat sitting right on his brow under the hairline.

'Jesus, Frank,' Doug called from the edge of the green. 'Any time before Christmas, yeah?'

Frank, way back on the fairway, couldn't actually hear Bryan and Mike snicker, Mike already on the green with Doug, Bryan sitting up nicely on the apron, all three holding putters. But he knew they'd be snickering. The 17th was an uphill dogleg par 5, Frank with six already played and still a good eighty yards short of the pin.

It was okay for Doug, blissed on Nervocaine, Frank handing over the pills in the dressing room before they went out. Frank, though—Frank was stressed, had been from the first tee, the insurance forms still unsigned in the breast pocket of his jacket, Doug getting interrupted when Bryan and Mike arrived together ...

He broke it all up, dragging an arm across his forehead to catch the bead of sweat. Then bent to it again, setting his feet, lacing his fingers. Telling himself to relax, it's all in the timing ...

He held his breath and drew back the wedge, smooth and easy, up over his head. Swayed into the downswing, fingers still nicely laced, feeling his shoulders pulling through gently. And then, just as the head of the wedge dropped past his kidneys, Frank got a mental flash, the club pro begging: *Don't slice it. All I'm asking is, for once, you don't fucking slice it.*

So he shanked it instead. Cutting across the ball and driving it low, hard and left at head height, so it caught Doug just behind his right ear, Doug going down in a welter of arms, legs and putter, choking out a strangled scream as he hit the turf.

Frank dropped the wedge and sprinted up the fairway, thinking, *that'll teach him*, standing so close to the green, fucking smart-arse playing off nine. But by the time he topped the rise and made the green, Frank was panting hard and his only thought was: *Don't sue, don't sue, don't sue ...*

MADGE

'Back then,' Madge said, sitting on the ground with her back against the couch, this to improve her posture, as recommended by Tamisha, 'there was no such thing as date rape.'

Karen sprawled on cushions beside the armchair, both of them angled towards the TV, the volume so low they couldn't hear it when they spoke. Not that Madge cared. The DVD was some Julia Roberts crap, Karen'd brought it over for laughs.

'Rape?' Karen said.

How they'd got into it was Karen'd asked, rubbing her tummy: 'Did it hurt?'

Madge snorted, handed the ashtray across. 'Frank, right?'

Karen took a hit off the joint. 'I thought he'd blow his wad telling me. Like, right there in reception, across the desk.'

Madge could imagine it, Frank licking his lips telling Karen about the piercing. Frank getting the news, she supposed, from Jeanie and Liz.

'He has a thing for belly buttons,' she said. 'I ever tell you that? The honeymoon's the first I hear of it. He must have spent, I swear, half an hour digging away at it the first night. Anyway, that's why I got it pierced, I knew it'd drive him insane.'

'Can I see it?'

'Sure.'

Karen crawled around the low coffee table. Madge hiked up the front of her sweater. Karen giggled. 'It looks a bit raw,' she said.

'It takes a few weeks for the swelling to go down. But it's okay to touch. Just don't go ripping at it.'

Karen tugged and pushed, still giggling, then sat back and reached for the ashtray. 'I don't know,' she said. 'It looks great, but I don't know.'

'If it looks great, then what's to know? Some day, when *you've* got an ass like mutant prunes, you'll appreciate those words of wisdom.'

Karen crawled back around the coffee table, sprawled out on the cushions again. 'This is after I've had kids, right? Twins.'

'And married some asshole who likes to play belly buttons.'

They both enjoyed that one. Karen wiped away a tear. 'Seriously, though—was it painful?'

Madge took a deep draw on the joint. 'I've had worse,' she said, considering. 'I mean, once you've had your first kid, everything else is a breeze.'

'Except you had to go and have two at the same time.' Karen thought for a moment. 'So who was the first, Jeanie or Liz?'

Madge watched Julia give some sappy-looking sack the full ninety-watt beam. 'Neither,' she said.

'Say again?'

'Neither.'

'You're saying,' Karen said carefully, 'there's more than Jeanie and Liz?'

'Just the one. Scary thought, isn't it?'

Karen wasn't to be diverted. 'And what—it died? I mean, he or she died?'

Madge shook her head, then shrugged. 'Being honest, Kar, I don't really know. It didn't die during labour, if that's what you're asking.'

Karen, Madge could tell from her expression, wasn't entirely sure what she was asking.

'I was sixteen,' Madge explained. 'I mean, we're talking thirty-five years ago. Things were different then.'

'Yeah, but—'

'Let me put it this way,' Madge said. 'Back then, there was no such thing as date rape.'

'Rape?' Karen's eyes widened, and then her shoulders slumped. 'Oh, Madge. Shit.'

'Not far off. Being honest? I wouldn't even wish it on Frank.'

'At least,' Karen said dolefully, 'he wouldn't have to worry about getting pregnant after.'

'This is true.' Madge felt light-headed, floaty, trying to work out if it was the dope or the unburdening that was making her feel that way. 'The worst of it was,' she said, 'I got blamed. For seducing the guy.' She snorted. 'We're out in the sticks, in his father's car, I'm sixteen. Yeah? I'm saying no for like three hours, and all the time I'm wondering how I'm getting home. But he won't quit. So, okay, I go with it. I mean, the guy's saying if I don't then he'll tell everyone I did. But if I do, he'll keep it quiet.'

Karen just stared. 'Like I say,' Madge said, 'things were different. Back then, if a guy got a boner, it was your fault for having boobs. Then I'm pregnant and my father starts looking up dictionaries, finding new words for slut. Then the priest, my mother called him in … Although, in his defence, he's already fucked up, else he wouldn't be a priest.'

'Anyway,' Madge continued, 'they shunted me off to this convent. I mean, no shit, your actual convent. First night I'm there, I hear the word fornication. By now I can see where they're coming from. I mean, if everyone called it fornication, no one'd be interested in getting their jollies, right? That's one seriously ugly word.'

Karen, fumbling, asked how it felt to be pregnant in a convent.

'Cold. Even in July it was always cold. And I knew, from day one, that I was giving it up, boy or girl. That was the whole idea. But the nuns were fine. Some of them were really sweet, actually wanted to help. One of them, Sister Concepta they called her'—Madge with a wry grin—'was actually interested in the physical process, how it felt, all that kind of thing. She was the one, when the baby was born, who asked if I wanted to give it its name or leave it up to the adoption board.'

'So what did you have—boy or girl?'

'A boy. Eight pounds, seven ounces, everything where it should be and nothing where it shouldn't.'

'You get to see him?'

'For about twenty minutes. They cleaned him up, brought him back in, gave me some time. Sister Concepta pulled out a camera, wanting to know if I wanted a picture taken.'

'Oh yeah?' Karen brightened. 'Have you got it?'

Madge shook her head. 'If they'd asked me before they brought him in, I'd have told them not to bother.'

'But Madge—'

'I didn't even want to screw the guy, Kar. And I know you can sympathise, and I truly love you for that. But thank God you'll never really understand.' Madge flicked the lighter, got the joint going again; exhaled, handed the ashtray across to Karen. 'Then, that's not bad enough, I have to carry this thing around inside me for nine fucking months, ten if you want to be pedantic about it. Being blamed, all the time, for the way I am. And this is before it rips me open, I mean, *rips* me open being born. And you're wanting a Kodak moment? Next thing

I know,' she said, 'they're calling the father in. To name the baby.'

'You're joking.'

'Nope. The joke is, the guy doesn't have to put his name on the birth cert, but he's allowed to, y'know, propose the baby's name. This because the adoption board is infested with men.'

Karen, despairing, said: 'So what'd you call him?'

'I'm honestly not sure. Sister Concepta gave me a Bible, told me to pick something out, she'd do her best to work it in. So I found something in the psalms, except she didn't like it.' Madge shrugged. 'The good news being, after all that crap? The twins were a breeze.'

Karen had a pair of fat tears either side of her nose.

Madge held her arms open, hoping Karen'd crawl around the table. 'I don't know how much I can hold my arms out, hon,' she said. 'You want a hug, you'd better get over here before I wind up crucified.'

A giggle erupted, Karen snuffling up the tears. Then she crawled around the coffee table and Madge sank into a fierce hug that seeped through to her bones.

After a while they both lay back against the couch, Karen wiping her cheeks with the back of her hand, saying: 'What kind of joint are you running here, woman? I bring Julia Roberts, you don't even break out the Kleenex?'

'Kar? Bring Julia fucking Roberts over here just one more time, I'll stick the DVD where the sun don't shine.'

Karen sniffled. 'Where's that, up my belly button?'

They both enjoyed that one too.

DOYLE

'Rossi Callaghan,' Sparks said, sticking her head around Doyle's door. 'Ring any bells?'

'Sure,' Doyle said. 'Rossi Francis Assisi Callaghan. Script drugs. Got out yesterday after five years for blagging a chemist, his third time down.'

'Wow,' Sparks said. 'You're good.'

Doyle selected the thickest of the files that had been dumped on her desk that morning, waved it at Sparks. The name had caught her eye, unusual enough to stick out, Doyle just the latest in a long line of care workers, probation officers, psychiatrists and prison guards who'd been keeping tabs on Rossi Callaghan for nigh on twenty years.

'What's he done now?' she said.

'Unlawful detention. Attempted rape.'

'Really?'

'That might well be the first time,' Sparks observed, 'I've ever heard you surprised.'

Doyle shrugged. 'It just doesn't sound like his MO. There's nothing in there,' she nodded at his file, 'about sex crime.'

'People change,' Sparks said. 'Anyway, you want to take it? I can pass it on.'

'That depends.' Doyle'd been on her way home before Sparks turned up. 'Where'll I find him?'

'If it was that easy …'

'We'd all make Commissioner. Where'd the call come from?'

Sparks handed over a typewritten report sheet. The address wouldn't send Doyle too far out of her way, so she nodded. 'I'll take it,' she said.

'Doing anything later on?' Sparks wanted to know.

'Dancing the flamenco with Brad Pitt. But I'll buzz you once I get rid of him.'

'First see if he has any brothers.'

'I'll do that.'

Doyle found the address and took a quick debrief from the visibly relieved patrolman, sat on the couch beside Marsha.

'Hi,' she said, flashing a smile. 'I'm Detective Doyle and we're going to catch this scum-sucker and feed him to the pigs. What can you tell me?'

Marsha told her story, the tale punctuated by choked sobs, an occasional hiccup. Doyle scribbled furiously. 'He actually said he'd staple your tits together?'

Marsha closed her eyes to block out the memory. Doyle thinking how they'd need to be big staples, Marsha packing a pair of M&Ms in a training bra.

'Then he goes,' Marsha said, gulping, '"Here's the *real* bad news. I only got out yesterday, it's been ten years since I've touched a woman."'

'Ten?'

Marsha nodded, tears welling. 'Then he said, "Want to know what I was in for? It wasn't just rape."'

Doyle consulted her notes. 'According to his file, he fell asleep on a motorbike after necking some pills he'd boosted from a chemist.'

'You don't believe me?'

'Plus he only did five years. By the way, is that a gentleman's handkerchief?'

Marsha nodded. 'It's his.'

'So the guy's threatening to rape you but he gives you his hanky first?'

Marsha sniffled hard. 'He wanted me to mop up, y'know, where I'd wet myself. Before he got started.'

'Sick fuck.' Doyle made another note. 'So how come he left?'

'He wanted a phone number.'

'Go on.'

'Started raving about some bitch, he called her, who stole his Ducati. Said he wasn't going to hurt her, all he wanted was his bike back. Then he said if I played along nothing'd happen to me, except I'd maybe get a rash from sitting in my own pee too long.'

Doyle scribbled it all down. 'So who's he trying to contact?'

'Someone called Karen King.'

'A friend of yours?'

'Where I work,' Marsha said, 'out at Pheasant Valley? I'm a receptionist. So he wanted me to ring up and say there's some weirdo stalking Karen King, I need to warn her. Get her address and phone number.'

'Did you do it?'

'He said,' Marsha said, lower lip trembling, '"They might not want to give you the information. Against that, what you have to consider right now is I'm pulling down my zipper."' Marsha shuddered. 'Then he said he'd have to turn me around before we got started. Because of all the shit that happened him in prison.'

'What about this Karen King?' Doyle said. 'Did you get the information?'

Marsha nodded.

'And then he left?'

Marsha nodded again. 'How come he left?' Doyle said.

'I had a, um, gentleman caller.'

Lucky you, Doyle thought. 'And you were expecting this guy?'

Marsha flushed up puce.

'He's married?' Doyle said.

'Actually, he's more in the way of being Caitlin's fiancé.'

'Caitlin being who?'

'My sister. Although, according to Tom, he's her ex-fiancé.'

'Either way, this gentleman caller isn't so much the gentleman.' Doyle made another note. 'So what about this Karen King? You ring her after Callaghan left, let her know he was tracking her down?'

Marsha, confused, shook her head. 'There was just so much going on ...' she began, eyes wide. Doyle swore.

While she dialled the number, Doyle gestured towards Marsha's bruised cheekbone, the pencil-thin gash on her forehead. 'He knocked you around?' she said. 'Got nasty?'

Marsha choked back a sob. 'That was Caitlin.'

'Can't say I'm surprised,' Doyle said. 'You were my sister, we'd be doing this in ICU. Oh, hi—is that Karen?'

FRANK

Doug insisted he was fine to drive, holding up three fingers and saying: 'Three, goddammit. *Three*.'

But the paramedics suspected a hairline fracture, a touch of concussion, and the deal with the fingers—Doug holding up two fingers on his left, one on his right—only hardened their resolve. So Doug travelled in the back of the ambulance and Frank, it was the least he could do, followed on in Doug's Beamer.

He hung around A&E until they wheeled Doug upstairs, the X-rays inconclusive, overnight observation required, then rang Audra and told her what he knew, subtly emphasising Doug's flouting of fairway etiquette.

'I can wait,' Frank offered, finishing up. 'Until you get here.'

'Christ, no. Just leave the car keys at reception. I'll pick them up there.'

'You're sure?'

'Certain. *Please*.'

Relieved, Frank hung up and then rang Genevieve to ask her to collect him at the hospital. Gen just banged the phone down. Didn't even ask, Frank reflected bitterly as he waited for a cab, was Frank okay, or who was hurt. So they argued about that when he got in, and then they had a row about Frank wanting to stay home.

'On a Friday night?' Gen said. 'You're kidding.'

'I've had a long day,' Frank pleaded.

'Me too, waiting for it to get to Friday night. Besides, you left the Merc out at Oakwood. So you need to pick it up.'

He had two stiff belts of bourbon waiting for Gen to get dressed, pacing his study, unable to sit still. Trying to convince himself it wasn't a bad omen, Doug shipping a stray Slazenger. Then, as the bourbon filtered through, the bad omen became karma, bouncing back on Doug for trying to play it cute with Frank over the insurance forms.

Frank wondering, with everything that was coming down the pike—divorce, the Medical Ethics Committee, inevitable bankruptcy—if someone wasn't trying to tell him something.

Like, how it might be coming time to bolt.

The phone rang. 'The Dolan residence,' Frank announced. 'Doctor Dolan speaking.'

'This Frank?'

'Who's this?'

'You have the twenty? The good faith?'

Frank harrumphed, clearing his throat. 'Um, not exactly.'

'Then no deal. Take care, Frank.'

'I thought,' Frank said quickly, 'that *you* could stump up the good faith, if required.'

'Why the fuck would we put up our own good faith, Frank? Kind of defeats the purpose, don'tcha think?'

'Well, yes, now you mention it. But—'

'Can you get it?'

'Sure, yeah. Probably.'

'It's a simple question, Frank. Yes or no?'

'It's, ah, being arranged.'

'For when?'

'Monday morning, first thing. And once I get it, I can drop it off anywhere you want.'

'That's real generous, Frank. But we'll probably just drop around to the office and pick it up there.'

'The office?'

'The surgery. Where you have your office. We wouldn't want to, y'know, put you out or anything. Then, once we know you're serious, someone'll call to confirm.'

'Confirm? Confirm what?'

'That you understand how, if anything goes wrong, it all fucks up or for some reason or other doesn't happen, we still clear the good faith.'

Frank swallowed hard, bourbon thick on the back of his throat. 'You get twenty grand for doing nothing?'

'We got expenses, Frank. We got the guy doing the snatch, we got transport, we got logistics. You want to take care of all that, okay. Just say the word and you can go ahead and snatch your own wife.'

'She's my *ex*-wife,' Frank said, desperate to retain a sliver of dignity.

'I give a fuck if she's your X-rated porno flick, Frank. You make a commitment to us, welch out on the deal, it's 'til death do *you* part. We clear on this?'

'Crystal.'

The phone clicked dead. Frank built another bourbon, three fingers in honour of Doug, the bottle clicking against the rim of the glass. He poured it down fast before going to the study door and calling upstairs: 'Gen? Baby? If you want to leave it for just another hour, we might make it out to Oakwood in time for breakfast. I hear they do muffins.'

Gen strolled out of the bedroom, still in her bra and panties, the lime-green thong-and-push-up combo. Leaned on the balcony railing, sucked the tip of a middle finger, flipped it at Frank and sashayed back into the bedroom.

Frank shrugged and went back to the wet bar, poured another couple of fingers and sipped it slow, thinking, okay, Doug'll be fine, the intern on A&E is just taking precautions, covering his ass. Monday Frank'd get Doug to sign the insurance forms, then wait for the half-million to roll in.

And then, fuck it, Frank had always liked the idea of captaining a yacht through the Caribbean. He'd often thought about setting up practice on an island not too far from Florida, all the rich Jews flying in for cheap surgery, some island where they'd never heard of any fucking Medical Ethics Committee.

Haiti, maybe. Frank liked the name, Port-au-Prince, the way it just rolled off his tongue.

RAY

Ray cracked a beer and settled in on the couch, watched some *Simpsons* and then a DVD, *Blood Simple*. What he liked about that was how long it took Marty to die, the realism, the guy shot and then buried alive, being battered with the spade. Ray in his time had seen two men die and neither went easy, one guy gut-shot, Ray still had nightmares once in a while hearing the glugging screams.

When the movie was over Ray got the Tindersticks going on the stereo, the TV still on, the sound down. He opened another beer and stripped the Glock, cleaning and oiling, building it back up, dry-firing. Then he flicked through the channels, wound up; sitting in on a Friday night, it wasn't natural.

Over the Tindersticks he heard the distant whizz-bang-crack of fireworks going off, a sad sound, the only way the kids could make themselves heard. It put Ray in mind of the time he'd seen this graffiti, the word 'sex' scrawled on a wall, that single stark word—Christ, how frustrated would you need to be?

Ray trying to distract himself from his main concern, whether Karen'd been feeding him a line when she said she was tired, didn't want to go three-for-three. Then thought about lunch, wincing as he remembered, shit, telling Karen about getting his arm broke three years in a row. Once, okay, maybe even twice would have bought him some oohs and aahs. Three made Ray a victim: a six-stone weakling, Karen'd called him. A loser, some bully's toe-rag.

He drank another beer, working it around, how maybe he'd let it all out because he felt he owed her something: Karen telling him about her father, the fork, all that shit. Laying herself open but getting the message through, how no one fucks with Karen.

Ray'd heard that one loud and clear. One thing he took pride in, why he did well in the Rangers, got his stripes, was no one had to tell Ray anything twice. Like the first time he ever heard the Tindersticks, he *got* it, Staples really pouring it on now in that quavery, heartbroke voice. Although, it wasn't so much the words as the way he sang them. What Ray got from Staples' voice was, when it came to women, you took that little bubble of joy for what it was, for as long as it ran, and when it was over you sucked your bitter little heart dry of the poison and started over fresh again …

He cracked another beer but didn't touch it, still edgy, winding up tight inside. Needing to get out, maybe take a drive.

Three minutes later he was behind the wheel, Bruce on the stereo singing about yet another Mary, Ray humming along. Heading across town with the vague idea of running a little drive-by recon past the surgeon's ex-wife's place, see how the layout looked, if there was anything unusual he'd need to know, one-way streets, shit like that.

Curious, too, about the swimming pool. These days everyone but Ray had a pool.

KAREN

Karen poured the last of the wine and watched Julia slap some guy's face, then smile and cry at the same time, the guy with a look like he was only now hearing about Julia's fee.

'Fiona had this guy around,' Madge said, 'he's doing her downstairs.'

Karen giggled. Madge caught on. 'I *mean*,' she said, 'he's redecorating the place. Like a makeover? She says he's cute, has buns of steel, a sexy voice. Not her type, though, he's too skinny.' Madge snorted. 'Not her type. It was wearing a Rolex, Fiona'd get up on a carrot.'

'You're thinking of redecorating?' Karen said.

'Maybe,' Madge said, considering. 'With the divorce going through, I don't mind telling you, I could do with a good cheer-me-up.'

'A coat of paint's going to cheer you up?'

'Tight buns up a ladder, Kar—*that'll* cheer me up.'

'Ray paints, decorates. Has nice buns too.'

'Oh yeah? Because Fiona said, her guy didn't leave his number.'

'Then that's him. That's Ray.'

'Now I'm definitely having the place done. Does he bring his own ladders or will he need me to, y'know, hold a chair for him?'

Karen was about to retort that a chair'd be the *only* wood Madge'd be holding with Ray around when she realised she didn't know if Ray had ladders or maybe screwed his clients as part of the makeover. Realised she knew practically nothing about Ray except he liked rock 'n' roll and didn't give out his number, drove a Transit van. She wondered if she hadn't been a bit previous earlier, telling Madge about Ray's eyes, the butterfly tornado over lunch.

'Hon?' Madge said. 'You okay?'

'Yeah, I'm fine. Just tired. It's been a long day.' Plus it was in the post, her moods were overdue. Karen suddenly feeling weepy, quivery.

'Frank giving you a hard time?'

'No worse than usual. Although, he's getting frisky again.'

'Maybe you'll be getting another raise soon,' Madge teased.

'No offence, Madge, but I'd rather go down on you.'

'Can't say as I blame you. Does he still make that snuffling sound when he's about to come?'

'Seriously, Madge, I'd rather not think about it.' Karen wondering where Ray might be, what he was doing on a Friday night. 'I think I'll head for home,' she said. 'I've a lot on tomorrow.'

'Want a lift?'

'You're stoned. I'll ring a cab.'

'I'll let you play with the stereo.'

Karen grinned. 'Okay by me.'

RAY

Ray didn't much like tree-lined streets, leafy avenues, all that middle-class crapola: three seasons a year they'll cut down your sight lines, narrow your field of vision. Then, in winter, the leaves are lying all over, damp and rotting, making it dangerous for a man who might need to take corners faster than maybe he should.

So Ray wasn't too impressed with Larkhill Mews, lined on both sides with sycamores meshing overhead.

Ray rolled down the avenue in third thinking, okay, it's worse than we thought but this is good to know. Putting some spin on it, looking at it from the other end, how narrowed sight lines would apply to everyone, not just Ray. Trying to judge, as he cruised Margaret Dolan's five-bed semi-D, glancing up the driveway, how near someone would need to be to the front gate before they could know for sure something was happening up there that maybe shouldn't be happening.

He turned left at the bottom of the avenue, drove around the block, cruised Larkhill Mews again; pulled in opposite the driveway, had a good look, noting details. The drive gravelled and curving up and away to his right behind a high laurel hedge. A Chrysler Crossfire—a sweet three-door coupé with, if Ray wasn't mistaken, double-wishbone front suspension, the six-speed manual shift—a Crossfire parked near the front door, reversed into position beside three shallow steps leading up to a glassed-in porch.

Ray sat there scribbling notes, the avenue quiet, no traffic, no pedestrians; thinking, okay, other than the trees, it's not so bad.

Then the Crossfire swung out of the driveway, wobbling slightly on the left turn, its headlights flaring to strafe Ray before he had time to duck.

KAREN

'So what's on tomorrow it's such a big day?' Madge said.

'I'm taking Ray to see Anna,' Karen said, still fiddling with the stereo.

'Oh yeah?'

Karen wondering, Christ, what was wrong with her? First pouring it out to Madge about Ray, then seeing weird flashes of Ray in the head-lights, some guy minding his own business sitting out in his car, maybe fighting with his wife.

And now, from nowhere, some half-stoned delusion or perverse instinct, talking about bringing Ray to see Anna.

'I thought you liked him,' Madge said quietly.

Karen tapped her fingers on her knee, a Smiths number on the radio, 'Panic', how appropriate was that? Seeing Ray again as Morrissey, the fringe that was nearly a quiff ...

'Kar?'

'Tomorrow,' Karen said firmly, 'I find out if I like him.'

ROSSI

Still hard, it had to be some kind of record, six hours now and still no sign of relief. Rossi peeing up the wall behind a stand of some bamboo-looking oriental crap in front of Karen's apartment block, wondering if he shouldn't contact the *Guinness Book of Records*, see how long he needed to keep it hard to qualify.

Plus, while he was on, he could be asking about the pee-height record, he had to be hitting six feet at least. Then realised, shit, there'd probably be tests for performance-enhancing drugs, urine samples, all this. Rossi with a few smokes on was good to go all night.

Although, Rossi wasn't smoking any more until he saw Karen and laid it out: the cash, the bike, the .44—just hand them over. Playing it cool, laid-back, the way he'd run it with Marsha, asking her nice, do what I want and no one gets hurt.

Rossi *still* peeing, hitting four feet now, the stream easing off.

It was times like these, trying times, when Rossi drew on his heritage, the Sicilians. Those old guys, Rossi knew, wouldn't bitch about having to wait around a couple of hours. The Sicilians could wait up in the hills for years, sitting around polishing their shotguns and growing beards they wouldn't shave off until honour had been avenged.

Rossi, humming some James Brown—'Payback'—didn't hear the metallic screech of the security gates. So the first he knew of Karen's arrival was headlights flashing across the stand of bamboo, which caused Rossi to instinctively zip up, thus snagging his erection in his fly.

The only consolation there was that he could hear ABBA's 'Super Trouper' booming muffled from the car, a grey Crossfire that crunched to a halt on the gravel just as Rossi came down knees-first on the chopped bark behind the bamboo.

Which meant they probably didn't hear him scream.

KAREN

Karen went through to the kitchen and put the kettle on, made some instant decaf, brought it into the living room.

She checked the phone, which told her she had two messages; punched in her code and heard the Rossi alert, the cop sounding dry and practical, advising Karen to contact her at her first opportunity.

Karen thought it was a strange phrase, 'her first opportunity'; like they were hoping she didn't get tied to any chairs before she had a chance to use the phone.

Then, it was always the way, she heard her mobile chirrup from her bag, cutting across the detective's voice. She hung up and dug out the mobile, checked the caller ID, but it was just a number flashing. She picked up, thinking, if this is Rossi I'll fucking—

'Hello?' she said.

Then, it was always the way, the doorbell rang.

ROSSI

Rossi was impressed. Sicilian it was, the way he caught the Crossfire's tags even from on his knees behind the stand of bamboo with a zipper lodged in the fleshy undercarriage of his rapidly shrinking shaft.

The moment passed. Then came the panic, the searing pain, a warm stickiness that could only mean one thing. Rossi buckled, keeled over and lay on his side, sobbing. The very idea horrified him, but somehow he managed to squeeze a hand inside his belt, cup his marbles and relieve some of the pressure; then, the warm stickiness in the palm of his hand spurring him on, Rossi made it back up onto his knees and hauled himself to his feet.

He lurched across the car park, cradling the box of Belgian truffles.

Leaning against the wall, summoning the strength, the courage, to reach up and buzz Karen's intercom, Rossi thought about the old guys sitting up in the hills and how they'd never had to deal with a ripped undercarriage. Hunched over, shivering, Rossi just hoped his ancestors weren't looking down on from, where, Rossi didn't know, Sicilia or some shit ...

Another agonising jab ripped through his shaft. Rossi sagged at the knees, slumping against the lobby door, streaking the glass bloody and screaming: 'Kaaaaaa-*ren*!'

RAY

Ray was so intent on watching the driver's side when the Crossfire's interior light went on that he missed the passenger getting out. He watched the Crossfire all the way to the security gates, getting ready to follow, when something about the way the passenger moved came to him.

Some kind of gesture, that was it, the way she waved into the Crossfire as she closed the door. Ray's gaze came back to the apartment block, watching as the passenger fiddled in her pockets, shadowed, standing directly beneath the porch light.

And then he stopped looking at the passenger, took a look at the apartment block instead. Thinking, no fucking *way* …

Watching the Crossfire roll up towards the roundabout, Ray cursed his sloppiness, how he hadn't recognised the apartment block straight off. Okay, so he'd had no reason to expect the ex-wife was heading for Karen's place, and he and Karen had always been coming from the other direction, out of town. Still, Ray knew he should have copped it earlier.

Knew too, the first sign of a guy on the slide is he starts believing his own excuses. But what the *fuck* was Karen doing with the ex-wife?

It was too much of a coincidence: Ray could smell it, a setup.

He got the Transit in gear, checked his mirrors, the Crossfire hitting the roundabout. Ray hoping the ex-wife's next port of call might clue him in as to what Karen might be planning. Then, rolling off, Ray jammed on, tyres squealing; reversed back to where he could see the apartment block and the hunched-over guy he'd caught in the rearview, now easing himself up the apartment-block steps.

Ray watched the guy fold in half, then slide down the lobby door.

He thought it through fast, the consequences of letting Karen know he'd been outside her place, prowling her, then went for his phone, shouldering out the Transit's door, dialling up as he sprinted across the road towards the security gates that were already closing, his view of the lobby door obscured by a stand of bamboo.

'Hello?'

'Karen?'

'Who's this, Ray?'

'Yeah. Don't answer the—'

Ray could hear a buzzing in the background, Karen saying: 'Hold on, Ray. I need to answer this.'

'Whoa! That's what I'm ringing—'

Clunk.

The buzzing stopped, Ray hearing a static hiss at Karen's end. Then: 'Put that away, Rossi. Don't *point* that fucking thing at me.'

Ray took the steps three at a time.

KAREN

'Shit, Rossi,' Karen'd been saying before the buzzer sounded again, 'that looks like it's going to need stitches. Maybe some metal pins to straighten it out. But you're definitely, I'd say, looking at tetanus shots. Two, minimum.'

Rossi moaning, Karen enjoying herself, Rossi exactly where she wanted him, helpless and in pain. So she wasn't impressed when her buzzer sounded again. She marched across to the intercom, wondering if she was going to strike it lucky two-for-two, find another guy at her door in pink pinstripes crying about his double-stitched dick.

Sitting back now in the rocking chair beside the artificial red-brick fireplace, sipping a tall vodka, Karen watched Rossi and Ray, the way they knew one another but didn't know how. She'd seen it before she didn't know how many times, two guys sniffing around waiting for the chance to piss up the other guy's leg. Except Rossi was more interested in gobbling Nervocaine, sucking hard on the joint Karen'd rolled for him, than staring Ray down. Ray, Karen could tell, wondering why Karen was entertaining the scumbag with his dick stuck in his zipper.

Not that it was any of Ray's business *who* Karen entertained.

'Rossi?' she said.'I'm calling you a cab. No way you're bleeding to death on my couch. I don't need the grief right now.'

'No hospitals,' Rossi gasped.'They'll only call the cops.'

'For a guy with his schlong stuck in his zip?'

'How come you were outside?' Ray wanted to know.

Asking, as it happened, the very question Karen wanted to ask Ray, Karen starting to wonder how come Ray'd just happened to be passing. He'd already told her, he lived way over on the other side of town.

'Karen,' Rossi pleaded, ignoring Ray, 'no kidding, I'll sleep on the floor. It doesn't have to be a bed or anything.'

'You think you're staying *here*?'

And, shit, there it was. The look. Rossi tilting his head, eyes wide, like a baby seal that just got clubbed.'Karen …'

'The lady said,' Ray cut in, 'she's calling you a cab.'

Ray sounding calm and reasonable, telling Rossi how it was going to be. Karen letting it go but wondering too where Ray got off calling the shots in Karen's home. Wondering how he'd feel if Karen wandered by *his* place late some night and started laying down the law, making his decisions for him.

'You don't want to take a cab,' Ray was saying, 'then fine, I'll drive you. How would that be?'

Rossi's face shrivelling up into a pinkish-looking walnut as he glared at Ray now with the look Karen'd seen too many times before. So she was glad, for Ray's sake, that Rossi couldn't make any quick moves, had his hand bandaged. When Rossi lashed out he hit like a snake, fast and dripping poison.

'Rossi,' she said, 'there's no way you're staying here. None. I'm calling a cab, I don't even mind paying for it, but either way you're leaving and never coming back. If you do, you won't have dick enough left to worry about it getting stuck in anything ever again. You hear that?'

A little dead-eyed now, the jay-Nervocaine combo starting to kick in, Rossi said: 'All's I want is the Ducati, Karen. The .44. The sixty grand, it's mine.'

There and then Karen decided Rossi could go whistle. Threatening rape, prowling Karen's apartment, packing a knife—the five years away hadn't done Rossi any good at all. The guy still fucking up.

'The bike I'm confiscating,' she said, 'along with the .44, for all the grief you've ever thrown my way. The sixty grand? That's Anna's, the going rate for losing an eye. How's that sound?'

Not good. Rossi looked to Karen like a deranged imp, the dead eyes suddenly thundery, flashing lightning. But even that one flash was enough to let Karen know she'd be moving on again, somewhere new where Rossi couldn't find her.

She rang a cab, thinking about the cottage out by the lake. Rossi'd never been too keen about what he called the not-so-fucking-great outdoors.

'Don't tell them he's going to hospital,' Ray whispered. 'The guy won't pick up if he thinks there's trouble.'

'Hi, yeah. Can I get a cab, please? To the city centre. Great, thanks. How long'll that be?'

Karen, giving her details, the address, felt a cold trickle in her stomach, a sensation she hadn't felt in nearly five years now. It meant, she knew, one thing: Rossi. The inevitability of him, how he'd track her down no matter where she went, how much trouble she took …

The things Karen was proudest about were how she'd nailed her father and tamed a Siberian wolf. Against that was the only thing she could never control, bring to heel—Rossi.

And what she hated most was the way Rossi made her feel she'd always be running.

RAY

What Ray couldn't figure out was how Karen was so calm, the scumbag in the Charlie Chaplin suit bleeding all over the room. Then, they get the guy into the cab and gone, they're back inside, she goes: 'How come you were outside?'

Ray thinking, shit, tough audience. 'I told you, I was just—'

'Yeah, right. "Out for a drive, just happened to be passing." That's about standard for some guy in a raincoat.'

'You think I'm a perv?'

'I'm not asking you to tell me what I think. I'm asking what you were thinking, hanging around outside my place when you're not supposed to be there.'

Rocking again in the chair beside the fireplace, a foot tapping fast on fresh air. Grim, like she'd dealt with this kind of crap once too often already. Holding the vodka like a prop, not sipping at it.

'Okay,' Ray said. 'I was out for a drive—'

Karen snorted.

'No kidding,' he said, 'I was out for a drive. It's something I do when I can't sleep. You see things, especially at weekends, they can be interesting.' No snort this time. 'So, I'm out, I thought I'd swing by this way, see if there were any lights on, maybe call in.'

'This even though I told you I didn't want to do anything tonight. And how'd you get my number, anyway?'

'In the laundromat,' he said sheepishly. 'When the woman rang your mobile? I could see her fingers when she dialled up.'

'So now you're peeping my number?'

'Yeah. Sorry about that.'

Karen brushed aside the apology. 'What'd you think, I'd have changed my mind by now? Spend a couple of hours away, I'd be mooning around thinking about Ray the sack-jockey?'

Ray thinking, shit, enough's enough.

'Hey, Karen—no offence meant, okay? I just thought I'd like to see you. And if that makes me some kind of pervert in your eyes, then maybe you might want to think about the kind of company you keep, makes you presume someone's a flake just because he thinks it'd be nice to call by, maybe surprise you.'

Laying it out there without mentioning the scumbag, Rossi in the pink chalk-stripes. But letting her know too that Ray didn't go calling on his lady friends with any hunting knives stuck in his belt. Hoping Karen'd take a good look at the difference between Rossi and Ray.

'Just so as you know, Ray. I don't like surprises.'

'Maybe that's the problem. Maybe you don't want to be surprised, find out every guy isn't like your father.'

Karen stopped rocking. Then she put the tall vodka down, got up and walked across to the couch. Ray was flinching even before it landed.

'Out.' Her palm was scarlet. 'Get the *fuck* out and don't come back. I swear, you even ring me again, I'll have you done for stalking.'

Ray drove for home, dabbing with a paper napkin at where Karen's ring had laid him open. Thinking, okay, it could have been worse; true or not, what he'd said had deserved worse.

He decided he'd give her a couple of days, time to cool off, then ring again to see if she was serious about the brush. Ray wasn't giving up that easy, not on someone like Karen, gets insulted and damn near breaks your jaw, draws blood. Ray, still bleeding from the narrow gash, had to admire the girl's panache.

Then there was the small matter of trying to figure out the hook-up between Karen and the ex-wife, the possibility that Terry Swipes was running a double cross, scheming with the shylock, the Balkan crew, looking to see Ray go down before he walked away from the life, maybe talked to someone he shouldn't be talking to ...

Soon as he got home, Ray rang Terry.

'Hey, Terry—what's with the surgeon? What's the twist?'

'Whaddya mean, twist? Why's there have to be a twist?'

'You tell me.'

Ray heard the clink-flick of a lighter, a short hacking cough. Then: 'All I know is, the guy's a surgeon, wants his wife snatched. Looks like there's some malpractice suit coming up, the guy needs to unfreeze some assets, let 'em leak away before the lawyers come calling. Why—you got a feeling about it?'

Ray in a bind. If Karen *was* in on the double cross, the last thing Ray wanted to do was tip Terry off that he'd tumbled. But if Karen was playing it straight then there was no double cross, which'd look bad for Ray, suspecting Terry. So all he said was: 'You ever hear of a doctor before wanting his wife snatched?'

'One time? This guy owns a circus came looking to have his mother kept on an island for a week. I mean, a fucking island. After that I stopped worrying about the whys.'

'Okay. But a plastic surgeon?'

'It's a funny one, Ray. I mean, the guy can't do any surgery anymore, but what he can do is minor stuff—skin jobs, Botox, that kind of crap.

Plus he can call himself a consultant, so the bigger jobs, he can refer them on, take some points off the top. But where the guy lives, with all he's got going on, I'm guessing he's finding it tight right now.'

'Where'll I find him?'

'You know St John's, the retirement home? Well, around the corner there's a street of Georgians, covered in ivy. The whole street's the same except with different coloured doors.'

'I know it.'

'He's number 24.'

'Where's home?'

'Place called The Paddocks. Up near Wood Grove, around the back of the lake. Actually has a putting green in the back garden with these dinky little flags. Why, what're you going to do?'

'Dunno. Drop by, maybe. Check the place out.'

'What'll that tell you?'

'Probably nothing. But Terry—I find anything that looks off, I'm taking a dive.'

'Yeah?'

'Yep.'

Ray waiting for it, Terry telling Ray he was paranoid, the pep talk that'd let Ray know Terry was offside.

But all Terry'd said was: 'Fuck it, we'll sting him for the good faith anyway. And Ray? If you find out the guy's trying something funny, I'll bung you a tenski. How's that?'

'Okay by me.'

SATURDAY

DOYLE

Doyle hated crowds, especially on her day off. So she got into town early, wearing new trainers and faded baby-blue jogging sweats, hair scraped back in a ponytail.

Leaving the chemist with a sackful of Clarins essentials, she suddenly remembered she was all out of legal pads back at the office—the memory jog happening, she'd later tell Sparks, mainly because she spotted the tall guy with the fringe walking into an office supplies outlet across the street.

She tossed it around, factored in the ponytail, the sweat pants, and thought, hey, no harm in taking a look.

She found him in the rear of the store checking out technical drawing pads, holding pages up to the light. Doyle sidled up. 'Hi, excuse me? Would you mind helping me find the legal pads?'

He turned, Doyle only now seeing the plaster strip under his eye.

'Sorry,' he said, 'I don't work here.'

'I know, yeah. What I'm asking is for you to come help me.'

He considered that, a slow grin starting, the eyes warming up. 'Yeah, okay,' he said, putting two pads back where he'd found them, tucking a third under his arm. They strolled up the aisle. 'You should probably know,' he said, 'I wouldn't know a legal pad if it puked on me. I'm Ray, by the way.'

'Stephanie. But most people call me Doyle.'

'So what are you, a lawyer? A brief?'

'Guess again.' Doyle picked up the five-pack of cheap legal pads from the usual rack. She had the eye going on with the guy behind the counter; Till Guy, she called him. He'd charge her low and ring it up high, hand Doyle her receipt with a wink. Doyle, who was it hurting, always winked back.

'You're never a cop,' Ray said.

'This is because, I'm presuming, you don't see so many gorgeous cops.'

'Absolutely,' Ray said, just as they arrived at the counter. 'Fact is, you're the best-looking cop I've ever met.'

Till Guy did a double take, from Doyle to Ray and back again. Doyle smiled sweetly as she handed over the legal pads and a twenty, saying: 'You have time for a quick coffee?'

Till Guy froze, swallowed hard, and glanced up from ringing in Doyle's purchase just in time to see Ray nod and say: 'You know anywhere we could get some Blue Mountain? That's some seriously fine coffee.'

Doyle checked her receipt while Ray paid for his pad, noting how Till Guy, the jealous prick, had billed her low even though she'd winked him a seductive one. She shrugged it off, figuring it was worth it; coffee with a guy who seemed good-natured, friendly, could handle a conversation. Worst-case scenario, it'd be a story for Sparks. Doyle tried to remember the last time she'd had any kind of date, or even just a good flirt, and hadn't managed to do so by the time Ray said: 'Ready?'

In the crowded coffee shop, sitting at a counter, awkward because the stools were close together and Ray had long legs, Doyle said: 'Your turn. What do you do?'

'You get right to the point, don't you?'

'It's a rare gift. So what do you do?'

Ray sipped on his mocha. 'Right now I'm a painter-decorator special-ising in murals. But I'm thinking of going back to college, getting into architecture.'

'Didn't someone once say architecture is manifest proof of Freud's theories?'

'What's that mean, towers are big dicks?'

'You can't see it?'

'What's worrying me are the homosexual connotations.'

'I can see how that could be an issue.'

'Oh yeah?'

'The fringe,' Doyle murmured, stirring her creamy chocolate.

'The fuck's wrong with my hair?'

'Nothing. That's the whole point.'

'This is what happens to every guy tells you you're the best-looking cop he's ever met?'

'See it my way. You been this close to many cops before?'

'Not many. And men, mainly.'

'I rest my case.'

'What's that, cop humour?'

'Yeah. Anyway,' Doyle said, her reserves of small-talk exhausted, 'how'd you fancy going for a drink sometime?'

Ray grinned. 'Straight to the point, right?'

'There's two possible options here, Ray,' Doyle said, still spooning her chocolate. 'One would be the act of a gentleman. The other'll get you parking tickets like you wouldn't believe.'

'A cop stalkeress,' Ray mused. 'You'd need to be unlucky.'

'You could nearly call it fate. So—yes or no?'

'You're serious?'

'Christ, Ray ...'

'Don't beg,' he said. 'Please. There's no dignity in that.'

KAREN

'Can you believe it?' Karen said. 'A fucking willy waver, hiding out in the bushes. The fucking creep.'

Madge, chewing toast on the other end of the line, said: 'Whadideday?'

'He *said* he was just driving by. Which is bullshit, he lives on the other side of town.'

'Maybe he wanted to see if you were still up, so he could parachute in,' a box of chocs under his arm. A little Friday night frolic. You can't blame a guy for trying.'

'Whose side are you on, Madge?'

'Yours hon, until you get some coffee inside you. I'm guessing the visit with Anna is off.'

Karen, who'd already found the box of Belgian truffles wedged behind a cushion on the couch, decided to skip the bit about how she'd warned Ray off, the calling-the-cops routine. Wincing now as she heard it again, Ray standing there with his cheek split, blood trickling. He hadn't looked angry, though; just disappointed. Like she'd spit in his face and hadn't quite missed.

'Last night,' Karen said, 'pulling out of your drive? You didn't happen to notice the guy sitting in the car across the street?'

'I barely noticed the street, Kar. Why? No, hold on—you think it was Ray. This because you're crazed on hormones. Am I right?'

Karen trying to spool the memory through her mind, freeze-frame the moment and see the face caught in the headlight flash. 'No,' she said, closing her eyes, a nervous tic Karen had when she lied to Madge on the phone.

'Bullshit, Karen. What you're trying to tell me, except you don't know it yet, is Ray did you a favour last night.'

'Did *me* a favour?' For a split second Karen wondered what Madge was talking about: she'd had Rossi all sewn up by the time Ray'd arrived, the guy in a state, his dick in a mincer. Then she realised, shit, she hadn't mentioned Rossi; never had, no point, there was nothing Madge could do about him. The guy was a force of nature, a plague of rats.

'Saving you a trip,' Madge said, 'out to see Anna this afternoon. Like, the guy's already gone, even before he sees Anna. How easy was that? And hey, try this—this time, *you* get to make the decision, show *him* the door. Jeez, Kar, counting them up, that's about four favours he did you.'

'Fuck you, Madge.'

'Karen, if you were the type that could, we wouldn't be having any conversations about anyone called Ray. But we are.'

'What am I, desperate? I have to take personal shit from a dope who paints cartoons?'

'All I'm saying is, if the guy rings, meet him. Slap him again if you want, get it all out of your system, and *then* ring me first thing in the morning to tell me you don't want to hear from him ever again.'

'What's that, some menopause wisdom shit?'

'Don't take it out on me, Kar. Either ring the guy or don't, do whatever you need to do. Call me later, tell me how it's going. And if it's going well, see if he'll do me a good price on a cheer-me-up paint job.'

'Will do. And Madge?'

'What?'

'About Anna? Me not wanting Ray to meet her? You're wrong.'

'Wouldn't be the first time. Bye.'

Karen blew a kiss down the line, hung up, poured herself a fresh mug of coffee; sat out on her tiny terrace, soaking up the warm morning and the faint scent of rhododendron. Wondering if Madge wasn't halfway right: Karen had been nicely stoned when she heard Rossi at the door, the guy bawling like a calf on acid. She'd been freaked, no doubt, and Ray had got the worst of it—no way she'd let Rossi know he'd spooked her, not that skinny prick.

So, yeah, she was feeling guilty about that, the way she'd taken it out on Ray. Then, finding the truffles after he'd left, that was the one that finally tipped her over the edge, started the weeping jag, her hormones dancing a reverse hornpipe ...

But even so, Ray right or wrong didn't have the right to say what he'd said. End of fucking sto—

She cramped and it was like someone yanked a rusty saw through her gut. The weakness left her light-headed, pukey, and she thought she'd faint. When it passed she made for the bathroom, the cabinet, then remembered, seeing again the last of the pills disappearing into the greedy maw of one Rossi fucking Callaghan, the half-wit who didn't know enough to tuck himself in before zipping up.

She skipped the leathers, just helmet and gloves, rode for town; taking it easy, a motorcycle being no place to start cramping at anything more than thirty kph. Thinking about how, okay, they were going different ways about it, but Madge and Ray were saying basically the same thing and for pretty much the same reason.

Not that Karen'd be telling Ray he had a good point, or anything like. If Ray called back, and called often enough, then maybe Karen'd let him apologise, see if she could work out if he really meant it. Then, afterwards …

Actually, Karen had no idea of what came afterwards. But she was going to find out pretty damn quick, turning now into the quiet street, the row of neat Georgians, seeing Ray standing there looking up at number 24, the one with the reddish-green ivy and yellow door, the shuttered windows of which were locked tight, Karen knew, because she'd closed them herself the evening before, leaving the surgery and heading for home.

ROSSI

Rossi woke up thinking, shit, the Germans are coming. A rumbling outside his lock-up like there was a tank on the towpath, a tank that was trying to eat itself.

He rolled over to see if he could peek through the gap beneath the lock-up's double doors and—*Christ*, the pain, like someone'd harpooned his dick and was dragging him up from two miles down.

Then came a pounding on the double doors. Rossi eased the sleeping bag off his legs and shuffled cautiously, one slow step at a time, to the doors.

'Shut that noise,' he bawled, 'or I *stab* some motherfucker.'

By the time they got him through A&E, stitched him up and pumped the tranks in, it'd already been getting bright outside. Now, after only three hours' sleep, he had a hangover like a blowtorch sizzling his brain.

The rumbling cut off, so Rossi pushed out the double doors. Big mistake. Sunlight lanced in, needles to gouge the back of his eyes. He stumbled back towards the rear of the lock-up, found a dark corner to huddle into, wondering, Christ, how come it's always *me*?

Sleeps strolled in, nodding appreciatively at the bare flagstones, the empty shelves, the rising damp on the rear wall.

'I like what you've done with the place. What they call minimalist.'

Always, Rossi thought, with the fucking education. Sleeps watched documentaries stoned and thought he was some kind of mastermind. Rossi wished he could spit. 'Whaddya want?' he snarled.

'You called me,' Sleeps pointed out. 'Last night? Wanting a bike, short term. So I brought a bike.'

Rossi remembered calling from the waiting room, hallucinating on a combination of pain and revenge fantasy.

'Fifty a day,' Sleeps went on. 'Any damage, you fuck up, leave a scratch, it comes out of your end.'

Rossi, if he hadn't had a dick like Frankenstein's neck, would've kicked Sleeps into the canal. Instead he gulped down three Nervocaine. 'What'd you get?' he said.

Sleeps walked back out into the sunlight, Rossi following, the sun warm on his shoulders and seeping through to his spine, Rossi starting to buzz. Then he saw the bike.

'A Chopper,' he said. A can-you-fucking-believe-it *Chopper*, leather strips dangling from the handlebars, orange flames up the side of the tank. 'What am I,' he demanded, 'a hippy? Born to be fucking wild or some shit?'

'It's fifty a day, Rossi. What'd you expect, a white limo?'

'I was expecting,' Rossi began, and then had to stop to think about what he'd been expecting. Yesterday he'd been expecting to be riding his Ducati, first time in five years. This before he got his dick mangled. Now the idea of throwing his leg over a kid's plastic tractor made him want to puke. Thinking, Christ, the leathers, folding up in his groin, catching his dick in the creases …

A wintry sweat broke out on his back. 'I'm riding no fucking Chopper,' he announced, 'and that's flat. I'll ride the *bus* before I ride any fucking Chopper.'

Sleeps shrugged, swung aboard the Chopper, kicked it to life. Rossi flinched at the roar, then waved his arms, gesturing to Sleeps, turn it *off*.

Sleeps cut the engine. 'What about you?' Rossi said.

'What about me?'

'What're you driving these days?'

'Sorry, Rossi, no can do. Last time around I got a suspended sentence, one of the conditions being that I don't drive for two years.'

'I'll make it two hundred. Two hundred a day.'

Sleeps considered. 'For how long?'

'Long as it takes. And when the job's done, you're in for two large. How's that?'

'Cash up front?'

'What'd you get, circumcised? You're gone all fucking kike?'

'It's a sellers' market, Rossi. You need the wheels. I can get 'em.'

'I'll make it five. Five big ones.'

'Can't do it, Rossi.'

Rossi couldn't catch a break, was getting screwed from all angles. So he played his ace, pouring it on about FARC, the ex-cons' co-op. Except, first he needed his sixty grand back. Sleeps was intrigued. 'I'll cut you in,' Rossi promised. 'Ground-floor rates. You can reinvest your three grand.'

'I thought you said five.'

'This is a whole different deal.'

'Make it five and we're on.'

Sleeps left, to return later with wheels. Rossi went back inside, turned on the blackened hot plate. He put some water on to boil—in a fucking *can*, for Chrissakes; at least they didn't brew up in any old baked-bean cans inside—and rolled a fat one, the job awkward with the bandage on his hand.

He wandered outside and sat on the edge of the canal, bare feet dangling in the cool water. Wiggling his toes, thinking about how he'd have to ask Sleeps, how come your feet always look so white underwater? Wondering too if they had canals in Sicily, Rossi liked canals. You could dump anything in a canal, a shopping trolley, an old car; who's going to stop you, it's only a fucking canal …

Except something was bothering him, an idea buzzing like a wasp at the window.

He drank the sickly sweet tomato-sauce coffee, comparing his lock-up to Karen's place, how it'd been warm, comfortable. That black leather was one sweet couch; Rossi could see himself stretching out there, getting his head down …

The idea found a gap, snuck in. Rossi, excited, listened to it buzz— about how, the last he'd heard, Karen'd been working till-jockey in a supermarket. And okay, Karen worked hard, didn't complain about long hours, had stamina—but who lives in a flash apartment on what a till-jockey makes?

He could *feel* it—fucking Sicilian instinct, it was—that Karen had something going on, was bringing home serious scoots. Rossi wondering, sucking on the jay, what were the chances, pretty fucking good he thought, that Karen's scam needed transport, like say-for-instance a flame-red Ducati that belonged to one Rossi Francis Assisi Callaghan.

Which meant Rossi, fair's fair, was due points.

RAY

Ray waited while Karen tugged the helmet off, shook out her hair. Looking fresh, just out of the shower, skin still glowing. Staring at Ray now like she was waiting for an apology, some explanation. Except Ray was the one who'd been slapped, bawled out, threatened with cops.

So he kept it cool, the way Karen was playing it, still straddling the dirt bike, the high mudguards a fetching pink. Ray'd never seen a motorcycle before had pink mudguards.

'Now you're following me?' she said.

'Whoa.' Ray did a mock double take. 'You're the one pulled up on *me*.'

'Enough, Ray,' she said quietly. 'What're you doing here?'

Ray fingered the plaster strip on his cheek. 'Thought I'd better get a tetanus shot, just to be on the safe side.'

'Sorry, we're not open Saturdays. And even if we were, we don't do tetanus shots.'

Ray, not kidding this time, did another double take. 'Yeah? This is where you work? For the doctor?'

'Frank the Skank, sure.'

Ray struggling to get a handle on things: Karen working for the guy who wants his ex-wife snatched, except the ex-wife's dropping Karen home late on Friday nights …

Now, watching Karen haul the dirt bike up onto its stand, not straining, just using this neat little technique she had, all wrist and forearm, Ray said: 'You mind if I ask you something?'

Karen, sullen, not even meeting his eye, said: 'What?'

And then she gasped, eyes blossoming wide; folded over, dropping to her knees, right there in the street.

FRANK

Frank popped a Nervocaine, a vitamin C tablet and an optimistic Viagra, washing them down with a strong Bloody Mary. Then he brushed his teeth, patted down his hair and went back to the bedroom, shed his bathrobe and spooned in behind Genevieve, grinding his nascent erection against the base of her spine.

'Gen?' he whispered. 'Hon? You awake?'

'Touch me again, Frank, I'll put on Simply Red. I mean, full fucking blast.'

She would too. Frank cursed his throbbing head, his vibrating erection and then Genevieve, who wasn't so much throbbing or vibrating as snoring gently—faking it, Frank was sure. He eased backwards out of the bed, bitterly disappointed. Christ, Saturday morning was his *time* …

Padding downstairs, another Bloody Mary on the agenda, Frank found himself wondering, and not for the first time, what the actual point of having Gen around might be. Okay, so her presence in the Members' Bar every Friday night meant no one was talking any triple bogeys or fourteen handicaps when Frank's name came up in conversation. But Frank'd worked it out, he could be getting laid *twice* a week, with *twins*, for what it was costing him to keep her around.

He sloshed some vodka into the glass, dumped tomato juice in on top, stirred viciously. Wondering if he shouldn't arrange to have Gen snatched instead of Margaret. At least that way he'd never have to hear Simply fucking Red again.

He sat in the breakfast nook, sunglasses on, bathrobe open, belly hanging down over his dampish silk boxer shorts, the erection bumping his tummy, frisky as a Labrador pup. It was another glorious day, Frank noted gloomily, another idyllic fucking autumn morning, sunbeams angling down through the blinds to sear his brainpan. He stared out at the manicured lawn he'd had mowed to putting-green standard while he sipped his Bloody Mary, wondering how come Madge got a pool in her back garden, a twenty-footer, when all Frank had was a stone birdbath. In all the years the bath had been out there, Frank had yet to see so much as a one-legged wasp fall in.

He fired up a cigar, hoping to hell Margaret was enjoying her pool, a beautiful morning like that, cabana boys cavorting on the decking, Margaret flashing her pierced belly button …

And then Frank realised, with an adrenaline rush, that there was every chance Margaret was under surveillance right now, this very second, the snatch guy scoping the place, checking Margaret out through his binoculars. Margaret still hauling around some nice tits that, okay, could do with some lift but weren't bad for a woman of fifty-one, had breast-fed twins. Frank could feel his jaw screwing down tight, his scrotum prickling; putting himself in the kidnapper's place, Margaret blindfolded and tied to a chair with no way of knowing it was Frank who was standing over her …

His erection began to hum painfully. He gulped down the last of the Bloody Mary and padded back upstairs and along the corridor to the bedroom, hoping Gen had kicked off the covers; she usually did when the mornings were warm. Slept naked, too, or wearing only a thong—Christ, yeah, now Frank remembered, she'd been wearing the little green number last night. And, *oh* yeah, there she lay, ass cocked at the ceiling, the scrap of green material disappearing between her buttocks just a tease.

He got himself set, leaning against the door frame, peeping between door and jamb; breathing faster now as he tugged his bathrobe open, the other hand already snaking across his flabby belly and down into the dampish silk boxers.

Hell, it was Saturday morning, his *time* …

KAREN

'And he lets you dip into the Nervocaine,' Ray said, 'like it's a cookie jar.'

'I don't know if *lets* is the right word,' Karen demurred. 'I mean, I take them. Frank just hasn't said anything about it yet.'

'And it's been going on how long now?'

'Pretty much since I got here. Couple of years, I'd say.'

'Ever think of going retail?'

'Nope. Don't shit where you live.'

Ray nodded. 'How's the cloth?' he said. 'Want me to soak it again?'

'That's okay. Seriously, I'm fine. It's happened before.'

Karen lying prone on Frank's over-stuffed couch of shiny green leather with dimples the size of saucers, Ray hunched forward on the chair he'd hauled out from behind Frank's desk.

The Big O

'And it's just the pain,' he said. 'Nothing else, y'know, more complicated.'

'No, Ray, it's just the pain. Just the cramps.' Karen working for sarcasm but losing it in the high, the pills washing through. Then she conceded, okay, she didn't have any monopolies on pain, not talking to a guy who'd had his arm broken as a kid, twice in a row. Or was it, shit, *three* times? She giggled.

'Hey, Ray? You think this is what they mean when they say a girl has the painters in?'

Ray nodding along, patient, like he'd heard it all before. Relaxing now, sitting back in the chair, the giggle convincing him Karen was fine. He didn't even protest when she removed the damp cloth from her forehead.

'Ray?'

'What?'

'Um, thanks.'

'No worries.'

'Usually I keep a bottle at home. But Rossi got the last of them last night.'

'Don't sweat it. I like it when women keel over in the street. Gives me the chance to act noble.'

Grabbing the opportunity, Karen'd noticed, with both hands. Like, literally—picking Karen off the pavement, hauling her up the steps, taking her keys and practically carrying her inside. Then getting her the pills, Karen directing him, and coming out of nowhere with a damp cloth, insisting she lie down. Christ, he'd have rubbed her tummy if she'd asked. Karen trying to remember the last time she'd felt that embarrassed—except Karen didn't do embarrassed.

Still, she conceded, it was all paying off now, the pain no more than a dull burn, an ache that was practically bliss.

'So what'd you want to know?' she said dreamily.

'Say again?'

'Outside on the street, you asked if you could ask me something. Just before I collapsed.'

'You remember that, huh?'

Karen didn't like his tone. Or maybe it was the way he was making her out to sound helpless, how she wouldn't even remember what they'd been talking about. Acting all superior, all manly and shit, with this smug grin.

Karen, coolly, heard herself say as much—sounding tinny, she thought, like she was talking from the room next door. Ray, grinning wider now, told her he was impressed at how women listen and remember stuff. How a guy, if he'd collapsed in the street, wouldn't be reminding anyone of the fact, bringing up questions they'd been asked just before, especially when there was a danger of something personal being proposed.

'Proposed?' Karen shook her head, taking a good five minutes or so to do it, her brain feeling a lot like fluffy cotton wool. 'It's a leap year, Ray. You don't *get* to propose.'

Ray jerked a thumb over his shoulder. 'Actually, I was wondering about the shutters. I don't suppose you know where Frank got 'em?'

Okay, Karen thought, so maybe I shouldn't have popped that third pill. And then, because she was about to die from mortification, Karen thought she'd fake a quick faint, have herself a little nap.

DOYLE

'It's not so much what he *says*,' Doyle told Sparks, sitting on the edge of Sparks' desk, dropping by the station with Danish and coffee, Christ, on her day off. 'It's what he doesn't say.'

'He doesn't say yes?'

'Last Wednesday night, in the bar? My birthday drinks? This is the night, of all nights, he meets someone.'

Sparks nodded sagely. 'And now he's getting his lumps, first time in ages, he doesn't want to fuck it up.'

'There's more to it than that.'

'She's pregnant already?'

'Apparently,' Doyle went on, 'she kicked him out last night. Busted him a good one too. I mean, cut him under the eye.'

'Go *girl*. So he's what, crying on your shoulder?'

'See, this is the thing. He's just telling me. Not looking for sympathy or maybe a quick blow job to pull him out of a hole.'

'He's telling you what, exactly?'

'That I'm not too sure about,' Doyle admitted. 'He said he'd been saying things to her he shouldn't, stuff he wouldn't usually tell anyone. This is the effect she's having on him.'

'So he doesn't tell you what he shouldn't be telling her.'

'Exactly.'

'Sounds like a marvellous conversation. How was the coffee?'

'The coffee was fine, thanks. *We* were fine, y'know? I mean, I'm sitting there thinking, this I could handle on a regular basis.'

'Except he's talking about someone who's just chucked him out.'

'Nobody's perfect, Sparks.'

'Girl,' Sparks bridled indignantly, 'have you *looked* at me lately?' She mulled the situation over. 'Here, what if the reason she kicked him out was he's crap in bed?'

'Nah. You'd give him a week at least. He might be the nervous type.'

'But he's not saying why she kicked him out.'

'All he said was, he behaved inappropriately.'

'He actually said that. Inappropriately.'

'Said it was all his fault. Said she was right, at the time, to show him the door.'

'Now I *know* you're shitting me.'

'He did say,' Doyle clarified, 'that he thought she maybe overreacted a little. That it wasn't as inappropriate as she made it out to be.'

'That sounds more like it.' Sparks nodded at her PC on the desk. 'You check him out yet?'

'Haven't had the chance. Want to?'

They huddled around the PC. Sparks, being the junior, did the hard slog. Forty minutes later they had nothing.

'Not even a birth cert,' Sparks said.

'So what have we tried?' Doyle said.

'Raymond, Raphael, Ralph, Ray and Reynaldo. And Rainier, naturally, in case he's an illegitimate prince from Monaco. You're sure his second name is Brogan?'

'That's what he said.'

'Which means he's lying or he's gone to a lot of trouble to get himself invisible. No driving licence, no social security number …' Sparks tapped at a tooth with the end of a pencil. 'Either way, he could be the straw that breaks society's back, starts riots in the streets. I mean, it's your duty as an officer of the law to get the guy legal.'

'It's a dirty job,' Doyle sighed.

RAY

'So that's Anna,' Ray said.

'Want to guess what she is?' Karen said.

'Guessing, I'd say some kind of wolf.'

'Husky-wolf cross—mostly wolf. Born to hunt. To kill.'

'Is she ever let out of the cage?'

'It's a high-security kennel, Ray. And of course she gets out, she's exercised twice a day. Otherwise she'd crack up.'

'What's she on, a seal a day?'

Karen with her face against the reinforced wire mesh, the wolf rubbing its nose against Karen's, its tongue lolling.

'She likes to eat alright,' Karen said. She winked at Ray. 'In the wild, she ate whatever she liked.'

'Reared wild, huh?'

Ray liked the warm smell of fresh straw and pretty much nothing else about the setup. The hound had a skull that was bigger than Ray's, the snout alone a foot long. Ray could see it, Anna roaming the steppes, bringing down mammoths as the mood took.

Plus, whenever she stopped snuffling around Karen, looked away towards Ray, he got the distinct impression the monster was laying on a baleful eye, this amber glare. To Ray's way of thinking, the growl going on low down in its throat was showing off.

'Hear that?' Karen giggled, still a little high from the Nervocaine rush. 'I always think I'm hearing a Harley when she does that. So what d'you think—should we let her out?'

'Fuck no.'

'C'mon, Ray. You'll have to meet her sooner or later. I walk her two, three times a week.'

Karen slid the bolt back, pushed in the wire-mesh gate. The wolf backed off, nipped around the gate and lunged across the walkway to plant a Yeti-sized paw either side of Ray's ears. Ray staggered back and fetched up pinned against an empty kennel, afraid to breathe, the wolf doing enough for both of them, huffing and puffing sour gales in Ray's face, upper lip curled back in a snarl, fangs the size of Ray's thumbs.

Karen patted the monster on the back of the head, tugged its ears. 'Anna,' she said, 'meet Ray. Ray, Anna.' Then: 'So what do you think?'

Ray, hoping Karen was speaking to him, said: 'I like the eye patch.'

'Really?'

'Absolutely. It's rakish.'

'Isn't it though? So Ray, last night—what were you doing outside my place?'

Ray knew as well as any man that when a woman gives you a gold-plated opportunity to come clean, that's the one time you need to lie like a priest in a convent dorm.

'I was just passing, Karen. What I told you.'

'How about Larkhill Mews? How come you were there?'

Ray gagged on Anna's sour breath. 'I did some work up there last month,' he said. 'I've been back a few times to collect but the fuckers'd pass gallstones quicker. But I wasn't up there last night, if that's what you're asking.'

'Why would I be asking about last night?'

'Last night's what we're talking about. Why I showed up at your place.'

'Swear?'

'Swear.'

While Karen thought that over, Ray squeezed his luck. 'So what's the deal with Larkhill Mews—someone saw me up there?'

Karen tapped Anna on the back of her head. 'Down, Anna. *Good girl.*'

The wolf dropped to all fours, its muzzle six inches from Ray's groin, the bushy tail whipping against Karen's leg.

'Don't flatter yourself,' Karen said. 'It was someone you priced a job for, she recommended you to Madge. So Madge was wondering if she'd seen you around.'

Ray held his breath, thinking, *You cannot be serious ...*

'Oh yeah?'

'Yeah. Madge thinks she might have her place redecorated for a cheer-me-up. She wants to know if you can you drop by, give her a quote.'

MADGE

Madge left the Crossfire running and strolled up into the high-hedged driveway, grinning when she saw Bryan in the khaki Bermudas, the Moses sandals, whistling off-key as he hosed down the Merc.

'Well *hello*, big boy,' she said breathlessly.

The way the water went spraying off in all directions, Madge couldn't be sure if Bryan had actually wet himself or not. He definitely had the look, furtive and guilty, as he twisted the nozzle to shut off the flow, glancing back at the house as he advanced towards Madge.

'Jesus, Madge—what're you *doing* here?'

Madge stepped back out of range, nudged the hose to one side. 'You're dripping, Bry. Didn't your mother ever teach you to shake?'

Bryan tossed the hose away in a flower bed, where it continued to dribble. 'What's up—what's *wrong*, for Chrissakes?'

'I'm pregnant, Bry. Isn't that nice? You're going to be a daddy. I'll bet you thought you'd never get the chance again so late in life.'

As it happened, Bryan wasn't that much older than Madge. But looking at him now, in the Bermudas, the white hairs on his shins, his shoulders hunched, Madge realised Bryan *was* old. He'd been born old, born to worry about money and only money, because everything else—class, position, prestige—could be bought, sold, rented or leased, Bryan didn't care how he got them so long as he wasn't the one looking in from the outside, slavering. A sad, miserable, pointless …

'But you *can't* be pregnant,' he said in a furious whisper. 'You're on the *pill*.'

'Did I tell you that? Really?' Madge tapped her pursed lips with a forefinger. 'I'm taking pills alright, vitamin supplements, Prozac … But *the* pill? No, I don't think I ever said that.'

Bryan ran a hand through his coiffed hair, revealing grey roots. 'But Madge, you're—'

'Too old? But Bry, don't you remember telling me I could easily pass for forty-five, y'know, depending on the light … Oh, *hi* Fee.' Madge waved past Bryan at Fiona. 'Sorry I'm late hon, but the traffic's murder.'

Fiona teetered down the driveway on the kind of heels that'd give Madge a nosebleed, maybe even vertigo. Wearing, Jesus, some kind of three-quarter slacks in bright pink, Madge didn't know what they were calling them nowadays but they used to be pedal-pushers back in the day.

Fiona brushed by Bryan, leaned in to air-kiss Madge. 'Don't worry about it, babes, I'm running late myself.' Then brayed a coarse peal of laughter that shattered the avenue's quiet. Behind her, despite his more pressing concerns, Bryan shuddered.

'That's okay, hon.' Madge glanced at Bryan. 'It's a lady's prerogative to be a little late sometimes. Isn't that right, Bry?'

Bryan nodded, swallowing hard. Fiona pecked a quick hard kiss on his cheek, putting Madge in mind of robins in winter.

'Don't forget, babes, dinner's at seven. It's Italian, Alfredo's, so pick out a dark shirt. Oh, and after lunch? Madge and I are off shopping, I need to pick up a few things.'

Bryan nodded again, caught between glum and distraught as he tried to digest all the bad news at once. Madge, leaving, waggled her fingers flirtatiously. 'Good to see you again, Bry. Don't be a stranger.'

Fiona lit a cigarette as the Crossfire pulled off. 'So how's Bryan keeping these days?' Madge said.

'Fine, I think. Why?'

'No reason.'

'Yeah well, he's fine … Listen, though,' Fiona said, half-turning in the passenger seat, wedging herself into the corner, 'never mind about Bryan. Did you hear about *Doug*?'

'Ugh? No. What's he done now?'

Madge keeping an eye on her mirrors, unable to guarantee herself a straight face if she looked at Fiona, the girl wearing a tight blouse patterned with what looked to Madge like orangey-green parrots and open to where Madge and anyone else who cared to look could see the little bow on Fiona's pink bra.

'Oh God, Madge,' Fiona said. 'Doug's in ICU.'

'Intensive *care*? But that's terrible, Fee. What happened?'

Fiona sucked hard on her cigarette. 'Frank happened.'

'Frank?'

Madge thinking, Christ, she really should get back out to Oakwood for the Friday night cabaret that was the infidelity waltz. The last time she'd been there Fiona had confessed, in the ladies', how she'd slept with Frank before the separation became official. 'I'm so sorry, Fee,' Madge'd said. 'After all these years, you finally get him into the sack and he goes and falls asleep.'

'No,' Fiona'd said, frowning, pink-faced from double gins. 'I mean, when I say slept, I mean—'

'Oh, it was *you* who fell asleep. Is that it?'

At which point Fiona—overcome by the moment and the effort of explaining to Madge how her ex-husband had finally availed himself of the most available comfort known to the male members of Oakwood—Fiona had slid down the wall and passed out on the damp tiles. Madge had told a waitress and gone home, swearing never to return to Oakwood again.

Fiona, sucking hard on her cigarette, said: 'D'you think he meant it?'

'Meant what?'

'Belting Doug with the golf ball like that. D'you think he might be, y'know, jealous?'

'Frank hit Doug with a *golf* ball?'

'Knocked him out. Audra says Doug's jaw is broken, said they might have to sue. But now they're talking brain damage, Doug isn't responding, and they don't know if … if …'

Madge, thinking how Frank couldn't hit his own knee with his pee if he was aiming for it, said: 'Fiona, hon—this isn't your fault.'

'It's *not* my fault. You *know* that.'

'You can't help it, Fee. *Men* can't help it, what you make them do.'

'But Madge—if something happens to Doug, if he doesn't recover …' She sniffled hard. 'It could be manslaughter, Madge. I mean, if they can prove Frank did it on purpose, that he knew about me and Doug, they could put him in prison for *years*. I can't have that on my conscience, Madge.'

Madge made soothing noises while Fiona dabbed at her eyes with some tissues Madge found in the glove compartment. Madge wondering, idly, waiting for the traffic to start moving again, where it was, Bali or Australia, or maybe somewhere mid-Pacific, that tantalising point on the globe that was farthest away from where she was sitting right now.

KAREN

How Karen met Madge was, she was working on the till in a super-market downtown.

'So the assistant manager, Bob, he asks me out.'

'Impeccable taste,' Ray murmured.

'Absolutely. So I say no, thanks all the same. I didn't like the idea of us working together, the guy's my boss, he can tell me what to do.'

'I can see how that wouldn't work,' Ray whispered.

Anna stirred any time Ray spoke in his normal voice, looking up from where she lay sprawled on the grass, her huge head on Karen's shins. Watchful even when Ray so much as turned his head. So Ray kept his voice low and stared straight ahead out over the valley at the picnic area on the bank of the river below.

'I wouldn't mind,' Karen said, tugging on Anna's ear, 'but he wasn't bad-looking. Anyway, the next thing I know is I'm a super bitch, I'm frigid, I'm a cock tease. I can't keep up. Half the time I'm asking, "Hey Bob, what am I today, a lesbian feminist or some shit?"'

'Can I sympathise in sign language?'

'I wouldn't. You start waving your hands around ...' Karen pat-ted Anna, who whined and raised her head so Karen could scratch her throat. 'Anyway, this graffiti shows up on the washroom wall, the women's, I should point out—"Karen King, Blowjob Queen". Which gets me thinking, I could earn as much off three blow jobs a day as I'm making behind the till, taking all this crap from Bob. I mean, in theory. So I'm back at the till and there's this rich bitch giving me grief, wants me to bag her stuff while it's going through, in case she breaks a nail or some shit. I tell her, "Sorry, it's against regulations, in case we miss an item." Trying to be reasonable, like. So she goes, "I'd like to see your supervisor, miss." I say, "That's him over there, he's called Bob. Feel free to call him over, I can't remember if I'm supposed to be a slut or a total cunt today."'

'Classy,' Ray observed.

'So Bob arrives over and by now the rich bitch is having a stroke, she's propped up on her shopping trolley, hasn't heard the like of it in all her born days. Bob wades in, starts fanning her, all this crap. Says he's giving me an official warning. Doesn't even wait to hear my side of the story.'

'Probably just as well.'

'Not the point. Anyway, I get out from behind the till and say, "Hey, Bob—you know what?" He says, "Wha—" and there it is, I've busted his nose.'

'Busted?'

'I kind of jumped in the air, it's what they teach you in class, so you're coming down punching on top of the nose. It's like hitting a tomato.'

'Nice class. Needlework?'

'So I'm sacked. This is even before the general manager comes running. I know it, there's no way I'm keeping the job. Which I'm happy about. Meanwhile Bob's on his knees pumping blood, Rich Bitch is on the mend, learning to breathe again. A crowd gathering around. I go, "Bob, you're a turd molester." I say, "You're the most God-awful excuse for a sick monkey that ever fell out of a tree and I've taken just about all the shit I'm ever going to take from you, them and every other fucking bastard on the planet. But I'm starting with you. If you're not out of my way when I start walking, I swear I'll bite your fucking throat out."'

'You really should be in politics.'

'The whole place is dead. I mean, for a supermarket, it's tumbleweed time. Everyone looking at Bob, Rich Bitch, then me. So this woman pushes forward, with her hand up? I say, "Yeah, what?" She says, "Can you type?"'

'And this is Madge.'

'She wanted to know where I'd learned the jump-in-the-air thing. Drove me home, told me about Frank, she wanted someone to keep an eye on him in the office, Frank the philanderer. This is back when Madge gave a shit. Saying how I'd be right up Frank's street with me being the, y'know ...'

'Blowjob Queen?'

'The boobs, Ray. Frank likes 'em perky.'

'So now, instead of whaling on Bob, you torture Frank.'

'Frank tortures himself. It's not my fault I'm curvy.'

'God bless random genetics.' Ray forgot himself, rolled closer for a quick squeeze and got a head butt for his troubles, Anna capable of little else while wearing the muzzle. Ray'd seen smaller masks on ice hockey goalies.

When his vision cleared again he said: 'What d'you say we dump the sabre-toothed tiger and go somewhere quieter?'

Karen scratched Anna under the chin. 'Okay by me.'

ROSSI

'Christ up a lollipop, now she's *petting* it.' Rossi poking his head out of the Volkswagen's window to train the binoculars up the side of the valley. 'Last thing you want with a hound like that,' he fumed, 'is to soften it up. I don't mind telling you, first time I saw it, I damn near shit myself.'

A sailor choking the beast down the gangplank, the chain as thick as Rossi's arm. The hound dragging the sailor all over, a leather belt around its snout, growling like it was about to explode. The sailor didn't speak much English, talking in this voice that sounded to Rossi like he was all the time hawking a spit, but Rossi got the message—the hound's *evil*.

'How much did he want?' Sleeps said, taking the binoculars.

'Five hundred. I threw down a ton. So the sailor chains the hound to a container, tells me to wait. This is three in the fucking morning, I'm hoping the Russians take better care of their choke chains than they do their ships, the rusty pieces-a-crap.'

The monster straining at the choke chain, amber eyes blazing and fixed on Rossi.

'So the sailor comes back with this other guy, this one sounds like he's coughing up coal. He says his piece. I put down four hundred there and then.'

'It's more than evil?'

'It's a four-legged Panzer,' Rossi said, 'that doesn't mind the cold.'

'She's tugging your Panzer's ears now,' Sleeps reported. 'Scratching its throat.'

'*Fuck*.'

The Russian reckoned Stalin had been about a year old, year and a half, when it got caught in a bear trap, the trap breaking its right hind leg. The hunter laid it out with a rifle butt between the ears, the hunter with a connection in St Petersburg who was always looking for guard dogs for the gangsters, something exotic. Trouble was, after two years, three different owners, using whips, chains, iron bars and cattle prods, no one had broken Stalin.

'The way the sailor told it,' Rossi said, taking the binoculars back, 'the hound became a game, one gangster passing it on to another, a gift of respect. Except every time someone passed Stalin on, they sat back and pissed themselves laughing, thinking about how the new guy'd have to feed the beast half a cow every day, maybe lose an arm in the process.'

Rossi watching Stalin fawn on Karen, the three of them walking down the hill now towards Pheasant Valley. Rossi wishing the hound'd make a dive for the weirdo with the voodoo stare, wondering what Karen was doing hanging out with some asshole with a *quiff*, for Chrissakes.

Wondering too how the staff at Pheasant Valley might treat Stalin if they knew she was a man killer, twice over according to the Russian, ripping out these guys' throats who thought she was out for the count, beaten down.

One thing about the hound Rossi liked was, it never complained. You could whale on the fucker for hours, use a chain, whatever came handy, and all the fucker'd give you was the juju yellow eye, daring you to come in close, just once, meet it halfway.

The only time Rossi'd ever seen it cry was the night he popped the eye, digging the fork deep into the socket and levering back—that night she'd howled like a pneumatic drill, baying pure hate. Which, to Rossi, represented progress. Except now Rossi had to deal with all this crap: Karen adopting the hound, just because she was the one who renewed its licence. Then, getting an eye patch so you couldn't see the ragged pink hole when the whole *point* with a monster like Stalin was you didn't want to think about what a wolf with a ripped-out eye might do to *you* ...

He watched Karen and the Elvis guy, Ray she'd called him, coming out of Pheasant Valley; crossing the car park now, heading for the beat-up Transit. He watched them pull off, then said, enjoying it: 'Follow that van.'

Braced himself for the takeoff and then realised, shit, Sleeps was on the nod, slumped down in the driver's seat, head against the window, snoring. Shaking his head in despair, Rossi spotted the needle on the dimpled mat between Sleeps' feet. He swore aloud, shook Sleeps' shoulder, pinched him under the ear, then punched the side of his head. No joy.

Rossi sat back and rolled a fat one. Thinking, this is my fucking luck, I get the only junkie wheelman who shoots up on the job ...

FRANK

Frank was sweating hard, hunched over the barbecue on the patio that'd been designed as a sun-trap. All day he'd been dreading Doug's call. The nasal tone, the gloating, the snide humour—first the jibes about Frank's golf, Doug asking if Frank had a licence for the sand wedge, how it could be a lethal weapon in the wrong hands.

Then, the pleasantries out of the way, Doug'd start in with the horse-shit: the hospital bills, the trauma, how he might never play golf again, was feeling agoraphobic just thinking about it. Then the dental work, Doug's jaw needing rewiring, a whole raft of restructuring and realignment ... *Jeeeeeesus.*

Frank jumped back from the grill, the steaks spitting molten fat. He rubbed his forearm as he reached in with the fork to turn the steaks, their undersides smouldering, blood still bubbling topside.

'Gen? Gen hon?' Frank cupped his mouth, aimed for the kitchen. 'Gen!'

She appeared at the window. Frank made a drinking motion, as if he were holding a bottle of beer. Gen nodded, then made precisely the same gesture, except she waggled her tongue in her cheek. Frank swore and turned back to the grill, poking desultorily at the steaks and wincing as globs of fat flew.

The *real* problem, Frank knew, wasn't that Doug was going to ring; it was that Doug hadn't yet made the call. That meant he was genuinely out of commission, flat-out fucked in ICU, or was keeping his powder dry, holed up with some shyster buddy putting together a dynamite civil action case against Oakwood that would, at the very least, see Frank's membership ripped up and thrown out.

Except, if Frank was Doug, he'd be bunkered in with Bryan right now plotting a civil action against Oakwood *and* how best to pursue Doug for damages. Frank couldn't even ring the hospital, for Chrissakes; making the call was as good as admitting liability, signing on the dotted line. And Frank was afraid to call Bryan, in case Bryan was Doug's shyster lawyer of choice.

So Frank paced and sweated and worried until the steaks were charred beyond recovery, then went inside and rang for pizza. Then, hoping against hope, he rang the hospital.

'I'm sorry,' the receptionist intoned, 'but I'm not at liberty to disclose that information.'

'But I'm *family*,' Frank said. 'His *brother*.'

'And this is why you can't tell me your name.'

'I'm, ah, the black sheep. There was a falling out.'

'In that case, I suggest you contact another family member and fall back in.'

'Is he that bad?'

'Like I said, I can't say.'

Frank swore and slammed down the phone, already tugging his wallet free, trying to remember the guy's name. Tony, he thought, dialling the number, peering at the scrap of paper. No, Tommy. Tucker? Tommy Tucker?

The phone brr-brr'd. Sweat coursed down Frank's back, leaving his skin cold and clammy. Feeling nauseous now, the sensation he got in his nightmares when he realised he'd taken one step too close to the edge of the cliff and was already pitching forward, spiralling away down into a black void.

Terry? *Terry* …

Brr-click. 'Yeah?'

'Terry? Terry, it's me, Frank.'

'Fuck.'

KAREN

They'd had Chinese and tidied away the cartons, washed up and opened a cold bottle of white when it finally arrived, just before the movie came on, *Taxi Driver*, Karen a De Niro fan even though Rossi liked him too.

She came back in from the bathroom saying: 'Ray? Listen, no offence, but if you're thinking of staying over you should know those painters have finally turned up.'

Karen explaining how she wasn't squeamish as such, she just couldn't help feeling unsexy, tired and drained, a little bloated. So she was relieved when Ray said those three little words she'd been hoping to hear, 'Okay by me,' Ray shrugging it off like he was surprised she thought it'd be a big deal, scooching over on the couch to make room for Karen to cuddle up.

Now, the movie over and sprawled on the couch, lying back on Ray, Karen couldn't help but notice that no matter where she looked there was some of him, the guy wide as well as tall. Tom Waits on the stereo,

Closing Time, Karen blissed on pills and white wine and a drag or two on Ray's joint. She said: 'I should probably tell you about my father.'

'That's okay. You already told me.'

'Don't patronise me, Ray. I mean, after he got out.'

'Oh.'

'By now he's got religion. "Oldest one in the Good Book," he says. I mean, the guy's telling jokes. This excuse for a crippled frog, he's killed my mother, and now he's cracking wise.'

'Karen, you don't need to—'

But Karen felt she did. She'd brought her father in, sat him down in a comfortable armchair, then went to the kitchen and came back with a steak knife.

He didn't panic. He just told her that she'd be as bad as him if she tried it, and he didn't want that because he'd repented and repenting means acknowledging the sin, its enormity, the consequences. He knew in his heart that no matter what the priests said he was doomed to burn; his wickedness was beyond God's salvation, may God forgive him for saying it. All he craved was Karen's forgiveness, and for what he'd done to Karen, not her mother, because that mercy wasn't Karen's to give. Not that being forgiven would save him, but at least his daughter's pardon would be a pure, cool drop in an eternity of pain.

'And that's all you want,' Karen'd said.

'I know,' he'd said. 'It's a lot to ask.'

'Not at all. You can have it.' Karen seeing the light in his eyes, the hope rising. 'The day Mum touches my face again,' she said, 'you'll have it.' Then slashed him across the eyes with the steak-knife ...

'Christ,' Ray said. 'You blinded him?'

'He ducked,' Karen said. 'I split him across the forehead instead. But what I was thinking after was, I should've allowed him to stay over and let him fall asleep.'

'I was hoping you'd have brought him to see Anna.'

'And what—poison her?'

'Fair point.' He kissed the back of her hand. 'Listen, when I asked the other night if you'd forked anyone else—'

'It was a steak knife, Ray.'

'See, that's what I'm wondering. Do I need to go through *every* kitchen utensil, ruling them out one by one?'

Karen smiled, then grew serious again. 'Ray, what you have to appreciate is—'

'No, I don't. I don't have to understand anything.'

Karen tingled. 'That's cute, Ray. It really is, and I hear what you're trying to say. But you couldn't understand anyway, even if you wanted to.'

'Why's that—I'm not a woman? I don't have feminine intuition or some shit?'

Karen took a deep breath, let it out slow. 'You're not an orphan, Ray. Y'know? You can go home any time you want, see your mother and father. You've got brothers, sisters … Want to know how many Christmas cards I got last year? Two. One from Madge, the other from Frank, and I only got that one because I'm the one types up his mail-shot.'

'Except,' Ray said, nodding along, 'I don't go home that often.'

'But that's your *choice*. It's a whole different thing when it's your choice.'

'Maybe. Anyway, there's no brothers or sisters.'

'I thought you said—'

'I was adopted, Karen. And Ma and Pa Brogan—they're nice people, don't get me wrong. But they didn't adopt until after they'd tried everything else, which meant they were pushing fifty by the time I was ten. It was like having grandparents, not parents. Not that it was their fault, I'm not blaming anyone. But still, it was fucked up. And maybe I don't understand it all, not the way you'd like me to. But I've accepted it.'

'So why'd you lie? About having brothers and sisters?'

Ray reached his smokes off the coffee table, lit two and handed one to Karen. He exhaled, saying: 'Same reason you got the eye patch for Anna.'

'How is that the same thing?'

'Think about it. You might be surprised.'

'I already told you, I don't like surprises. Although,' she went on, 'that was cute last night, with the truffles. How'd you know I like Belgian chocolate?'

'I thought everyone,' Ray said slowly, 'likes Belgian chocolate.'

'They're still in the fridge. Want some?' Karen stood up and drank off the last of her wine. 'I need to get some more plonk anyway. Want a beer?'

'Sure. And Karen?' Karen paused in the doorway, something different in his voice; Ray looking anxious, perturbed. 'While we're being honest and all, there's something you should probably know.'

'About what?'

'Madge.'

MADGE

Stooooooooned. Like, totally fried, seeing double and laughing at her reflection, saying to the hall mirror: 'You talkin' to me?'

Catching her reflection on the way to the kitchen, Madge with a bad case of the munchies, riffing now off the guy from the movie she'd watched on TV, some basket case with a mohawk waving guns around and talking to his mirror. 'I don't see anyone else here,' she said sternly, then giggled.

'You think that's funny?' Mirror-Madge said, sounding a little prissy to Madge. 'I mean, is that supposed to be funny?'

'Yep,' Madge said, and dissolved into another fit of giggles.

'See,' Mirror-Madge said, 'it *might* be funny. Y'know? If there was anyone else here, there's every chance it'd be funny. But there's no one else here.'

Madge, straightening out, giggles subsiding, said: 'I don't get you.'

'For something to be funny, it needs an audience. Like a tree falling in a forest. If there's no one around to hear the punch line, how can we know it's funny?'

'*I'm* laughing,' Madge said, even though she wasn't, was feeling suddenly ratty, paranoid.

'You're stoned. Stoned and alone. On a Saturday night.'

'So what? I can't sit in on a Saturday night? There's a law against that?'

'No law,' Mirror-Madge conceded. 'No actual *law*. But a crime doesn't have to break any laws to be wrong.'

'I'm a criminal? For not going out on a Saturday fucking night?'

'Let me put it this way. Audra, yeah? She's sitting in the hospital right now talking to a vegetable. But at least if she wants to she can reach out and squeeze a hand that has a pulse.'

'There's a point to all this?'

'Try this. How do you feel—honestly, now—about Jeanie and Liz going off to college?'

Madge considered. 'Like someone broke into the aquarium and freed the sharks.'

'That's all? You don't envy them just a little bit?'

'Maybe. A little.'

'Okay, now we're talking. What about Karen?'

'Sure, I'm jealous. Is that what you want to hear? She's keeping company tonight, so I'm jealous.'

'Bullshit. You're not jealous of Karen at all, are you? I mean, even if she's lucky and the guy comes good, she's facing thirty years of heartbreak and grief. Am I right? What if Ray turns out like Frank, the way they always do, chasing everything in a skirt, Christ, everything except men in kilts. And then there's that baby you gave away, the one with the weird name. What'd you call him?'

Madge, feeling it all bubble up hot as lava, said: 'You're one dead-hearted bitch, Madge Dolan.'

Mirror-Madge nodded, pleased. 'At last, we're getting somewhere. Now—what about Frank?'

'Frank? Why should I give a shit about Frank?'

'You mightn't,' Mirror-Madge said. 'But there's thirty years that do. I mean, those thirty years, they're hanging around in time-limbo, purgatory, because they were wasted. Lived empty. Y'know? Shot through with Valium, Prozac, you name it, Frank prescribed it. You should hear those thirty years scream, Madge.'

'I want Frank to die.'

'Yeah, but enough about you. What're we going to do about Frank?'

ROSSI

'Narcolepsy,' Rossi said.

'Can happen any time,' Sleeps confirmed, 'anywhere. You don't even have to be tired.'

'Tired? You're *asleep* half the fucking day.'

'It's not *proper* sleep. Mostly it's like you're sleepwalking.' Sleeps thought about that. 'You never wondered where I got the name?'

'I got better things to do,' Rossi growled, 'than give a shit about where people got their fucking names.'

The Volks parked up in the shadow of a big oak fifty yards back from the wrought-iron gates, giving Rossi a good view of the apartment block. Karen's window to the front, a light on behind the lowered shades.

'What I used to do,' Sleeps said, 'this is when I'm still getting gigs as a wheelman, I'd boot up on crystal meth. Be *wide* awake, for days, shit, it was hard fucking going. You can die, y'know? From not getting your forty winks.'

'You don't mind me asking,' Rossi said, 'with all the nodding off and all, how you thought of wheelman for a career? I'm only asking.'

'When I was at school? They kicked me out. Sent me off on this training scheme, forklifts. How to reverse with the load up, all this shit.

The first day, the guy running the scheme gets everyone to try and lift a pallet, these sacks of cement on it. We're all pulling on a corner of the pallet, pretending we're trying to lift. The guy says, "See that? The world will always need forklifts."'

'And?'

'I'm *trained*, man. It's what they trained me for. Driving.'

'Forklifts,' Rossi said, shifting his weight from one buttock to the other, grunting even before he felt the stabbing in his shaft. He took a hit off the jay and held it down. 'So when'd they move you up to, y'know, the getaway mopeds?'

'Hey—I took one nap, okay? A few zeds. Always happens after I've had a jab. And you told me, no sweat, you know where she lives. So what's the problem?'

'The problem,' Rossi began, then shook his head. Christ, where to start? Rossi depending on some zombie fucking forklift jockey, a diabetic to boot, to keep him close to Karen, the Ducati. Rossi had his eye on the underground car park with the sliding gates; the Ducati was in there, he could nearly smell it.

First, though, Rossi'd be needing to root through Karen's apartment, see if he couldn't stumble across the sixty grand, *his* sixty grand. Plus, the .44—Rossi, it was a matter of principle, of ethics, wasn't giving up on the Mag.

'By the way, Rossi? This con you're running? The advice centre?'

'FARC, yeah.'

'That's just it. There's something you should know.'

'What's that?' Rossi said, opening the door to take his second piss in an hour, Rossi paranoid about letting pressure build up on his stitched shaft.

'There's already a FARC.'

'You're kidding. Who the fuck're FARC?'

'Colombians. Leftist rebels, they're into coke, all this.'

'Fuck.' Rossi thought fast. 'What d'you think, will they want points?'

Thinking, shit, that was the pope and the Colombians already, all he needed now was the Revenue taking a bite out of his ass.

'Unlikely. But there's every chance they'll, y'know, blow you sky-high for taking the piss.'

'They'd blow up a charity?'

'These boys are hardcore, Rossi. I mean, they're jungle fighting the CIA, mortaring whole fucking towns, assassinating nuns and shit. You think they'd draw the line at a charity?'

'I wouldn't. I mean, if I had their firepower.' Rossi handed the joint across. 'Duck-ass this one and you're walking home. And get thinking about a new name.'

He went behind the Volks and got down on his knees before unzipping; the first time he'd tried to piss standing up, the pain had been so bad he'd *fallen* down, letting go all over the trousers, the pink pinstripes glowing up red. This time there wasn't much more than a dribble. He got back to his feet, zipped up, went around to the passenger door, eased in slow.

'We'll give it another hour,' he said. 'If they're not out by then, they won't be coming.'

And got a little snore in return, Sleeps with his chin on his chest. Rossi swore and plucked the joint from Sleeps' fingers, fired it up. Then saw the flashing blue light pulling in behind the Volks that could mean only one thing.

FRANK

Frank dumped more bourbon in his glass, splashed in some ginger ale, staggered across to the stereo. Trying to remember who he was listening to. Puccini, it sounded like. Or maybe Mozart. Earlier on, he recalled, he'd had a hankering for *Die Fledermaus*.

But, no, it was definitely Italian—shit, was it Verdi? He squinted down at the title on the record, the LP revolving on the turntable, Frank getting dizzy, vision blurring, shit, the whole *room* was spinning now …

He staggered, bumping up against the stereo, scratching the vinyl. The needle wound up in the middle of the record making a wuhf-wuhf noise that sounded none too operatic to Frank. By then, though, he had other things to worry about, bouncing as he was off the stereo cabinet onto the desk and jabbing the phone with a wayward elbow before ricocheting away again to stumble on the edge of the carpet and sit down, hard, jarring his spine.

Frank sat there awhile listening to the wuhf-wuhf, trying to remember when he'd decided to sit down, and why he might have wanted to sit on the ground when there were so many plush armchairs dotted around his study. Although, the way the armchairs seemed to be shimmying, Frank reckoned he was probably safer on the floor.

He noted that the heavy jolt hadn't cost him a drop of the ginger-bourbon, then drank it off fast in case he wasn't so lucky the next time. He burped loudly, tasting stale cigarettes, bourbon and cheap pizza, then heard a voice, faint and tinny: 'Who's this?'

Frank looked up and around, expecting to see Gen, but he was alone in the study. 'Hello?' he ventured.

'Who the fuck *is* this?'

Frank, who vaguely remembered the story of Samuel from the Bible, Samuel hearing the voice of God, scratched divine intervention off his list of possible sources for the intrusion. 'It's me,' he said tentatively. 'Frank.'

'Oh *Christ*,' said the tinny voice, Frank hearing it from somewhere above his right ear. He untangled himself and made a desperate lunge for the edge of the desk, grabbing the receiver that lay on the blotting pad, then slumped back onto the carpet, horizontal, saying: 'Terry? Did he ring?'

'I already told you. He rings when he rings.'

'So why're you calling?' Frank said, bewildered.

'*You* rang *me*. Despite express fucking warnings to the contrary. So this better be good, Frank.'

Frank realised he must have hit the redial button when he elbowed the phone. But, accident or not, and now the opportunity was there …

'Terry, I just want to clarify somethi—'

'We've been through this already, Frank. What'd I say?'

'You'll have me killed?'

'Christ no. Why do that and be out twenty grand good faith? Okay, yeah, we might call around and break your knees, I'm not saying we won't. Then again, we might not. As long as you're making vig every month, why would we want to put you out of business?'

'Vig?'

Terry sighed. 'I hear what you're saying, Frank. You're not, if this thing fucks up, entirely responsible. So what I'll do is, worst case scenario, I'll split the vig. All I'll call in is two. But don't go spreading that around. Word gets out I'm doing two for twenty, it'll be Black Friday all over again.'

'Two?'

'Two grand, Frank. Per month, every month. Whenever you want to pay off the capital, the twenty grand, come talk to us and we'll see what we can work out. Okay? Now—ring this number again, I'll personally come around and feed your balls to the guppies.'

'But I don't *have* guppies.'

'I'll bring the guppies, Frank.'

Click-brrrrrrrrrr …

DOYLE

'You're leaving? But it's only twelve-thirty.'

'I could do with an early night,' Doyle said.

'Couldn't we all,' Sparks said, smacking her lips. 'Plus you're pining for cuddly Ray.'

'I never said he was cuddly.'

'Saturday night, they're all cuddly.'

'Like any of those,' Doyle said, pointing across the bar at the group of guys clustered around the juke. Sparks checked them out: four of them, wearing stripey shirts and Chinos, clutching bottles of import beer.

'Student doctors,' she said, 'don't qualify.'

'Except, inside the club? That's what you're looking at. Guys who still want their toast soldiers cut without the crusts.'

'Harsh,' Sparks observed, 'but probably more than fair.'

'Anyway, I'm working tomorrow. You don't mind if I scoot off?'

'Of course I mind.' Sparks nodding across at the rest of the crew on the other side of the table, their heads together, hair being flicked, the girls copping the eye from the interns at the juke. 'This lot wouldn't score on a fucking oil rig. Plus, I've seen better dancers in bouncy castles.'

'I'll make it up to you,' Doyle promised. 'Next weekend, we'll rip it up.'

'Unless by then you've tracked Ray down and blackmailed him into pushing your knees up around your ears.'

'I'm disappointed to hear,' Doyle said, standing up, 'that you think it'd take blackmail.'

'Bring a gun,' Sparks called after her. 'Just to be on the safe side.'

Making for the cab-rank at the top of the street, Doyle heard the guy coming, one of the stripey-shirt brigade, she'd caught his reflection in the closing door as he followed her out. The guy calling: 'Hey? Yeah you, the gorgeous one.'

So she stopped and turned to face him. He sauntered up with a wide cheesy grin, about to make Doyle's night with an offer she couldn't refuse. 'I was just wondering—'

'Don't.'

His smile barely wobbled. 'But you don't even know what—'

'Whatever it is, it'll be some bullshit designed to get your rocks off. Am I right?'

'Jesus, I was only—'

'Only five-six, I'd say. Sorry, stud. I like 'em tall.'

The guy squaring his shoulders now, puffing out his chest.

The Big O

'Don't sweat it,' Doyle said. 'Napoleon was a midget too.'

The smile long gone by now. 'Sorry,' he said, harshly. 'Looks like I made a mistake.' He turned to go, then turned back. Doyle tensed. But all he said was: 'Good manners cost nothing.'

'*What* did you say?'

'I said, good manners cost nothing.'

Doyle fumbled in her bag, flashed her badge. 'I'm a cop,' she said.

'I don't care if you're Dirty Harriet,' the guy said defiantly. 'Manners are manners.'

Doyle, on the verge of karate-chopping the guy to the shoulder, grinding his face into the concrete, heard herself say: 'Yeah, maybe you have a point there at that.'

Then took his number, saying she'd ring in a few days, she had a job she needed to finish up first. 'That's cool,' the guy said, Doyle impressed by the way he wasn't fazed she was a cop.

'A word of advice,' she said. 'You want to chat a girl up, do it when she's in the mood. If she's already left, she's probably not in the mood anymore.'

'I hear you,' he said, sauntering off, hands in pockets.

Doyle got in a cab thinking, okay, he's no Ray, but maybe things are looking up. Then realised, the guy being five-six, five-seven at a stretch, he'd be looking up too, at Doyle. So she crumpled the number, tossed it out the window.

ROSSI

One cop stood on the pavement, the peaked hat pushed back on his forehead, hands on his hips. The other one rapped his knuckles on the driver's window. Rossi leaned across Sleeps and wound down the window, wincing at the burn in his groin.

'Whaddya want *now?*'

The cop, leaning in, wrinkled his nose. 'Sir, you're parked on a double yellow line.'

Rossi sucked on the cigarette he'd lit to cover the smell of herb. 'It's Saturday fucking night and you're handing out *parking* tickets?'

'The law never sleeps, sir.'

The other cop got a bang out of that one.

'Yeah, well,' Rossi said, 'that's your problem right there.' He jerked a thumb at Sleeps. 'This guy's got, he calls it, narcolepsy. Fell asleep ten minutes ago. So we pulled in.'

'You pulled in *after* he fell asleep? Sir, driving a vehicle under the influence of sleep is considered undue care.'

The other cop damn near slapped his thigh.

'He got tired,' Rossi explained, 'said he needed a few zeds. So he pulled in. *Then* he fell asleep.'

The cop staring Rossi down. 'Okay,' he conceded, 'I'm not smelling any alcohol. But I'm getting something. You want to tell me what that might be?'

'It might be him,' Rossi said. 'I mean, the guy ate three chilli cheese-dogs, a double curry-chip, earlier on.' The cop grimaced. 'But it might be, too, my condition you're getting.'

'Condition?'

'Manic depression.' Rossi tried to recall some of the phrases he'd learned inside, greasing up the shrink for some early release. 'Severe mood swings,' he hazarded.

'You can *smell* mood swings?'

The other cop gurgled.

'I mean, the treatment, the doc prescribed it, is a marijuana cigarette.' Rossi pronouncing it marry-jew-anna. 'Taken in moderation.'

'I see. And this doctor of yours, you can tell me where I can find him.'

'Sure. He's in Paris.'

'Paris.'

'He's a specialist. I mean, for depression. And, I think, toxic shock.'

'Sir, would you mind stepping out of the car?'

The cop raised his head, made a smoking gesture to the guy on the pavement. Rossi shook his head in despair, how fucking cruel is life; dropped his cigarette into the ashtray and got out slow, assumed the position against the car.

Then, it was Rossi's luck, the security gates across the way rattled back and the Transit swung out, turning up towards the roundabout so Rossi couldn't see who was in the cab. He said to the cop, the chortler patting him down: 'Seriously—I'm just out, three fucking days. You think I'd be stupid enough to be carrying something?'

'Yep.'

The cop ran a practiced hand up the inside of Rossi's left leg, then all the way down the right, skipping, Rossi was relieved, his groin. Rossi watching the first cop coming back from the squad car, the guy throwing this casual swagger.

'Tell me again, sir, how come you just happened to be sitting here.'

'The guy felt tired. Ask him. He's the fucker was driving, not me.'

'Less of the foul language,' the chortler told Rossi. 'I won't remind you again.'

'Okay,' the first cop said, 'if Rip Van Winkle here ever wakes up, we'll ask him how come he got tired around this spot in particular. Also, we'll want to know where he was about one-thirty this afternoon.'

Rossi winced, knowing what was coming.

'When,' the cop continued, 'this car was stolen.'

Rossi nodded. 'Hold up,' he said, bending down and leaning into the car, fishing the still-smouldering cigarette from the ashtray. He popped it into Sleeps' ear, then ducked back out of the car again, nodded at the cop. 'Okay,' he said. 'Go on.'

RAY

'Know who'd get a bang out of this?' Ray said. 'Anna. Am I right?'

Karen nodded. 'That's the general idea, yeah.'

Ray looked back across the clearing from the wooden jetty. 'Place like this, you'd think it'd be going cheap. I mean, the state of it.'

'It's the lake you're paying for, the view.' The lake limned with moonlight. 'And it's not just the cottage. There's three acres goes with it.'

'I know. But still, I don't know.'

Ray working hard to keep it all together. He'd expected Karen to blow her top, sitting her down on the couch to tell her about Madge, first making sure he was between Karen and the cutlery drawer; waiting for her to erupt, throw slaps, left-handed side-kicks, the works—except Karen'd listened in silence, glowering, arms folded.

When she was sure he was finished she'd said, in an even, dead tone: 'Three times, Ray. I asked you, be honest, three times in a row, and you lied straight to my fucking face.' Then, the killer: 'Of all people, you should know how three-in-a-row feels.'

So Ray'd skipped the last confession, the bit about the Belgian truffles, figuring it'd keep for another day. The twist in Karen's jaw giving her face a sinister cast while she chewed on her lower lip. Then she stood up, saying: 'Okay, come on. Get your coat.'

Bringing him way out into the sticks, up around the lake, Ray wondering if she wasn't planning to stick him and dump the body where it'd never be found. Ray, when he first caught a glimpse of the cottage on the shore, did a double take—no doubt about it, it was the place he'd seen in Terry's portfolio, Ray starting to wonder again if Karen and Terry weren't somehow hooked up.

Except it was Karen who brought it up, how she'd been to see an estate agent, a guy called Terry. How he'd quoted her three-fifty for the cottage and three acres, finance to go with it …

Ray shivering, a chilly breeze chopping up the lake. He flipped away his cigarette and walked in off the jetty, up the incline towards Karen.

'Talk me through it,' she said.

'What's to say?'

'The snatch. How does it work?'

Ray gave it to her in broad strokes. Karen said: 'And what happens if the ransom isn't paid, it goes missing?'

'It's never happened. Most people, the kind we snatch, they're at the high end of the scale. Insured against everything, icebergs falling on the yachts, the full nine yards. Why wouldn't they pay? It's not even their money.'

'But just say it happens. What then?'

'You're worried, I can appreciate, because it's Madge. But the thing is, Frank wants Madge snatched. So it's going to happen. The guy's made up his mind. But if you know it's me that's holding Madge, then you know nothing's going to happen her.'

'All due respect, Ray, but what the fuck do I know about you? I mean, we only met three days ago.'

'Five if you want to be technical about it.'

'Technical? Ray, three fucking times I asked what you were doing outside my place last night. Yeah? And you fed me this horseshit about how you were just passing. Now it's because you were stalking Madge, and you want to get *technical*?'

'Karen—'

'You lied to me, Ray. Straight to my face you lied, three fucking times. Although, I can understand why. I mean, what's a good way to tell someone you're kidnapping their best friend?'

'You knew what I did, Karen. I told you straight off, first night we met. Now because it's Madge you're getting moral?'

'Fuck moral! This is *Madge* we're talking about.'

'I hear you. But you're presuming something'll go wrong, that Madge'll be exposed to some kind of threat.' He shook his head emphatically. 'We've pulled a lot of these jobs, Karen. Never once has there been a problem.'

'Except this time there's already a problem.'

'You can't stop it, Karen. And even if you could, if you tell Madge, what does that achieve? Frank arranges to have the twins snatched instead, by someone you don't know. How would that be any better?'

'Even Frank wouldn't sink that low.'

'With half a million on the line?'

Karen considered. 'Actually,' she said dolefully, 'Frank'd sell tickets to an abortion if he thought he'd get away with it.'

Ray nodding along. 'So you see where that leaves us. Look, Karen, you're telling me you want this place for Anna, right?'

'Mostly, yeah.'

'And you'll be a long time knocking over bookies before you put together three-fifty.'

'So?'

Ray took a deep breath, plunged on. 'So I say we do it, snatch Madge, then take our cut and—'

'*Our* cut?'

'You're in it, Karen. Whether you like it or not, you're in it now and it's bigger than you or me. Or Madge.'

Karen closed her eyes and swore softly. 'Go on.'

'I know this guy, he runs finance. You put up the basics, he'll punt you the difference. He won't screw you on points either.'

'You know him that well.'

'He's a businessman, he won't do me any favours. But yeah, he'll be okay.'

'And you're arranging all this out of the goodness of your heart.'

'Hey,' Ray said, stung by the acid tone. 'You want this place or not?'

'Not,' Karen said quietly.

'Because,' Ray said, nodding again, 'it's blood money, earned from snatching Madge. But what you have to realise is—'

'Because,' Karen said, 'Rossi'll find it, track me down, and then it starts all over again.'

'Fuck Rossi.'

'I got a better plan.'

'There *is* no other plan, Karen. It happens this way or—'

'First tell me,' she said, 'when it's happening.'

'If Frank stumps up the good faith and doesn't change his mind, then it happens Tuesday.'

'Good faith?'

'Twenty grand. So we know he's not a messer.'

'He's a messer. How long will it take once you have her?'

'That all depends on Frank. If he has everything sorted and the insurance claim goes through fast, then a couple of days.'

'And once Frank pays up, Madge goes home safe.'

'Absolutely.'

'So who gets the money?'

'Frank, mostly.'

'Mostly?'

'We take our cut. Maybe, depending on circumstance, a little extra. What's he going to do, ring the cops?'

'What's to stop you taking it all?'

'Frank's big mouth and five-to-ten inside. Maybe a shiv in the ribs because my guy had to take some heat from the cops.'

'Okay. But what if Frank manages to lose the cash, I mean before he pays you off—your guy can't blame you for that, can he?'

'Karen—'

'And like you say, Frank can hardly go crying to the cops.'

'No,' Ray said slowly, 'I don't suppose he can.'

'How d'you think your guy would react to that?'

'How do think Madge would?'

'Pretty fucking badly at first,' Karen conceded. 'But stinging Frank for half a million? I think she'd see the lighter side of it in the end.'

'Long as he gets his points,' Ray said, 'my guy's rinky-dink.'

'Which leaves us,' Karen said, 'splitting about four hundred grand. I mean, me, you and Madge.'

'If, for example, Frank fucks up and loses the ransom.'

'Our problem,' Karen said grimly, 'will be getting to Frank *before* he fucks up and loses the ransom.'

DOYLE

'So you just let him go,' Doyle said.

'The other guy,' Moran insisted, 'kept falling asleep.'

Doyle consulted the arrest record.

'Says here they were booked at two-thirty in the morning. Why wouldn't he fall asleep?'

'Let's just say it wasn't your normal kind of sleep.' Moran round-shouldered, forty-plus with a salt-and-pepper crew-cut going thin at the sides. Dull-eyed now, on his way home after the graveyard shift. 'He'd wake up, fall asleep. Then wake up again.'

'And then—let me guess—he'd fall asleep again.'

'Right. Bobo in the clown suit said the guy was narcoleptic *and* diabetic, could start having fits. Said claustrophobia, being in a cell, brings it on. Says he goes, and I quote, spastic he don't get his fuckin' zeds.' Moran shrugged. 'No way's any fucker clocking off on my watch.'

Doyle's buzz long since punctured. She'd been up early, feeling bright and zesty, the intern's come-on—clumsy though it was—giving her the impression something new was on the horizon.

Then, on her way through to her office, checking the night's arrests at the front desk, she'd spotted the name of one Rossi Callaghan. Doyle getting excited, it wasn't often a collar just dropped into her lap like that. Except Moran had signed Callaghan out, along with his narcoleptic buddy, forty-five minutes before Doyle got in.

'Okay,' she said. 'You're letting the spastic go. That much I understand, he's more trouble than he's worth. But what about Callaghan?'

'It was the spastic stole the car,' Moran said patiently. 'Callaghan was just an accessory after the fact.'

'Says here,' Doyle going back to the arrest record, 'there was enough grass in the trunk to stun a hippo.'

'He says it must have already been there when the car was stolen. Or it was planted.'

Doyle raised one eyebrow. Moran shrugged.

'You didn't think to check him out?' Doyle said. 'I mean, the guy's only wanted for attempted rape.' Although, Doyle had her doubts about that, a gut feeling telling her Marsha was working for sympathy by creating a diversion after getting caught screwing her sister's fiancé. 'Not only that,' she went on, 'he gets himself nabbed prowling the domicile of an ex he's been stalking since he got out.'

'How the fuck would we know that?'

'Like I say, you could've had him checked out.'

'In the middle of a stampede. How long's it been,' Moran wanted to know, 'since you worked the Saturday night desk?'

'Couple of years,' Doyle admitted. 'But even then, way back in the Dark Ages, we had computers where you could type in a name, see if anything snagged.'

'What I do is book 'em in. That's what they pay me for. What they *don't* pay me for is standing around all morning taking grief from detectives who need other people to do their jobs for them.' He looked at his watch. 'Now, if it's okay by you, I have a wife and three kids back home. Who're *entitled* to give me grief.'

Doyle watched Moran's back as he walked away. The weekend day-shift desk jockey, a red-cheeked rookie busy typing, looked up and said: 'That spastic? Says here he has six outstanding parking tickets.'

'Whoop-de-fucking-doo,' Doyle said.

KAREN

Karen rolled over, nudged Ray. 'You awake yet?'

'Nope.'

'Pity. Can you eat breakfast while you're asleep?'

'Sure.'

'Scrambled eggs okay? Some toast?'

'Sounds good.' Ray opened one eye, felt for Karen's thigh under the covers and squeezed it. 'Want me to make the coffee?'

'What'd I tell you, Ray? Stop trying so hard.'

'Okay by me,' he said, snuggling down under the duvet again.

Making a guy breakfast in bed wasn't really Karen's thing but she'd woken up feeling, what ... oppressed, that was it. Sensing him, his warmth and bulk even though he was curled up way over on the other side of the bed, Karen telling him going to bed how she felt hot and prickly in her moods. Ray taking up a space that, okay, Karen didn't actually need right there and then but might, hey, it was a girl's prerogative to roll around in her bed on a Sunday morning ...

But even as the resentment grew Karen had to acknowledge she was being self-destructive, freaking about Ray screwing with her space, going out of her way to make things difficult, digging up potential problems so she'd have a little something to trip over if things got complicated. She cracked some eggs into a bowl, flicked the kettle on to boil, laughing at herself—Christ, she was into a kidnap caper, snatching her best friend, and was worried things might *get* complicated?

It wasn't Ray's physical presence, she knew: it was more what his being there meant, how Karen was into something she couldn't control, map out all the way. Ray she couldn't trust, not now. Whisking the eggs, Karen knew she had to accept that fact, make it her bottom line: for all Ray had to worry about—doing time if the snatch went wrong, maybe taking a shiv in the ribs like he said—Karen had other concerns.

She felt guilty about Madge, for sure—although the deal depended, Karen had insisted, on Madge saying yes; otherwise no dice—but Karen knew Madge, or Ray for that matter, didn't have someone depending on them the way Karen did. No one else would get turfed out on the street and starve, or get a bullet in the back of the head, if Karen let them down. Anna, though—she needed Karen, needed Karen at the top of her game, and Karen at the top of her game meant not trusting Ray another inch. Hey, she said as the guilties came eating at her again, he'd had his chance. *Three* fucking chances ...

Karen had taken him out to the lake with a little speech in mind, to show him why she'd go through with the snatch; not because she wanted the cottage, not anymore, not with Rossi on the prowl, but because she wanted something *like* the cottage—a place for her and Anna, somewhere safe where they wouldn't be hassled and poked up the ass by a world that couldn't get enough of that poking.

Ray, if he'd baulked, Karen'd been ready to tell him she'd blow the whistle, turn him in. Not because she wanted to do it—not because she'd *do* it, end of story—but because she wanted him to know how big it was for her, how much it mattered. That she was prepared to stitch him up to make it happen.

Karen shivering now, even in the warm kitchen, trying to imagine half a million in cash ... And then caught herself, still mulling it over, halfway to the kitchen door on her way back to the bedroom to ask Ray if he liked Tabasco in his eggs. She decided there and then that Ray liked Tabasco in his eggs or he got used to the taste; Karen was too old to go changing her eggs now. You start by leaving out the hot sauce and next thing you know you've become your mother, or Madge, fifty-one years old and trying to remember, *Shit, didn't I used to put something tasty in my eggs once, just to give them a kick?*

She popped some bread in the toaster, nibbling on a sneaky Belgian truffle; thinking, okay, it had to happen sooner or later, if not with Ray then with someone else—the tipping point, the breaker. It was inevitable, with the stickups, that the law of averages had to kick in: some day, somewhere, someone'd call her bluff, even after she'd waved the .44 around, racked the slide. She drew the line when it came to pulling any triggers; had tried to picture it, standing there braced with both hands on the butt, squeezing one off into someone's face ...

No. Not that there'd be much point squeezing any triggers: Karen'd never even loaded the .44. The first thing she'd done after lifting it from Rossi's lock-up was dump the ammo in the canal. Armed robbery was one thing; anything more was a world of pain. Karen's plan, if some guy thought he was a hero, made a grab for the gun, was to break the bastard's nose, lash him in the face with the barrel, then call it a day. Get gone. Put the guy down, drop the .44, walk away. Karen wasn't too clued up on forensics but she was pretty sure fingerprints didn't have a best-before date, and Karen hadn't touched the gun without wearing surgical gloves since she'd pinched it from the lock-up. The one good thing about Rossi being back on the streets was, if Karen did have to drop the gun, Rossi's prints were all over it. Christ, there was a time when the prick couldn't *stop* playing with it, Roy fucking Rogers, twirling it and dry-firing it, all this shit.

Except, she knew, it wouldn't happen as easily as that. It *hadn't* happened like that. When Ray came up out of the freezer into her peripheral vision, Karen had turned and dry-fired without thinking, right in his face.

Maybe, she pondered, just maybe, the fact that it had been Ray was an omen of sorts.

She put three scoops of coffee into the pot, a little perk-me-up, Karen still groggy from the pills and the wine. Arranged the tray, trying to picture Ray twirling a gun; hearing him again, his voice low and growly, looking her straight in the eye: *I don't have to understand anything …*

Karen smiled, thinking, yeah, maybe you could do things with a guy who thought that way. Especially if you were coming from a place where you didn't have to trust him.

But when she pushed through into the bedroom, nudging the door open with the tray, Ray was gone. Leaving a note: *Things to do. Catch you later. x Ray.*

An *x?* After all they'd been through last night, all she got was a fucking *x?*

FRANK

'You're a persistent little bugger,' Terry said grudgingly. 'I'll give you that.'

'He still hasn't called?'

'It's Sunday morning, Frank. Even Koreans don't do business on Sunday fucking morning.'

'But you're saying, he'll definitely call.'

'Definitely, yeah. But not until Tuesday. On Tuesday he'll be up with the larks, ringing me. Why would I lie to you on this?'

A building site went off in Frank's head, the stress causing the hangover to finally kick in. He plucked the deck of smokes from his desk, lit a fresh one from the old despite the shake in his hands, resumed pacing.

'I just want you to know, Terry, that I've said it. In case anything goes wrong. There's no point in—'

'Why would anything go wrong?'

'Just let me say it. So there's no confusion after.'

'It's clear as a bell to me right now, Frank. So anything you might say would only start messing things around. And I hate it when things get messy.'

Frank sucked on his front teeth, then quit when he felt something wobble, the loose crown. 'Can I at least ask a question?'

'That depends.'

'Depends on what?'

'On what the question is.'

'But how will you know what the question is,' Frank said carefully, the building site dancing a rumba in his head, 'until I ask it?'

'Sorry, Frank. I don't do philosophy Sunday mornings.'

'But say something does go wrong,' Frank said hurriedly. 'No, *wait*— say he goes ahead with the snatch and for some reason the ransom isn't immediately available.'

'He waits, Frank.' An edge to Terry's voice like a saw before it begins to buzz. 'He's good at waiting.'

'Okay.' Frank swallowed, downed his bourbon before he went on.

'Now say the ransom is likely to never become immediately available.'

'He goes on waiting.'

'That's it? He keeps on waiting?'

'What *he* does isn't your problem, Frank. It's what *you'll* be doing should worry you. Anyway, what'd I tell you already?'

'That we'd only cross that bridge,' he mumbled, 'if we burned it down.'

'So, there it is. Frank—when he rings Tuesday morning, I'll get him to double-check with you everything's kosher. What're you worried about?'

Terry hung up. Frank dumped another bourbon in his glass and began pacing again. What was he *worried* about? Christ, down twenty grand already, and looking at two grand a month interest for the fore-seeable future or kneecaps like, Terry'd said, punctured fucking gerbils. Then, with Doug sticking his fat face in the way of Frank's Slazenger, Frank had no one on the inside at Trust Direct to sign off on the insurance forms. This on top of Doug getting ready to sue.

His hand shook uncontrollably, splashing bourbon up his wrist. Even in the depths of his misery Frank diagnosed the symptoms: the excess of adrenaline, the fight-or-flight reflex; time for Frank to stand up and be counted or slope away fast.

He waits, Frank. He's good at waiting …

Mopping up the bourbon with a tissue, Frank crossed the study to the French windows, went out onto the patio.

'Gen? Uh, Gen?'

Prone on the lounger, from behind saucer-sized shades, Genevieve said: 'What?'

Frank advanced towards the lounger trying to gauge her mood. 'Say we were to go on holiday,' he said. 'Where would you most like to go?'

'Acapulco.'

That one caught Frank broadside. 'Acapulco? How come?'

'Palm trees. Tequila. Banditos. Trumpets.' She made a lazy V-for-victory sign. 'Viva.'

'Acapulco it is, then.'

She sat up fast, one hand holding up her bikini top, the other above her saucer-sized shades. 'Really?'

'Yep.'

'No shit. Acafuckingpulco. When?'

'Tuesday. But listen, Gen, there's something else. Before we go?'

'To Acapulco. On Tuesday.'

'First class. But Gen, what I need to ask is—Are you listening? Gen? How much do you want to go to Acapulco?'

But Gen, dancing topless around the patio in what looked to Frank like a Hawaiian rain-dance, was too busy squawking 'La Cucaracha'.

ROSSI

'You could do with a maid,' Rossi noted. 'Driving,' he added, 'a bulldozer.'

The place a crummy one-room littered with sandwich wrappers, pizza boxes, empty beer cans, foil cartons. A damp patch on the back wall, behind the fold-down couch, that looked to Rossi like a map of the oceans. A carpet made of damp socks.

'A maid?' Sleeps lifted his head from where he lay sprawled on the couch, squinting at Rossi to see if he was serious. 'On disability cheques?'

"Course,' Rossi said. 'You're on disability for the narcolepsy.'

Sleeps shook his head. 'They call it a lack of motivation. It's a clinical ailment now. I'm certified.'

'So they pay you,' Rossi said, shifting gingerly in the busted deck chair, 'to stay home and get stoned.'

'Pretty much.'

'Sweet.' Rossi passed the joint across, took a slug of Sleeps' home brew. 'Good wine, too. What is it, raspberries or some shit?'

'Elderberries. But yeah, it's a good year.' Sleeps deep-sixed the joint, held it down. 'So what's the plan now? I mean, we can't go prowling Karen's place again, right?'

Rossi scowled. 'See those fucking cops? Time they had me spread on the car, I look down—there isn't even any yellow fucking lines. You see what I'm saying?'

'Harassment.'

'Perxactly.'

Rossi bitter, worn down after a night in the cells staying awake to nudge Sleeps every time he nodded off. Rossi still couldn't believe the cops had fallen for it. Except here they were, back at Sleeps' dump, watching *Little House on the Prairie* on the black-and-white portable.

'Fight fire with fire,' Sleeps advised.

''Cept we don't have any—'

Sleeps dug under a cushion, felt around, pulled out a .22. Rossi hunched forward. Shit, it even looked real; nickel-plated, a pearl handle. 'Where the fuck did you get *that*?'

'Right now,' Sleeps said, enjoying the moment, 'I got it from under the cushion. Originally, if that's what you're asking, the Internet. Eighty, ammo included.'

'Yeah? How many rounds?'

'Just the six. I mean, there's six chambers.'

'You'll be wanting them all. Gimme a look.'

Sleeps handed the .22 across. Rossi broke it, checked the action. 'Soft-tops,' he announced. 'Blunts in a lady-gun.' He snapped it shut, lobbed it back onto the couch. 'You might want to think about bringing along a kazoo,' he said sourly, 'in case the soft-tops don't blow him away first try.'

Sleeps nodding along. 'If I get picked up carrying that, what'll happen?'

'The cops'll bust a gut laughing, put you away five-to-ten.'

'Because the gun's a fucking joke.'

'Piece a crap,' Rossi confirmed. 'Now your .44—that's a rod. Cop goes up against that, he gets a hole in his head you could watch a movie through.'

'For which,' Sleeps countered, 'you're doing life.'

'If you get bounced, yeah.'

Sleeps got up from the couch and lurched unsteadily towards the kitchen. 'See, this is what I need to tell you,' he said. He opened the fridge, took out a bottle of wine, lumbered back through the pizza boxes to the couch. 'The rod? The whole *point* is it's a piece of crap.'

Rossi's brain made five or six efforts at absorbing Sleeps' words before they finally filtered through. 'You *want* to go back inside?' he said, aghast.

Sleeps made a half-hearted wave around. 'The fucking walls're damp, man. I mean, they're actually leaking. See last winter? I fucking cried. That's how cold it was. Meanwhile I can drive forklifts except I fall asleep, just like that. So I can't even make minimum wage. And anyone says you can live on disability cheques, I dunno, maybe in fucking China. I mean, Rossi—you see what I'm saying.'

Rossi, saddened, said: 'This is the whole point of FARC, Sleeps. To get people back to—'

'First off, it can't be FARC no more. We talked about this.'

Rossi nodded. 'I'm thinking about FARCO,' he said. 'Same as before, only with Organisation on the end. What d'you think?'

'I dunno. It's not all that different when you say it fast. And then there's that movie.' Sleeps shrugged. 'Anyway, being honest, the reason I boosted the Volks …' He took a deep breath. 'Rossi, straight up, I'm hoping to get pinched. And the way I see it is, if I stick with you, it's bound to happen. I'm hoping it's a soft fall so I do good time, but the way things are now, I'll take any pinch I can get.'

'You're banking on *me*,' Rossi said, outraged, 'to get you put away?'

'No offence, Rossi. But you're not exactly Little Caesar, y'know?'

'Sleeps—Rico gets wiped. Eddie G goes down, riddled by cops.'

'Okay, so maybe you're more like Rico than I thought. The point being, when the shit hits the fan, I'll be there.'

'I don't follow.'

'I mean I'll go down. Do your time. What it is you fuck up for, I'll take the rap.'

'You're serious.'

'Never seriouser. I know how we can do it, too.'

'Do what?'

'Get your sixty grand, the Ducati. Get me back inside in some halfway house doing soft time.'

Rossi, despite himself, was intrigued. 'Go on.'

'Okay. You said, Friday night, you caught the tags on the Crossfire that dropped Karen off at her place.'

Rossi nodded, wincing at the memory, a twinge in his shaft.

'So why don't you run a trace on the tags?' Sleeps said. 'Get an address for the Crossfire, nail the owner. Then buzz Karen, tell her you're up for a swap.'

'Sounds solid to me,' Rossi said after thinking it through for precisely four seconds. 'What'll it cost, this trace?'

'This one I do for free,' Sleeps said, waving it off.

DOYLE

Ray glanced up from his paper, then grinned when he saw who it was.

'Don't shoot, detective,' he drawled, putting his hands up.

'Mind if I join you?'

'By all means.'

'Put your hands down, Ray.'

'Yes, ma'am.'

The coffee shop was busy, most of the tables taken, conversation buzzing. Doyle'd been so dispirited after the Rossi Callaghan fiasco she'd decided to take an early lunch of decent coffee and a wedge of carrot cake, extra cream. Not expecting to see Ray, alone and hunched in the corner reading the sports page.

He folded the paper as she sat down, put his mocha to one side, elbows on the polished glass. 'So, Stephanie,' he said, 'what can I do for you?'

Doyle was jazzed he remembered her name, liking the way he said it, cool but not slick. What she didn't like was the way he held the advantage.

'For starters,' she said, 'you could tell me your real name this time.'

'You ran my details?' He tut-tutted. 'That's not strictly legal, is it?'

'Not strictly,' Doyle admitted. 'Unless I have valid reasons to believe it might be worth my while.'

'And I looked like I might be worth your while.'

'Everyone's guilty, Ray. Until they can prove otherwise.'

'Whatever happened to innocent until?'

'We lost that one the day defence lawyers started to make more than the prosecution.' She forked home some carrot cake. 'So how come,' she said, 'you have no record? I mean, not necessarily a rap sheet. I'm talking no record at all, not even a birth cert.'

'It's out there. You just didn't look hard enough.'

'And it's definitely Brogan.'

'Ray Brogan, yeah.'

'The Ray bit being short for something else?'

'Yep.'

'Rumplestiltskin?'

'Close. Keep working it, you'll get there.'

Doyle sipped her latte, forked up another chunk of carrot cake.

'Let me help you out,' Ray said. 'The murals?'

'What about them?'

'I picked that one up inside.'

'You were in prison?'

'The stockade. I was in the Rangers, yeah? Got in a court-martial. Refusal to obey direct orders.' He grinned. 'I thought they'd kick me out, y'know? Fuckers put me away for six months. Insubordination.'

'Six months is a long time for insubordination.' Doyle thinking, *the Rangers?*

'They were looking to make examples,' Ray explained. 'There was a lot of it about at the time. Plus, this particular deal? Had to do with the OC's wife, her dog, this fucking Chihuahua. Nasty little shit. Got a firecracker up its wazoo one Hallowe'en night.'

'And you …?'

'Wasn't me, no. But I knew who did it. And they knew I knew. I mean, at the court-martial. But what're you going to do, squeal?'

'And this,' Doyle said, wondering why he was telling her, 'is where you learnt murals.'

'Among other things, yeah.'

'Like what?'

He kept it brief, no names. How the guy he'd celled with put him wise to the kidnap routine, a percentage deal, low risk. The guy giving him the name of this guy on the outside who ran the show.

'You're telling me,' Doyle said, a forkful of carrot cake poised halfway to her chin, 'you *snatch* people?'

Ray nodded.

'Except,' she said, 'if I believe you, you're naming no names. I mean, this conversation never happened.'

Ray nodded again.

'So why're you telling me?' she said.

'I'm unburdening,' Ray said. 'Can't live with the guilt anymore.'

'Try again.'

'You're thirty-one, right? Thirty-two?'

'Thirty-one.'

'Okay. So how long's it been since you realised no one else gives a fuck except you?'

'I honestly couldn't tell you.'

'Doesn't matter. What matters is, the first time you said it, to yourself, why should *I* give a fuck, that's when you started sliding.'

Doyle didn't like the way Ray was assuming a lot. On the other hand, he'd let her skate by on claiming thirty-one without so much as batting an eyelash. 'Go on,' she said.

'There's a job coming up,' he said. 'You keep an eye on me, a close eye, maybe you'll see something you shouldn't. Piss off the boys down the station by closing their files.'

Doyle put down her fork, stared at Ray. Ray stared back. 'You're saying,' she said, 'you'll take a fall so I can piss off the boys?'

'What I'll do is go down on a sample charge. Cop a plea for one snatch.'

'Giving me what?'

'Names, dates, places, amounts. That way you get to wipe about fifteen cases off the files.'

'Except this guy who runs the show, the legit guy—you're not shopping him, right?'

'Wrong. I'll hand him up wrapped in a bow.'

'And you get what?'

'The money from the snatch. What else?'

'How much?'

'That's nothing to do with you. Anyway, it's insurance money.'

'No chance.'

'Hey, Stephanie—you're getting fifteen scores, plus you're pissing off the boys down at the station. And you're telling me you're worried about some insurance company's loot?'

Doyle chewed slowly on some carrot cake, trying to get her head around what Ray was saying. 'So how much time are you thinking of doing?'

'I'll go two years.'

'Two actual years or, y'know, two years?'

'Two years.'

'So you're back out in what, nine months?'

'I do good time.'

'What's to stop me pulling you in now, obstruction of justice, accessory before and after?'

Ray just grinned.

'Okay,' Doyle conceded. 'But throw me *something*.'

'Like what?'

'The guy, the legit one, running the show. What's his front?'

'It's a beaut. In a million years you wouldn't guess it.'

'Pretend I've just spent a million years guessing.'

Ray leaned in. 'He's a doctor. To be precise, a surgeon.'

'Jesus B. Christ.'

'Sad, isn't it? Listen—you want another latte? I'm ready for more of that mocha.'

Watching him order the coffees up at the counter, Doyle congratulated herself on her stroke of good fortune, stumbling across Ray. Then heard the high-pitched giggle, even over the buzz of conversation, and caught the girl behind the counter laughing at something Ray was saying.

Heard him again, with the growly drawl: *Don't shoot, detective.*

And got to wondering, shit, if Ray, sitting there in the coffee shop nearest the cop station, just reading the sports page on a Sunday morning, hadn't wanted to be found.

MADGE

'Hey, Moms, what's up?'

'I'm on the Internet, Jeanie. Having a little trouble making a purchase.'

Jeanie's sigh was meant to be heard. 'Don't worry about it. Just close the whole thing down and start over. I'll talk you through it.'

'Jeanie—'

'It's *easy*, Moms. Come on, just try it.'

Madge groped through the dull, cloudy fog of the dope hangover to find the glass of red, had herself a fortifying gulp. 'The *problem*, Jeanie, is that—'

'Have you closed it down yet? Logged off?'

'Jeanie? Can you just listen for a sec?' *Christ.* 'The problem is that I'm up to where I input my credit card details.'

'Oh.'

'Exactly. Where's my credit card, Jeanie?'

'You gave it to us, Moms. Remember? To get stuff for the ski trip.'

'I remember. What I also remember was, you were supposed to give it back.'

Madge heard the receiver being covered at Jeanie's end, some muted mumbling. Then: 'Liz has it, Moms. Hold on.'

'Moms?'

'Hi Liz. Rumour has it you have my card.'

'Sure thing.' The twins even sounded identical, even to Madge. 'What're you doing, buying books and shit? On Amazon?'

'That's right. Give me the details slowly.'

Liz recited the numbers. Madge tapped them in. 'Okay,' she said. 'And Liz? If you try to leave the country with that card, I'll have you arrested.'

'I hear you, Moms.'

'And for Christ's sake stop calling me *Moms*.'

A static-filled quiet. Then: 'Mum? You okay?'

'I'm hungover, Liz. Hungover, pissed off and drinking Sunday lunch alone. How're you doing?'

'Okay,' Liz said, sounding subdued, 'I guess.'

'Good for you. Now—am I going to see you two before you go?'

'Sure. We'll call over … Hold on.' More muted mumbling. 'You want to meet in town, Moms? For a coffee or some shit?'

'I'd prefer a coffee. When?'

'How's tomorrow? I mean, we need to get that cheque for five grand anyway, for the trip. It should have been in on Friday.'

'I thought it was next Friday.'

'No, *last* Friday.'

'Okay. One o'clock.'

'Sure thing, yeah. The usual place?'

'That'll be fine.'

Liz hesitated, then said: 'Moms, are you sure you're okay?'

'I will be as soon as you stop calling me Moms. And bring that card tomorrow. I don't want to hear about you forgetting it, or losing it, or any other excuse. Okay? Give my love to Jeanie.'

Madge hung up and drank off the rest of the red. An hour later, upstairs, trying to decide if it was worth bringing the floppy sunhat or if Karen would make her life a misery for wearing it, Madge realised she still hadn't rung Karen.

She got the metallic-sounding answering service, waited for the beep.

'Hi Kar, it's me. Listen, you'll need to start packing, we're off on a cruise, two weeks in the Aegean. Just the two of us, hon, sorry, but they have these weird rules against bringing wolves. And don't worry about money, it's all expenses paid, my treat. Well, Frank's treat. Anyway, we're flying out Thursday night, eight-thirty. And if Frank gives you any grief about taking time off, tell him talk to me. Love you, 'bye.'

FRANK

Frank, tapping gently on the distressed pine of the walk-in wardrobe, found himself wondering if maybe life wouldn't be simpler if he was gay, didn't have to handle women all the time.

'You're going to have to talk to me, Gen. You'll have to come out of there sometime. Gen?'

All afternoon she'd been in there. Frank had panicked half an hour into the siege, trying to remember if the walk-in had a window through which she might have escaped. So he'd charged downstairs and out into the garden; no window. Then, thinking she might have bolted while he was away from his post, he'd charged back up the stairs again. All of which was as much intensive exercise as Frank had voluntarily taken in about three years. His heart was still pounding, sweat prickling up in his confined regions.

Plus he was wondering how she was getting by without a pee, Frank concerned for his new Italian loafers.

'Gen? At least let me explain. Allow me that much, babes.'

The first time he'd tried, she'd screamed and punched him flush on the nose, catching him off guard so he toppled backwards across the sun lounger. By the time Frank got his bearings again, she'd already barricaded herself into the wardrobe.

'This is just ridiculous, Gen. We're going to, at some point—'

'You're going to jail, Frank.' Her voice came muffled. 'Prison.'

'Hon,' he crooned, getting down on his knees to paw at the distressed pine, 'no one's going to prison. Okay?'

'*You* are. I'll testify.'

'You can't.' Frank had checked it out. 'A wife can't testify against her husband.'

'Christ, Frank—we're not even engaged.'

'You're common-law. It's the same thing. I mean, in court.'

'Horseshit, Frank. Complete fucking horseshit.'

'If you'll just open the door and let me explain … It's foolproof, Gen.' He heard a muffled snort. 'No, seriously—these guys are professionals. They know what they're doing. No *way* are they fucking up a half-million deal.'

Frank, still pawing at the door, fell forward when Gen jerked it open. She looked down at him, surprised. 'What the fuck're you doing down *there*? Praying?'

She was dressed in a beige jogging suit, brown piping down the seams. Frank struggled to his feet and reached out for her. Gen held up a warning forefinger.

'I swear, Frank—touch me once and I call the cops.'

She pointed to the far corner of the room. Frank backed away until he felt the bed at the back of his knees, then sat down heavily on the rumpled duvet. Gen tossed her hair back, head tilted, the better to peer down her nose. Frank understood a little of what it might be like to be a specimen in a petri dish.

'Now,' she said, lighting a cigarette. 'What's all this about half a million?'

RAY

Crossing town in the Transit, late evening, the traffic light, Karen—quiet until now—said: 'Bad news.'

'Oh yeah?'

'I got a call from Madge. Looks like we're off on holiday.'

'You're kidding.'

'Nope. Cruising the Greek islands, her treat. We're supposed to be, I think, Thelma and Louise. Except with deck chairs.'

'And this is happening …?'

'We fly into Athens on Thursday night.'

'Fuck.'

'So that's it, right? It's all off.'

Ray lit a cigarette, trying to work out Karen's tone. Did she sound hopeful, but wanting Ray to make the decision for them? Or sad-but-glad, relieved the choice had already been made for them? Ray wondering, not for the first time, where she was coming from, where she was going.

'I told you, Karen. It's off if you want it to be off.'

'Yeah.' Silence. 'See, Ray—I don't think that's fair.'

'I hear you. But that's how it is. I mean, I'm game. Terry's game. Frank's putting up the cash. So you can spike it, sure, but this late in the game, you're the only one who can.'

'Except for Madge.'

'Yeah, she can spike it too. But you're saying you think she'll play along.'

'What I said was, if it was me, I'd probably play along. But I'm not Madge.'

Ray nodded. Karen said: 'I'm the one has to look her in the eye, Ray, telling her the news. And by the way, thanks for making the effort. I mean, we're only going to Oakwood, trying to impress Madge.'

Ray glanced down at his T-shirt, the Pistols, *Never Mind the Bollocks*. He indicated and turned onto Larkhill Road. 'You want to go to Plan B?' he asked.

'There's a Plan B now?'

'Always.'

'Good. Because I have a Plan C.'

'Go on.'

'What I'm wondering,' Karen said after a moment or two, 'is if it'd work if we let Madge go off on her cruise but we still sting Frank. Like, we'd be away for a fortnight. How long do these things usually take?'

'It varies. A job takes as long as it takes. But, on the cruise idea, I don't know. You're going to need Madge around for if they want to talk to her, make sure she's safe. They usually do.' He gave it a half-beat, then: 'You think she's going to freak, don't you?'

'Freaking's not exactly encouraged out at Oakwood.'

'But if she does?'

'She mightn't. Not if we say it the right way.'

'What way is that?'

'How she's helping to screw Frank for half a million. Only let's not get into it straight away.'

'Sure thing.'

'Let her meet you first, get to know you. Maybe roll her a joint and shoot the breeze a while. Chill her out.'

'I get it.'

'It's the next left, then—shit, who am I telling?'

Ray turned off, the paint pots clanking in the rear. Karen said: 'You're not worried? I mean, about telling Madge what you do?'

Ray shrugged.

'I get it,' Karen said. 'You want to meet her first, see if she's the kind that's likely to freak.'

He shrugged again. 'If she doesn't want to do it,' he said, 'we don't do it. If she does, we do. Either way, that's me done. Stick a fork in my ass.'

'That cute ass?'

Ray grinned. Karen said: 'You're really done?'

'Yep.'

'But if it's so easy—'

'I never said it was easy. I said we never got caught.'

'But how come now?'

'I told you. The new shylock. I don't trust the guy.'

'And that's all it is?'

Wanting more than logic, pushing it now, not letting it go. Ray'd be the first to say he knew jack-shit about women, but even Ray knew enough to appreciate that Karen wouldn't have let the moment build up to where it was if she didn't have an inkling as to how Ray was thinking, maybe even feeling the same herself.

Problem was, Ray was too sure how he was feeling. What it felt like, when Karen was around, was tingly and soft, like being electrocuted by cotton wool. Except Ray didn't know how to make that sound the way a woman might like it to sound.

He pulled in opposite Madge's place. 'Answer me this,' he said. 'How come women always have to be asking big questions all the time?'

Karen, opening the door, getting out, said: 'You wouldn't know this, Ray. But when a girl's out with a guy? Mostly she needs to make her own fun.'

MADGE

'Pull in,' Madge said.

Ray indicated, parked up in the slow lane, set his hazard lights flashing. Madge looked at him long and hard, then twisted to look at Karen in the rear of the van, Karen perched on a big paint pot.

'So just to clarify,' Madge said. 'You're abducting me.'

'Not right now,' Karen said. 'And not me, exactly. Ray'll be looking after the actual logistics.'

'Logistics?'

'Picking you up, showing you where you'll be staying. That kind of thing.'

'Look, Madge,' Ray said, 'it was Karen's idea to tell you. If it was just me, I'd have gone ahead and done the snatch. So if you have problems with the concept, blame me. Karen's just trying to make it easy on you.'

'The *concept?*'

'All you have to do is say no,' Ray confirmed. 'Being honest? I'd rather you said no. Seriously.'

'That's sweet, Ray. Really it is. Makes all the difference. My ex-husband wants me kidnapped and my best friend's helping out, but you'd rather I said no. Now I'm all happy again.'

'This isn't us, Madge,' Karen said. 'It's Frank. And if we don't do it, he'll get someone else. Or maybe have the twins snatched.'

Madge had a toke, considering. 'Could that be arranged? Ray? You feel like working a little freelance?'

'I know it's a bit of a shock, Madge,' Karen said, 'but—'

'*Shock?* Christ, I knew he was a lousy bastard, but kidnap?'

'No one gets hurt,' Ray said. 'No one ever gets hurt.'

'You think?' Madge was outraged. 'Try this, Ray. I'm fifty-one years old, I have a husband who wants me kidnapped and two kids who'd care less if I wound up a whore in a Karachi slum. How much hurt do you want, exactly?'

'See,' Karen said, 'this is what we were thinking. About turning it around. Hurting Frank.'

'Hurt him? Hurt him how?'

'With hammers and shit,' Karen said. 'Like in *Misery.*'

'I told you,' Ray said. 'No one gets hurt. Not on my watch. That's a good way to go about pulling hard time.'

'Okay,' Karen conceded. 'Then how about we just rip him off for the half-million and turn him over to Terry, tell Terry that Frank was trying to scam us all?'

'What's to stop Frank going to the cops?' Madge heard herself say.

'He'd incriminate himself,' Ray said. 'Intent to defraud, the works.'

'Neat,' Madge said. 'Very tidy.' She handed Ray the joint.

'Ray? Mind if Karen and I get a little space here?'

'Sure thing.'

Ray got out and strolled away up the hard shoulder, the tip of the joint glowing orange in the headlights. Karen said: 'Madge—'

'Hold up, Kar. There's something we need to be clear on.'

'What's that?'

'The date-rape thing? That was Frank.'

'*Frank?*'

'He was already at college, three years in. No way he could've finished out, not back then, with some bastard running around at home. So my father did him a deal. We hand up the baby, and then Frank swings around again when he's qualified, marries me.'

'Fuck.'

'Pretty much. I mean, Kar—they signed a fucking agreement. I'm in the middle with no say, I'm a piece of fucking meat.'

'The bastards.'

'Yeah, well. That was then. This is now.'

'You're going to run with it?'

'Only if Frank gets hurt.'

'How hurt?'

'Let's not tie ourselves down,' Madge said, leaning across to flash the headlights at Ray, 'to specifics.'

FRANK

'You just missed the off-ramp, Frank.'

'*Fuck.*'

Frank wouldn't have minded so much but they were travelling south on the bypass at the time. So he had to wait ten minutes before another exit came up, then another twenty to get all the way around and back on the road out to Oakwood.

'You think next time,' he said, gritting his teeth, 'you could let me know *before* we pass the exit?'

Gen just exhaled and turned up the stereo—Christ, some Bobbie Williams moron, sounded to Frank like a bomb gone off in hell's cutlery drawer. Frank was in the mood for a little Rossini, something smooth and full to take the edge off. Except Gen had listened to about three minutes of *The Barber of Seville* and then frisbee'd the CD out the window.

Rossini in the gutter: a metaphor, Frank thought bitterly, for my world.

Frank hadn't even wanted to go out, had things to think about. Like say Gen cutting herself in for exactly half the swag, telling Frank it'd be a good idea to lock up any whistles he had lying around the house in case she felt like blowing a few. Frank had agreed fast, except now he was wondering if he hadn't set himself up for a double cross, giving Gen all she needed to leech him dry if she ever got around to considering blackmail.

Then that started him wondering, shit, if maybe the pros, the kidnappers, mightn't try to run the bounce on Frank too. Maybe it was just Frank, but it made perfect sense to him that criminal types would pass up a one-off percentage deal for a lucrative, never-ending sting.

'But we *have* to go out,' Gen had insisted. 'Tonight of all nights.'

'I'm not feeling so good,' Frank'd mumbled, quailing at the prospect of the inevitable jibes, the cracks about his golf, Doug still tubed up in ICU.

'Tough titty, Frank. Because everything has to look normal. First thing the cops'll look for, if they drop around asking questions, is anything out of the ordinary. A change in pattern, your routine, that kind of thing. And we always go out on Sunday nights.' She'd finished her martini in one long draught, patted back a tiny burp. 'More to the point, if you don't turn up tonight, you're as good as admitting liability for busting Doug's skull.'

Frank, while accepting the logic, had caught himself wondering, while getting dressed, how come Gen was such an expert on what cops might or mightn't do when they turned up to ask questions ...

It started early, while they were still crossing the foyer towards the

Members' Bar. Grimes, this spongy excuse for a speckled turd, buttoning up coming out of the gents', saw Frank and grinned, then scuttled across the foyer to intersect with their path, wiping his damp hand on his ass. An air-kiss for Gen, a furtive fondle of her hand; then: 'How goes it, Frank?'

'Fine, Grimes. And you?'

'Great, great. I hear Doug's on the mend.'

'Really?'

'Yep. They have him on horse tranquilisers now.'

Gen rose to the bait. 'Horse tranks?'

'Apparently,' Grimes gurgled, 'it's to keep him in a stableford condition. Geddit? A *stable*ford condition.'

'Hilarious,' Frank fumed, gripping Gen by the elbow, pushing on through the double doors of the Members' Bar. A warm wave of unsweetened sweat washed over them, and it was only then that Frank began to understand how hellish his evening was going to be. Because Margaret was holding court at the bar, gin in hand, resplendent in a slinky green dress of some kind of shimmering material …

And oh Christ, no—who the fuck let *Karen* in?

ROSSI

'I've been thinking,' Rossi said. 'This soft time you want to do?'

'What about it?'

'You've what they call put it all into perspective.'

'No shit.'

'No shit. I mean, what are we at, Sleeps? Really, what are we at?'

They were parked up on Larkhill Mews, diagonally across from Margaret Dolan's place, nobody home. Sleeps said as much.

'Okay,' Rossi said patiently. 'But I'm talking about the big picture. You see what I'm saying.'

'Not really, no.'

'Look around you, man. The fucking houses, the cars …'

'That Crossfire's a tasty motor,' Sleeps agreed.

'Meanwhile we're sitting in this piece-a-crap.'

A '92 Corolla Sleeps had boosted earlier on.

'Beggars can't be choosers, Rossi.'

'This is my point. How come we're beggars?'

'Because we are.'

'Okay. But try this—maybe we're beggars because we're the only ones who don't look the part. I mean, legit.'

Sleeps considered that as he sucked some tangerine Slurpy Joe through a straw. 'Maybe,' he conceded. 'So what?'

'Couple a days back I was in this charity shop,' Rossi began. 'Where I got the threads.'

'This wouldn't happen to be,' Sleeps said cautiously, 'the charity shop that got knocked over?'

'Same one.'

'No way, Rossi.'

'No way what?'

'No way am I taking the rap for blagging a charity shop. It'd be like going down for prowling little girls.'

'Perxactly,' Rossi said. 'Everyone, don't ask me why, but when it's charity? They want to believe it's all above board. I mean, it's like they're kids. Walk into a charity shop and it's like a magic fucking bubble, no one ever got screwed in a charity shop.'

'It'd be bad form,' Sleeps agreed.

'Wait for it,' Rossi said. 'Now the thing with charity shops is, no one'd be seen dead in one of those holes unless everyone knew they didn't need to be there in the first place. I mean, have *you* ever bought anything in Oxfam?'

'Not fucking likely.'

'See, it's the folks that live up here,' Rossi said, nodding out at the sycamore-lined street. 'They'll drop in, buy some shit, take it home.'

'Easing their conscience.'

'Then, next fucking week, they'll drop it off on some other charity.'

'So it's the same shit,' Sleeps said, starting to see it, 'doing the rounds all the time.'

'Perfuckingxactly.'

'And you want to …'

'Buy a load of scabby shirts, get stocked up, open the doors.'

'Except,' Sleeps said, 'in a case like this, it's the punters who bring *you* the stock.'

'You're seeing it?'

'Fucking A I'm seeing it, man.'

'Sleeps?' Rossi said, feeling choked up. 'I want to tell you, what you said this morning, about taking my rap—that's the noblest fucking thing I ever fucking heard. And I'm here to tell you right now, that I want *you* to be president of the Francis Assisi Rehabilitation Concern Organisation.'

Sleeps put down his Slurpy Joe. 'You're serious? You're actually going legit?'

'All the way, Sleeps. Some day,' he added, gesturing out at Larkhill Mews, 'all this will be yours. Well, some of it anyway.'

'I don't know what to say, Rossi.'

'The less said the better. Soon as we get my sixty grand back from Karen, we're in business. Get stocked up, rent an office, start applying for grants and shit. Scam 'em blind.'

'Don't forget the Ducati,' Sleeps said.

'And the .44,' Rossi said. 'I mean, it's a matter of principle.'

FRANK

'Y'think,' Gen murmured, swirling her gin-and-tonic, 'if I was to dump you, I'd be having that good a night out?'

'For the last fucking time,' Frank growled, his back to the room, elbows on the bar, 'I dumped *her*. Okay?'

'Sure, Frank. Whatever you say.' Gen sounding bored, insolent—Christ, Frank could get that kind of shit at work, or from the twins. 'But it looks to me like she's having a pretty good time for a woman who's been dumped. Wouldn't you say?'

'You think people come here to have a good time?' Frank, grinding out the words, felt his incisor crown wobble. 'Jesus.'

'Chill, Frank. Relax. I mean, we're supposed to look natural, like nothing weird's going on.' Gen swivelling on the bar stool, puckering up and making kissy noises. 'Why don't you kiss me or some shit?'

'I hardly think that that would constitute acceptable behaviour in Margaret's presence.'

'Y'know what? We could start a dwarf conga on her table and she wouldn't notice. That guy she's with? He's hot.'

Frank was about to reply when he felt himself skewered by a high-pitched trilling, a peal of laughter that pierced the plinkity-plonk muzak and set his marrow a-shiver. The noise coming, he could tell without looking, from Margaret's table, where the hilarity was bordering on hysterical. Even the guy—some freak with a fringe, in T-shirt and jeans; Christ, on a Sunday night at Oakwood?—even the toy-boy seemed to be enjoying himself. Frank couldn't work it out. Unless, it was possible, the guy was on drugs. Why else would he be boffing Margaret?

'I'll say one thing for her,' Gen said. 'That's a serious dress. I mean, she's mutton dressed as mutton, but if she was twenty years younger … Hey, isn't that Bryan?'

'Thank fucking Christ,' Frank said, turning from the bar. 'Oh, *shit.*'

Bryan strolling over to Margaret's table, Fiona in his wake; Bryan shaking hands now with Karen, being introduced to the toy-boy, all the while smiling sadly at something Margaret was saying. Frank wondering how long it'd take Bryan, the acid-fried asshole, to let something slip …

'Stay here,' he ordered, dismounting from his stool.

'And miss this?' Gen giggled as she slid down off her own stool and staggered slightly on her spike heels. 'We're partners now, Frank. Remember?'

Frank gritted his teeth, wincing as the loose crown danced a fandango. 'Okay,' he conceded. 'But let me do the talking.'

Gen teetered as she took Frank's arm. 'Y'know what I like most about you, Frank? You're so dynamic. Virile. You make me feel … Ooops,' she said as her dangling handbag walloped the back of an unwary head. 'Sorry.'

'Just try to stay on your feet for ten minutes,' Frank urged. 'That's all I ask. And perk up them tits.'

The toy-boy nudging Margaret now as they approached, the guy meeting Frank's stare.

Frank cleared his throat. 'Margaret.'

'Frank.'

'Fiona.'

'Frank.'

'Karen.'

'Hey, Frank. Nice tie.'

'Yes, well …'

'How goes it, Frank?'

'Good, Bry, good. And you?'

'Not great, Frank. I just heard about Doug.'

'It's tragic,' Frank agreed. 'But accidents will happen. And if the guy hadn't been, y'know, standing on the edge of the green, he'd have been well out of—'

'Not that.' Bryan peering curiously at Frank now. 'You haven't heard?'

Frank's stomach pitched sideways. 'Heard what?'

'About Doug.'

Frank's guts yawed in a gale. 'What about him?'

'Bryan?' Margaret put her hand up. 'Can I answer this one?' She turned to Frank. 'Doug slipped into a coma earlier this afternoon,' she announced. 'You didn't know?'

'But Grimes said he was on the *mend*,' Frank barked.

'They say it's touch-and-go,' Margaret went on.

'Although,' Karen added, 'they're also saying you should get away with,

I think, third-degree manslaughter. If Doug doesn't come around, like.'

Frank, in shock and already weaving unsteadily on his feet, wobbled as he was brushed to one side, Gen leaning in across the table with her hand outstretched. 'You're Margaret, right?'

Margaret arched an eyebrow. 'And you might be …?'

'Genevieve. Gen. Y'know, Frank's partner?'

Frank watched, horrified, as Gen extended her hand again. Christ, he'd known she was drunk, maybe a little mopey on gin—but how could he have failed to spot that the girl was actually suicidal?

Except, Jesus, now Margaret was taking Gen's hand and shaking it, looking her up and down. Frank wobbled again, even though no one had touched him; the room starting to swirl, Frank feeling a tremor in the floorboards. He nodded at the toy-boy in one last desperate bid for dignity. 'And who might this young man be?'

'Jesus, Frank,' Gen snapped, 'lighten the fuck up.'

Margaret hooted. Karen snorted. The toy-boy grinned. Frank wished the ground would get on with swallowing him whole, just plunge him into a dark and silent cellar. Except Gen was still pumping Margaret's hand, giggling now, saying: 'No offence, but I just had to meet the woman who, Frank says, has the sexiest belly button since Raquel Welch.' She shrugged. 'I mean, whoever the fuck, Raquel Welch—'

There was a moment's stunned silence. Then, as if in slow-motion, the storm broke. Everywhere he looked Frank saw grotesquely distorted masks of hilarity—Margaret bawling tears of joy, Karen red-faced and whooping, the toy-boy suppressing a sneaky grin, Bryan tugging at his nose, Fiona with her thin-lipped Botox smile. Even Gen, the traitorous bitch, was chortling along.

Frank gritted his teeth so hard he popped the loose crown off his incisor. It shot onto the table, bounced high as a dice, and skittered off the edge into Margaret's lap. Margaret shrieked, setting them all off again.

Frank bowed his head and found himself wondering, for the first time in his life, how he might go about getting a gun.

The Big O

RAY

Ray glanced at the scrap of paper Karen had placed by his coffee mug, then crumpled it into a ball and dropped that in the ashtray. He wiggled his thumb, indicating she should set it alight.

'Because,' Karen said, 'if anyone finds it, I mean here, then I'm an accessory.'

'Yep.'

'What'd we decide, Ray? We're in this together. Yeah?'

Ray knuckled his stubble. 'Yeah, but it was my idea in the first place. At least, it was Terry's. Plus you have Anna to worry about. So if anything fucks up—'

'I thought it never fucked up.'

'You said it yourself, about the stickups, it's the law of averages. It's only a matter of time.'

'Okay,' Karen conceded. 'But how come you're thinking negative all of a sudden?'

'Just looking at the options. And the worst-case scenario is, the gig fucks up.'

'Sure. But—'

'No buts. Look,' he said placatingly, 'it probably won't. But if it does, I'll do okay. It'll be Frank and me, unlawful detention, conspiracy to defraud. No,' he said as Karen made to protest, 'wait a minute. Terry's got good lawyers, they're sharks. And Frank's the scumbag who wants his ex-wife snatched. Me, I'm just the fuckwit he pulled in to do his dirty work. That way no one else gets touched. Not Terry, not Madge, and not you.'

'How come not Terry? I mean, it was his idea.'

Ray just stared.

'You'd do time for him?' Karen said.

'Some.'

'And that isn't a problem for you?'

'I don't *want* to do it. But we need someone, if it all fucks up, they can put away. And looking around, I'm the logical option. The one with the least to lose.'

'There's still time. We can ring Madge and tell her it's off.'

Ray with a little speech prepared. 'Say it does work out,' he said, 'the way it usually does. You and me, we're splitting three hundred grand. And that buys a place, maybe not the cottage at the lake, but somewhere Anna can live the way she should.' He held up a hand to forestall Karen's protest. 'It sounds freaky, I know, because we're only hanging out a few days. But that's actually the beauty of it. Because if I do go down, why would anyone come to you looking for the insurance money? Especially after Terry's washed it, left it bright and shiny new.'

'What happens after?' Karen said. 'When you get out?'

'Christ, you don't make it easy, do you?'

Karen looking him straight in the eye. 'I'm not looking for someone who needs it to come easy, Ray.'

Ray lit a cigarette. 'Okay,' he said, 'this is how I see it. If I go down I'll take two years, which'll work out at around nine months. Then, when I get out, if things are different between you and me …' He shrugged. 'I say we deal with that if it happens. I don't know, maybe you remortgage, hand me my cut, I'm gone.'

'Either way, I'm sitting pretty.'

'Or even prettier than usual. Put it this way—it'd be like you doing me a favour, holding my stash. In property, where it's gaining points every day.'

'I'd be the one,' Karen said, deadpan, 'doing you the favour.'

Ray nodded. Karen reached for his lighter and picked up the crumpled ball of paper, still meeting his eye. She lit a stray corner and dropped the ball into the ashtray again. They watched it burn up, Karen tamping the ashes with the butt of the lighter, this expression in her eyes, defiant longing.

'So we're on,' Ray said.

'Okay by me.'

FRANK

All night Frank had had this nightmare where a giant golf ball chased him down the 14th fairway out at Oakwood, Doug perched atop behind a steering wheel, a Jolly Roger fluttering, Doug laughing like Scooby Doo on helium.

Now Frank was haggard, drawn and damn near quartered, the razor in his shaky hand slicing divots out of his jawbone. A disaster in the making: Frank had long ago discovered that a forgotten dab of toilet tissue on a surgeon's chin could cause a stampede in a cosmetic surgery waiting room. Two mornings in a row could ruin a man for life.

'Frank?' Even from downstairs, through two sets of closed doors, Gen's voice was shrill enough to set Frank's crownless tooth shivering. 'Babes? You ready?'

Frank groaned, towelled off the last of the shaving foam, splashed on some Pasha and began buttoning his shirt. He trudged downstairs knotting his tie and found Gen sitting at the kitchen table, smoking. By some miracle she was actually dressed at nine-thirty in the morning, although Frank was quick to acknowledge, as he headed for the coffee pot, that such miracles usually didn't augur well for one Francis Xavier Peter Dolan.

'Hey, babes,' Gen said brightly. 'You nearly ready yet?'

Frank sipped at his coffee, holding the cup steady in both hands. 'Ready for what?'

'To drive me into town. I'll be needing some new outfits for Acapulco.'

Frank's stomach churned at the prospect of Gen on an impromptu spree. Plus, the coffee was barely tepid. 'Gen, we really don't need—'

'Maybe *you* don't. But if you think I'm flying into Acapulco wearing russets and tans, you've another think coming. So don't even think it.'

Frank steeled himself. 'How much do you need?'

'*I* don't know. Jesus, Frank, I don't even know what I want yet. It's not just outfits. I'll be needing—'

Coffee erupted as the phone rang, each peal a piercing drill in Frank's ear. He snatched up the receiver. 'The Dolan residence,' he croaked, 'Doctor Dolan speaking.'

'Doctor? It's Detective Doyle.'

Frank sagged at the knees. So this is how the end comes, he thought bitterly; without so much as a hot coffee to sustain him.

'Yes,' he said, hearing his doleful tone, realising he was admitting to guilt before being officially accused.

'I interviewed you on Thursday,' she went on. 'After the mugging?'

Frank's knees failed him. He sank to the floor, eyes closed. 'Of course you did,' he mumbled.

'Good news, Doctor. We've located your briefcase.'

'That,' Frank said, opening his eyes to see Gen glaring at him, 'is fantastic news. You have no idea of how good that news is right now.'

'Well, unfortunately the briefcase was empty. But you probably expected that.'

'It's the world we live in,' Frank agreed. He hauled himself vertical, levering against the marble worktop, hands shaking.

'So when can you come down to collect it?' the detective said.

'Collect what?'

'The briefcase. You want it back, don't you?'

'That's okay. You can keep it.'

'I'm afraid I wouldn't be allowed, sir. That's not the way we do things.'

'It's good leather,' Frank said. 'And you deserve something for yourself. You've obviously worked very hard on the case.' He sniggered. 'The case.'

'Sir? Are you okay?'

'Fine. Marvellous.'

'Well, if you're sure …'

By now Gen was making slashing gestures across her throat, urging Frank to hang up.

'The thing is, Doctor,' the detective went on, 'we'd still like you to come down to the station and have a look at those mug shots I mentioned.'

'Do I have to?'

'No, sir, you're not obliged to help us in any way. But we would appreciate it greatly if—'

Frank heard a muffled brr-brr on the line. 'Sergeant Boyle? Can you hold? I have a call coming in.'

'It's Detective, sir. Detective Doyle. And I wouldn't advise—'

Frank punched line two. 'The Dolan residence, Doctor—'

'Frank?'

'Jeanie?'

'It's Liz. Where's Moms?'

'How would I know?'

'Well, we've been trying to ring her all morning to cancel for lunch but she isn't answering. You think she's, like, sick or something?'

Frank closed his eyes again, the better to block out the memory of a gin-soused Margaret handing over his lemming-like crown. 'Liz, I have no idea where your mother might—'

'Yeah, well, you'll do. Jeanie and me, we need that money for the trip to Aspen. Like, five grand. Today.'

'I thought you needed it for Friday.'

'Yeah. Last Friday.' Liz groaned. 'Don't tell me Moms fucked up again. Jesus, ever since she started smoking dope …'

Frank dabbed his damp forehead with a shirt cuff. 'Liz, hon, your mother and I discussed this. Didn't she tell you? We decided that it wasn't such a good idea for you and Jeanie to go skiing. Not with all the hijackings and suchlike these days.'

Liz laughed harshly. 'Yeah, but seriously Frank, we need that money today. A cheque'll do it. I'll call around to the office this afternoon to pick it up. What? Hold on, Frank.'

Frank heard a muttered conversation, then Liz came on again. 'Yeah, Jeanie wants to know what we should do about Moms. Should we, like, ring the cops or some shit?'

'No need. Hold on.'

He punched call waiting. 'Hello, Sergeant?'

'*Doctor* Dolan, I do *not* appreciate—'

'Yeah, I know. But my daughter is on the other line. Can you speak to her? She's worried about her mother.'

'What? I don't want to—'

Frank double-punched the buttons, hung up. Then dialled Margaret's number and let it ring until the answering machine kicked in; hung up again. He shivered.

'Something you want to tell me, Frank?'

He stared at Gen, his vision blurry, cold sweat oozing into the corners of his eyes.

'It's, ah, possible,' he said, 'that the guy who's supposed to kidnap Margaret tomorrow has moved a day early.'

'And that means what?'

'I'm not sure. But I think we'd better start getting the ransom together as soon as possible.'

'I hope you're not thinking that this might interfere with my shopping. I won't go without a new wardrobe, Frank. I *won't*.' She gave it a half-beat. 'And you don't want to leave me behind, Frank. Not now.'

Frank whimpered.

'And Frank?'

'Christ, what *now*?'

'If the cops want you to go see them, go see them. Remember—everything has to look normal.'

'As normal as you, say, shopping for new bikinis?'

But she was already gone. Frank collapsed onto a chair and slumped forward, head on his forearms. He stared into the darkness, fighting the impulse to pick up the phone and call Sergeant Boyle, confess all. Except it was cosy in the dark little world Frank had created, the mini-womb he had built from his folded arms; Frank thought of Doug, comatose and blissfully unaware, and felt a pang of envy.

Then, a flash of inspiration—Christ, inspiration? It was genius, sheer fucking *genius*. If, he allowed, he actually had the balls to carry it off …

The Big O

He grabbed his jacket and stumbled out of the kitchen, found the car keys on the hall table.

'Gen?' he called up the stairs. 'Hon? Can you call a cab to get into town? I've an emergency at the office that can't wait.'

Her shrill tone followed him out the front door but Frank wasn't listening. He was too busy trembling, shocked at the audacity of his genius, as he turned the key in the ignition.

ROSSI

Rossi woke already reaching for the little brown bottle, shards of pain shooting through his dick like someone had jammed a knitting needle up his Jap's eye, a fat knitting needle with little hooks on either side, each hook busy stitching barbed wire into his shaft.

The pain, he believed, was even worse than the night before, when he'd called off the surveillance on Larkhill Mews and bolted for home, the Nervocaine stash. Now he gobbled down three blue-speckled pills, wincing at each movement; then, when the numbing began, he slid off Sleeps' couch and made for the tiny kitchen, put the kettle on to boil.

He dressed slowly, careful not to snag the stitches—although, at least, they were already dissolving, less noticeable now—thinking about how it might be coming time to invest in a pair of clean skanks. He noticed the mobile on the ground beside the couch, the battery dead, so he plugged it in, turned it on and went back into the kitchen.

Sleeps stumbled through from the bedroom, yawning, just as the phone emitted a high-pitched beep-beep to let Rossi know he had a message. He flicked his head at Sleeps from the kitchen, indicating he should pick up.

'If it's that stupid prick again, wanting his phone back,' he said, 'we're tracking him down and sticking it where he won't be taking any calls unless he's some kind of contortionist fucking ventriloquist.'

Sleeps nodded, knuckling his eyes; dialled up and relayed the message to Rossi. Rossi came through to the living room stirring his coffee. 'Who the fuck,' he demanded, 'is Frank?'

'How would I know?'

'Give it me again,' Rossi said.

Sleeps dialled up, waited for the metallic voice, then recited along with the message: *Hey, Frank, we have Madge. You have twenty-four hours to get the half-million together. You know the drill—used notes, non-sequential, unmarked, no dye-packs. We'll be watching, Frank, so no cops. Contact no one. And don't turn the phone off, we'll be in touch to let you know where you can drop off the cash.*

'A half-*million*?' Rossi was gobsmacked. 'Christ on a fucking moped.'

'It's not *a* half-million,' Sleeps pointed out. 'It's *the* half-million.'

'So what?'

'So it sounds like this isn't the first time Frank's heard about it.'

'Yeah,' Rossi said, 'I can see that. But who the fuck is Frank?'

'Want me to try the last-caller service?'

No joy. 'It's blocked,' Sleeps confirmed.

Rossi had been expecting that. He grabbed the phone, dialled up; listened to the message, hearing the voice, this lazy drawl Rossi thought he recognised but couldn't concentrate on. Tears welling up in Rossi's eyes. All his life he'd been waiting on a big score, the one to kick him upstairs into the big leagues so he could arrive on Sicily a major player, a *bona fide* family member in the greatest family of them all.

Only for Sleeps, slumped in the busted deck chair with his legs apart, his equipment pouring out of his loose-fitting skanks, Rossi would have said he was dreaming. But Rossi's dreams, when he dreamt, were of Sicily, where the sun always shone down out of clear blue skies on bee-buzzing orchards of olives, oranges and, shit, maybe even some honey trees, Rossi'd always had a sweet tooth.

'So what do we do?' Sleeps said, scratching his undercarriage.

'Nothing,' Rossi said, averting his eyes. 'You heard it yourself, the guy said he'd ring back, let us know where to drop the cash.'

'Then what?'

'Then we roll with it. Play along. Muscle in.'

'But—'

'But fucking nothing, Sleeps. Half a million? Christ.' Rossi's palms were damp. 'First we nail this Margaret Dolan tart, get the .44 off Karen. I mean, this is hardcore shit. We're muscling no one with any lady-gun .22s.'

Sleeps stared at the mouldy carpet.

'What's the matter now?' Rossi said. 'Christ, man, you're in for a half-mill split.'

'That's just it. You said, last night, we were going legit.' Sleeps, doleful, met Rossi's eye. 'I mean, we nail a half-mill, there's no way we're going legit after that.'

Rossi scrabbled through the makings on the table, started building a jay. 'Make me a fresh coffee,' he said. 'This one I need to think through.'

KAREN

Karen wasn't even sure if Frank, after getting Ray's message, would turn up for work. She'd been hovering by the phone, half-expecting Frank to ring with a mumbled apology, sounding like sick seaweed.

But, though it looked to Karen like Frank had shaved with a cheese-grater while kneeling in puddles of coffee, he seemed upbeat when he arrived. Karen had expected him to be a couple of twitches short of a fit, wrong-footed by the change in plan, Madge snatched a day early. But he marched up to the desk swinging his briefcase.

'Morning, Karen.'

'Frank.'

'I trust you had a good night last night?'

'Great, yeah. How's the tooth?'

'Oh fine, just fine. And Margaret? She enjoyed herself, I hope?'

'I guess.'

'Marvellous.' Frank dry-washed his hands. 'Is there any fresh coffee?'

'Can be in about five minutes.'

'Excellent. Drop it in when you get a chance. Any calls?'

'None so far.'

'Wonderful.'

He crossed to his office and let himself in. Karen frowned. It was possible, she reckoned, that Frank was putting on a charade, trying to pretend he hadn't been humiliated when the ditsy mooch went public with the belly-button baloo. But no—Karen knew Frank better than that. If Frank was in a good mood, especially on a Monday morning, somebody somewhere had to be suffering.

She put on a fresh pot of coffee, wondering if she wasn't looking at things from the wrong end; how maybe Frank was elated *because* Madge had been snatched a day early. That at least made sense. Frank was the kind, Rossi was the same, he could never concentrate on more than one problem at a time; and, being a man, Frank wouldn't be able to let the problem go until he'd solved it. Or, Karen acknowledged, what was more likely, offloaded the grief onto someone else.

She poured the coffee, added sugar and a dollop of cream, knocked on the office door and pushed through. She noted the open wall-safe, the framed *Barber of Seville* reproduction poster hanging at an angle, Frank behind the desk riffling through a sheaf of papers. Karen craned her neck as she put down the coffee, unable to make out what the papers were; desperate, she nudged the coffee cup, splashing the creamy liquid onto the mahogany surface.

'Ooops, sorry Frank. I'll just grab a cloth and—'

'That's okay.' Intent on the papers, Frank didn't even look up. 'Leave it, I'll get to it in a minute.'

Karen frowned again. Usually it was the highlight of Frank's working week, Karen bending in low to mop up spilt coffee—Frank, she decided, was either high or coming out of the closet. She turned for the door.

'Oh, Karen?'

'Yeah?'

'I don't want you to think I'm prying or anything, but …' He selected a sheet of paper, glanced at it and smiled grimly, then looked up. 'I don't suppose you'd know where Margaret might be?'

'No idea, Frank. Why?'

'I'm just wondering if she went home last night. Or if she might have gone off somewhere with, y'know, the guy in the T-shirt. I know it's none of my business, but—'

'I'm sure it's not.'

'Yes. I know. But Jeanie rang this morning, she was trying to contact her mother. She was worried.'

Karen let her sigh of relief out slow. 'Maybe she's hungover, has the phone off the hook.'

'Maybe that's all it is,' he agreed, going back to his papers. By then, though, Karen had tumbled—Frank was asking dumb questions to set up some half-assed alibi for later on when the cops called around. So he could say, *Hey, ask Karen, I don't know where Margaret is; but, yeah, now I think about it, I saw her with this guy last night, out with Karen …*

'Is that all, Frank?'

'Yes, that's all. Thanks.' Karen turned to go. 'Oh—one more thing.'

'What's that?'

'Can you call the mobile phone company for me? I need a new phone.'

Karen's blood froze. 'How'd you mean?'

Frank looked up. 'I mean, I need a new phone. Since the mugging. The bastard took my phone and the briefcase.'

'You were mugged?'

'I didn't tell you?' He nodded. 'Last Thursday, in town.'

'And he swiped your phone?'

'I'm pretty sure it was insured against theft,' Frank said, 'but don't worry about replacing it. It'll take ages, there'll be forms to sign, all that crap. Just get me a new one.'

Karen nodded, not trusting herself to speak.

'Thanks, Karen. You're a pet. And can you grab me some smokes? Marlboro reds. Thanks.'

Karen stumbled out of the office, dizzy, her mind awhirl, each thought fizzing like a faulty Catherine wheel.

Wondering, Christ, where the fuck was Madge?

MADGE

Madge checked the clock again, wondering what the hell was keeping Ray. She'd been ready for over an hour now, perched on the edge of the armchair, the television on, sound down, no way could Madge cope with morning TV and a gin hangover—Christ, the very thought of bouffant wigs and too much mascara, that early, made her queasy. And that was just the chaps.

Thinking one last coffee might help settle her stomach, she stood and headed for the kitchen. But halfway there, nerves jangling like a jester's bell, she detoured to the TV, reaching in behind for the small pottery jar. Then she went back to the armchair, laid out the makings and began to roll a joint.

Ray had sounded confident the night before, sitting in the very same armchair, laying out the plan. All Madge had to do was pack an overnight bag, he'd said, and be ready to go when he called. After that it was just a matter of waiting. Once Karen was sure Frank had kicked the cash free, they'd swoop on Frank, hold him. In case, Ray said, Frank got clever, started thinking about a double cross.

'We grab him *before* he gets the money?' Karen'd said. Ray nodding. 'So how do *we* get it?' Karen wanted to know.

'The waif,' Madge'd butted in. 'Gen. We get her to pick it up.'

Ray nodding again. One thing Madge liked about the guy, he kept quiet unless he had something to say …

The phone rang again. Madge leaned over, checked the caller ID—Jeanie, for the fourth time in less than an hour, the twins fretting about their five grand, the ski trip. Well, they'd just have to miss out on Aspen for this year, she thought, firing up the joint, taking a deep drag, closing her eyes as she waited for the tingle in her toes.

The doorbell bing-bing-bonged. Madge tamped the joint. Okay, she thought, here goes …

Except she'd opened the front door and stepped back into the hall before she realised the guy in the oversized suit with the pink pinstripes wasn't Ray. 'Oh,' she said, stepping forward again to block the doorway. 'Yes? Can I help you?'

'Margaret Dolan, right?' His voice sounded thin, nasal.

Madge, feeling the rush, the tingle in her toes, said: 'Are you with Ray?'

The guy frowned, his face puzzling up as he opened his mouth to say something. But then Madge saw his eyes brighten. 'Yeah,' he said. 'That's right. I'm with Ray.'

Madge felt her guts squeeze tight: wrong, wrong, *wrong*. She stepped back closing the door, saying: 'I'm sorry, but you'll have to—'

He jammed his foot between the door and its frame, wincing as Madge slammed. Then he pushed forward, shoving Madge back into the hall; came on limping slightly, closing the door with his heel. Madge felt her gorge rise. 'You're making a big mistake,' she said. 'I'm expecting—'

'Shut it.' He dipped into a pocket of the oversized suit and came up holding a gun that looked far too small for his hand. He pointed it at her face. 'I don't want to use this,' he said. 'But I will. No kidding.' Then he thought for a second. 'Actually, scratch that. I *do* want to use it.'

He gestured for Madge to turn around, then pushed her in the small of her back, propelling her down the hallway towards the kitchen, saying: 'Okay, so where d'you keep the tea towels?'

He made her rip some tea towels into strips, then lay them on the table. He turned her around, and she automatically held out her arms, offering her wrists. But when he touched her hands, her knees gave way and Madge pitched forward, grabbing for the table as she puked a torrent of coffee, bile and gin.

RAY

'Just like that,' the shylock growled, 'you're walking away.'

'That's right,' Ray said.

'You think it's that easy?'

'Why wouldn't it be?'

'You know shit you shouldn't.'

'Sure. About Terry.'

The shylock lumbering across Terry's office, shoulders hunched, hands in his trouser pockets. He stopped at the window to twitch the lateral bamboo and glance out into the car park. Then he turned to face Ray again.

'Terry's business is my business now,' he said. 'If Terry gets fucked, I get fucked.'

'Terry isn't my type. You got nothing to worry about.'

Terry glared at Ray. Ray caught the gist—don't get pissy with the shylock, the guy'll cause you problems. But Ray wasn't looking to antagonise anyone. The whole point of calling around to Terry so early in the morning was to put Terry in the picture, let him know the snatch was going ahead as discussed—okay, with a few tweaks here and there, but Terry's cut was safe.

Terry had shrugged. 'Play it how you need to, Ray. Do I look worried?' Then started kidding Ray about going legit, drawing cartoons.

'Murals, Terry,' Ray'd said. 'The oldest art form known to mankind. You've heard of cave paintings, right?'

'Yeah. I hear they keep them in caves. Ever wonder why they keep them in caves?'

Ray was about to answer when he heard, from over his shoulder, the shylock growl: 'Who's keeping what in caves?'

So then Ray had to explain murals to the shylock. This after Terry and Ray turned off their mobiles, in case someone might ring, incriminate the shylock in a dodgy deal. Then came the back-and-forth about how Ray owed it to Terry and the shylock not to walk away. How it could be dangerous having someone out there who knew what Ray knew, could put people away for serious time if he didn't keep his trap shut.

'First off,' Ray said, 'nothing I can say touches you, right?'

'Damn straight,' the shylock grunted.

'Okay. So now we're talking about Terry.' Ray looked across the desk. 'You worried about me, Terry?'

'Nope.'

'Why aren't you worried, Terry?'

'Because if you pull any shit that sticks to me, I'll have your heart cut out and fed to someone you're not so keen to see eating hearts.'

Ray said, to the shylock: 'Terry and me, we go back. Why would I want to fuck him over?'

The shylock came back across the office, a sour expression on his face; leaned back against the desk facing Ray, hands still jammed in his pockets. 'What kind of guarantee do I get?'

'What kind do you want?'

The shylock thought about that. 'I don't know.'

Ray stood up. 'Well, if you think of one, Terry'll know where to find me.'

But with the shylock and the traffic, the Monday morning snarl, Ray was running fifty minutes late by the time he turned into Larkhill Mews. He nosed the Transit up Madge's driveway and hopped out, leaving the engine running; jogged up the steps, rang the doorbell, heard the faint echo, bing-bing-bong. Surprised she wasn't waiting, Ray tried the bell again; when there was no answer the second time, he headed off around the side of the house.

If there was any problem, he reasoned, Madge would have rung, she had his number; Ray making a joke of it in front of Karen, handing it over the night before …

Ray stopped dead. He sprinted back to the van, grabbed the phone, powered up. 'C'mon,' he urged. 'C'mon …'

The beep-beep told him he had a message waiting. He dialled and heard Karen's voice, urgent: *Ray? Fuck … Ray, that call you made, fuck knows who got it. Frank had his phone stolen last Thursday. And Ray—Madge isn't answering at home. Call when you get this.*

He jogged back up the steps, tried the front door. It was unlocked. He checked the downstairs rooms, recoiling at the stench in the kitchen even before he saw the pool of puke. Then he went upstairs, even checking the bathroom, knowing all the while he was wasting his time.

He wiped off the door handle with the cuff of his sleeve, reversed out of the driveway, headed back towards town. Dialled Karen's work number, driving one-handed, hearing Terry again: *… someone you're not so keen to see eating hearts.*

Then remembered, shit, Terry knew Karen. Had her address.

KAREN

Karen told Frank she was going out to get his Marlboros and went around the corner to the small coffee dock. They sat on high stools at the counter along the wall, Ray facing the sunny, tree-lined street.

'You think,' he said, 'she might have changed her mind?'

'Doubt it. And even if she did, she'd have rang to say. She wouldn't just scoot off.'

'You tried to ring her?'

'I must've left three, four messages. The twins have been trying to get her too.'

'And you're saying Frank doesn't know where she is.'

'He asked if *I* knew where she was. But that could mean anything. He could be trying something sneaky.'

'Yeah,' Ray said, 'but *I'm* Frank's sneaky. I mean, if someone was going to snatch Madge for Frank, it'd be me. I'm his guy.'

Karen sipped her latte. 'You don't think,' she said slowly, 'that whoever got your message on Frank's phone, that it's them?'

'No chance. First they'd have to know who Madge was and where she lived. And that's presuming, and it's a pretty big presumption, that they'd have the balls to snatch someone. I mean, muggers? And even if they *were* the kind, they'd have to be lunatics to do it without knowing whose score they were fucking with.'

Karen lit one of Frank's Marlboros. 'And there was no sign at the house of, y'know, a struggle?'

'Apart from the puke, everything looked okay.'

'The puke's a big thing, Ray. Madge wouldn't just walk away from a puddle of puke. She'd clean it up.'

'So you're saying she left in a hurry.'

'Against her *will*, Ray.'

Ray filched one of Frank's smokes. 'What are the odds,' he said, exhaling, 'that she went shopping or something. Y'know, she was going to be away for a few days, maybe she thought—'

'Don't be such a patronising fuck. You think it's all women think about, how they look? Jesus.' Then it hit her. 'Hey, take me back to the house again. You're saying nothing looked out of place, right?'

'It looked fine to me.'

'Yeah, but … There was nothing there that shouldn't have been there. Apart from the puke.'

'I don't follow.'

'In the hallway, or maybe the bedroom—you didn't see Madge's bag? I mean, she'd have packed a bag. You told her to.'

Ray thought hard, squinting past Karen as he tried to remember. 'There was nothing left out, no. Unless she had it stashed under the bed or something.'

'She'd have had it ready to go.' Karen stubbed her smoke, grabbed her mobile. 'We need to ring her,' she said.

'I thought you already rang her?'

'The landline, yeah.'

'You didn't try her mobile?' Ray sounding incredulous.

'Madge doesn't *like* mobiles, Ray. She only ever turns it on for emergencies.'

Ray, sounding miffed now, said: 'So you're saying, hanging out with me for a few days—that constitutes an emergency?'

Karen, listening to the brr-brr, glared. 'This'd be a bad time to start getting sensitive, Ray.'

DOYLE

Doyle had been fuming, fantasising about how to nail Frank for wasting police time. So she didn't make the jump until the kid said: 'I mean, like, how long do we wait before ringing her in as a missing person?'

'Whoa. Who's missing?'

'*Moms.*' The whiney voice ground down on Doyle's nerves. 'We've already tried ringing her friends, not that she has many ... Anyway, no one knows where she is.'

'Maybe she went for a walk.'

'Moms? I don't think so. At least, nothing longer than a stroll to the drinks cabinet.'

'Could she have a friend—I mean, a gentleman friend—that you don't know about?'

'You're joking, right? Although,' the kid said thoughtfully, 'now you mention it, one of her friends, Fiona, said she saw Moms out last night at the golf club. She was with people, a girl called Karen and this guy Fiona says is a painter-decorator.'

Doyle felt the lucky-break shivers. 'You got a description?'

'Sure. She's about fifty, has a—'

'Not your *mother*. The painter guy. What'd he look like?'

'I don't know. I wasn't there.'

'Okay. Give me this Fiona's number. And sit tight, I'll call back. If you hear from her, call me.'

Two minutes with Fiona got Doyle all the description she needed—serious fringe, cute buns. She took the address and was turning into Larkhill Mews when the Transit swept out by her, Ray on the phone. Doyle had ducked down, pulled in, thought it over fast—training said check the house, instinct said follow Ray. She'd U-turned, peeled rubber.

Now, sitting across the street from the coffee dock, watching Ray through the big window, the girl—Karen, Doyle was guessing—making a call, Doyle started working it through. Ray was pulling a snatch, this much he'd already told her. Except it looked like his intended target, this Margaret Dolan, had gone AWOL—and wherever she was, she wasn't in the Transit parked up the street, Doyle'd already had a sneaky peek inside.

Meanwhile, Margaret Dolan was the ex-wife of Doctor Frank Dolan, who was reluctant to help the police with their enquiries on an apparently unrelated matter. And according to Fiona, the Karen who'd been with Margaret Dolan out at Oakwood was the doctor's receptionist.

Doyle gnawed her lower lip. Ray hanging out with the slicer's receptionist, both of them sweating it up—Doyle could tell that much even from across the street. Then you had the plastic surgeon getting mugged, but none too worried about losing his briefcase, this just before his wife goes missing. Doyle still wondering in the back of her mind about the Nervocaine, how maybe the doc was peddling pills to socialites worried about how liposuction might leave scars. The receptionist, Karen, talking now on the phone, getting agitated, stabbing the air with the forefinger of her free hand …

Karen? Nervocaine?

Something clicked. Doyle, still watching the coffee dock, went with her instincts again, rang Sparks.

'Hey,' Sparks said, 'you missed a great fucking night Saturday night. Wait'll you hear who—'

'Later, Sparks. I need a quick favour.'

'Shoot.'

'Can you run down to my office and dig out the file on Callaghan?'

'Sure thing. Hold on.' Doyle watched Karen jab the air some more, the phone conversation getting heated; hearing spasms of conversation on her own phone as Sparks moved through the station. Then Sparks said: 'Okay, I got it.'

'Flick through to known associates. Any Karens in there?'

A pause. Then: 'Yep. Karen King. Rossi Callaghan was living with her before he went away the third time.'

Another click—Karen King, the name Doyle had rung the night Callaghan terrorised the fiancé-screwing Marsha. The Karen King who'd never rung back.

'She have any previous?' Doyle said. 'Specifically, I'm looking for black-market scripts.'

'Doesn't say anything here, no.'

'Okay. Run a check on her, buzz me back if there's anything.'

'Will do.'

'Thanks, Sparks. That's another one.'

'I'm counting 'em.'

Doyle hung up, trying to decide if it was too early to call it in. Or, already, too late.

ROSSI

Rossi fumbled through Margaret's travel bag and finally found the phone, down at the bottom, under the green skimpies. He checked the caller ID—*Karen-Karen-Karen*—and realised it was all going to be easier than he'd even dared hope.

'Hey, Karen. How's tricks?'

He heard the sharp intake of breath, relished it. Then: '*Rossi?*'

'The one and only.'

For once in his life Rossi was on a roll. Being chauffeured around in a Merc, Sleeps' latest boost, and the Germans, give them their due, they built to last, paying particular attention to things like seats, suspension, comfort. Rossi hadn't had a jab in his shaft in what felt like forever.

Then, also on the plus side, was the way Margaret was behaving herself, not freaking out the way Rossi'd expected. He'd gagged her with a tea towel strip after force-feeding her three Nervocaine, but it wasn't just the pills. The way she looked at him, wide-eyed, with as much awe as fear—it put Rossi in mind of the way Kay had looked at Michael at the end of *The Godfather*, realising what he could do, what he'd done. Rossi believed he could get used to being looked at like that.

Then, the piece-the-resistance—Rossi recognising, as soon as Margaret said Ray's name, the drawl he'd heard on the answering machine: the freak with the fringe, Karen's new guy. Rossi couldn't believe how it was all coming together. Like, you start out wanting your .44 back, the Ducati, the stash, and the next thing you know you're riding around in a Merc with half a million in the post. *The* half-million.

Strictly speaking, of course, Rossi wouldn't be needing the stash now, not with the half-million coming through. All the same, he'd told Sleeps, there was still a principle involved. You start off letting small things like that slip, next thing you know, everyone's taking liberties. Besides, Rossi wasn't touching down in Sicily with any piece-a-crap lady-gun .22. A popgun like that might be enough to frighten the likes of Margaret Dolan from Larkhill Mews but any decent crew, a proper family, they'd laugh Rossi back onto the plane if he pulled a .22.

'Where are you, Rossi?'

'Right now I'm just driving around. Sleeps reckons the cops have this thing they call triangulation, it can pick up a phone signal and—'

'Where's Madge?'

'On the backseat.'

'Let me talk to her.'

'What's that, an order or some shit?'

'Rossi, I swear, if you lay one fucking finger—'

'You're threatening me?'

'You skinny fucking *prick*! I'll cut your fucking—'

Rossi, grinning, held the phone away from his ear so Sleeps could get in on the action. Sleeps nodded, bored already, and kept his eyes on the road. Rossi shrugged, went back to listening.

'—and feed it to *Anna*!'

'Yeah. Listen, Karen—don't get me wrong, it's been nice talking to you. But I'm thinking you're a little too worked up to discuss details. So when you're ready to chat nicely, ring me back, we can work out where you're going to drop off this half-million Ray's getting from Frank.'

He hung up and switched off the phone. Winked at Sleeps, then glanced into the backseat. Margaret lay bent at an angle, hands behind her back, the tea towel strip wound around the lower half of her head.

'Sounds to me,' he said, 'like Karen's pretty worried about you. So this should be over in no time at all.'

No response; just the wide-eyed stare. Rossi caught a flash of the green skimpies and cursed his luck, his dangling gear still out of sorts—this Margaret, okay, was pushing fifty, but she was curvy all the way round and Rossi still hadn't had a jump since he'd got out.

Maybe, he thought, turning around to face forward, just maybe, later on, he might even be in a position to give her some more reasons to look at him wide-eyed. Yeah, the way Kay had looked at Michael.

FRANK

'I'm not really sure,' the nurse behind the desk said, 'if I should allow you in. I mean, Mr Jennings is in a coma.'

'I understand,' Frank said. 'But I'm his doctor.'

The nurse, squat and frumpy, her arms akimbo, nodded. 'That's what I'm talking about. Like, what good can you do? He's already got specialist care.'

'As it happens,' Frank said, back-pedalling furiously, 'I'm actually here as his friend rather than his doctor. We golf together.'

'Oh yeah? Were you there when he got beaned with the ball?'

'I, ah, no. I couldn't make it that day. Emergency call-out.'

'Shame. Anyway, it's family only. Sorry.'

'Y'know,' Frank wheedled, 'maybe the sound of a friendly voice …'

'Now that is a good idea. Why don't you go away and tape yourself, I don't know, singing some Tom Jones maybe? I'll make sure your Mr Jennings gets to hear it.'

Frank stared. The nurse stared right back. Frank about-turned and trudged down the long corridor, turned right into the foyer and punched the button to summon an elevator. As always, when it was Frank waiting, the elevator wouldn't budge from the ground floor; Frank reached again and jiggled the button, feeling the insurance form crinkle in his breast pocket; stared off through the fire-exit doors, seeing but not really seeing the flat roof beyond, the car park, the poplars fringing the hospital grounds …

Frank rewound fast. Trying to work out what it might have been that flashed like a glowworm, once and faint, way back in his brain. The trees, the car park, the flat roof, the fire-exit doors …

Thirty seconds later, the fire alarm squealing like buzz saws on steel, Frank was crouched beside Doug's bed holding a pen upright in Doug's limp fingers and scrawling Doug's signature in triplicate on Frank's copy of the insurance form. It was a low act, for sure, but Frank—walking out now through the chaos in the corridor, the blaring fire alarm making it difficult for the evacuation orders to be heard—Frank was of the opinion that any insurance company not insured against bogus claims didn't really deserve to be in the business.

MADGE

As if things weren't bad enough—bound and gagged, the Nervocaine wearing off, a nasty tea towel taste in her mouth; Madge now needed to pee. The pee-burn turning into an actual pain.

'Mmm-mmmm,' she said. 'Mmm-mmmf-*mmmm*.'

The driver, Sleeps, said: 'We can't keep driving around all night, Rossi. At some point we're going to have to find somewhere to kip down.'

'We're not going back to your place?'

'No can do. People know I went looking for you the other day with the Chopper. So if anyone starts asking about you, I mean the cops, they'll get pointed straight to my place.'

'MMMMMMFFF!'

'You got any ideas?' Rossi said.

'I'm working on it.'

'MMMMMMM!' Madge screamed, kicking the back of Rossi's seat.

'Christ! What the fuck—' Rossi half-turned to glare. 'What's *your* fucking beef?'

Sleeps checked the rearview, then indicated and pulled onto the hard shoulder, turned down the volume. 'I'm guessing,' he said, 'she needs to take a whizz.'

Madge nodded frantically.

'Wouldn't mind a pit stop myself,' Sleeps said. 'Anyway, we need to fill up.'

'Okay,' Rossi said, still glaring into the backseat. 'Find somewhere quiet, pull in around the back.' Then he held up the gun for Madge to see. 'Any funny stuff,' he warned, 'you try to shout or some shit when we take the towel off, I'll blaze away. And it won't just be you. You want that on your conscience?'

Madge shook her head, closed her eyes and clenched every pore in her body. Ten minutes later she was squatting above a brown-streaked toilet in a one-stall washroom out back of a Shell station. Tears of relief rolling down her cheeks, big fat balls soaked up by the tea towel. Wondering, disgusted by her squalid surroundings, how it was possible in the circumstances to feel, ohmigod, horny? She'd heard, okay, of the Stockholm syndrome, captives falling for their captors, and she'd always fantasised about a bit of rough—but Christ, *this* guy? Some skanger in a clown's suit?

Back in the car, driving off, Madge with her hands bound to the front this time, a small concession, Sleeps said: 'Hey Rossi, why don't we take her down the country? Lay up somewhere quiet.'

Rossi shook his head. 'We don't want to be too far away when Karen gets the money, give her any time to think. Seriously, Sleeps, you don't know her. I mean, look what she did with my sixty grand.'

'Mmmmmm,' Madge said.

'What the fuck is it *this* time?' Rossi demanded.

'Mmm-mmmm.'

'I think she wants you to take off the towel again,' Sleeps said.

'Why?'

'I'm thinking, if you take off the towel, you'll find out.'

Rossi considered that, then reached into the back. 'If you do anything stupid,' he said, sliding the towel down, 'I'll notch your nose. Both sides.'

Madge coughed and spat.

'Go on,' Rossi said.

'I know a place you can go,' she said, 'out of town. It's not far.'

'Oh yeah? Where?'

'Three-Rock Woods. There's an old Forestry Commission cottage, no one ever goes there.'

'Except,' Sleeps said, glancing in the rearview, 'maybe the occasional woodcutter, wandering by looking for a Red Riding Hood to save.'

Madge shook her head. 'What you're presuming,' she said, 'is I want you to get caught.'

Rossi, intrigued, scratched the tip of his nose with the .22. 'You're saying you don't?'

'The money?' Madge said. 'This half-million? Guess where that's coming from. I mean, guess who gets screwed if you walk away with it all?'

FRANK

Frank found a parking spot and jogged around to Trust Direct so he'd be sweating, ruffled, when he asked to see Doug.

'I'm afraid Mr Jennings isn't available today,' the receptionist said. 'Is there anyone else who might be able to help?'

'There'd better be. Otherwise I'll be getting a finger in the post.'

'I'm sorry?'

'Not half as sorry as you'll be if my wife ends up paraplegic. Who's in charge?'

Twenty minutes later Frank was sitting in front of the deputy manager's desk dunking a chocolate biscuit into a cup of hot sweet tea, Frank pleading shock, needing a sugar rush. The deputy manager, Marie, a severely streamlined brunette who'd had a rhino, Frank could tell, and some bleph, said: 'Take me through it again, Doctor Dolan. You say you received the ransom demand this morning.'

'Correct. About nine-ish.'

'Okay. And according to this stamp, Mr Jennings counter-signed the insurance form only last Thursday. A form that includes kidnap insurance.'

'That's right.'

'Something of a coincidence, don't you think?'

'An unfortunate coincidence,' Frank said smoothly. 'But Doug was the one who said I had to sign for everything, the full nine yards, because it was only a week's worth of insurance.'

'This is what's confusing me,' Marie said. 'Why only one week's insurance?'

'I'm getting divorced on Friday.'

'I see.'

'The plan,' Frank explained patiently, 'was that I'd get a week's insurance just to tide me over. Then, once the divorce went through, I'd reinsure, except with my wife-to-be Genevieve on the policy instead.'

'Except someone kidnapped your current wife just days before the divorce goes through.'

'It's tragic.'

'Not to mention highly improbable.'

'Which is probably why,' Frank pointed out, 'the kidnap insurance premium was so low.'

'Hmmmm.' Tapping a pencil on the form, Marie said: 'I presume you've already contacted the police?'

Frank shook his head. 'They're watching me. The kidnappers, I mean, not the cops. For all I know they're bugging my phone. And they said, if I call the cops, I'd never see Margaret alive again.'

'Yes, well, this is all highly irregular. It's company policy to contact the police in situations like this.'

'Oh yeah? And is it company policy to go bankrupt after it gets itself sued up the ass for criminal negligence resulting in the death of an insured party?'

Marie stared. Frank reached for a fresh biscuit, dunked into his tea. 'I'll be needing the money in cash,' he said. 'Small notes, non-sequential, you know the drill. Half a million by tomorrow morning, first thing. So—chop-chop. Let's go.'

KAREN

Ray, on the other end of the line, said: 'How can it get any worse?'

Still stunned, Karen heard herself say: 'It's *Rossi*, Ray.'

'I know it's Rossi. And he's getting the money so we get Madge. Where's the problem?'

'No, I mean, it's *Rossi*.' Karen lit one of Frank's Marlboros, sucked hard. 'Madge told me the other night she'd had a kid, years ago, long before the twins. She gave it up for adoption.'

'So?'

'So last night, I didn't twig at the time, there was too much going on—anyway, last night she told me the father was Frank.'

'And?'

'There was all this crap about the kid's name. Madge was fucked around when the baby was born, she says the father—Frank—got involved in naming the kid. Madge wanted to call it Israel.'

'Israel?'

'Yeah, she said it was from the Bible. Anyway, Frank got involved—'

'You think this kid is Rossi? Jesus, Karen—it's long odds.'

'You're the one,' Karen shot back, 'said it'd be long odds that Madge would be snatched by someone we know. And Rossi came up in a home, never knew who his folks were.' Ray did some grumbling way down his throat, but Karen talked over him. 'Ray—Frank's an opera nut, it's all he ever plays, makes him feel like he's some kind of intellectual. Anyway, his favourite? It's Rossini.'

Ray, for some reason, sounded very far away saying: 'The William Tell guy?'

'The Lone Ranger guy, Ray. Look—Rossi'd be the right age. I mean, from what Madge was saying.'

'Okay.' Ray sounded infuriatingly patient. 'But even if that *is* the case, then—'

'Rossi's just out, Ray. After doing five years, he'd get up on a crack in a plate. And Madge, she has this thing for younger guys, a bit of rough.'

'Jesus.'

Karen heard a muffled brr-brr. 'Ray? Hold on, there's a call coming through. It might be Frank.' She punched in call-waiting. 'Hello?'

'Yeah, hi.' A woman's voice, sounding cool and firm. 'Can I speak to Doctor Dolan, please?'

'I'm afraid the doctor isn't here right now. Can I take a message?'

'That's fine, thanks. Has he got any other contact numbers?'

'Actually he's unavailable at the moment. Would you like to make an appointment?'

A stern chuckle. 'No thanks. Can you tell him Marie from Trust Direct rang? He'll know what it's about.'

'Trust Direct. The insurance company, right?'

'That's right.'

'I'll do that.' Karen punched call-waiting again. 'Ray?'

'Yeah?'

'Green light.'

'I'm on my way.' He took a deep breath and said: 'Karen? Don't worry about, y'know, what you were saying. Even Rossi isn't so dumb or crazy he'll fuck with half a million. We'll lose the money, sure. But Madge'll be fine.'

'Hey, Ray?'

'What?'

'Next time you're talking to Anna, when she's not wearing the eye-patch—try telling *her* how Rossi isn't dumb or crazy.'

RAY

'And you've been through all his files,' Ray said.

Karen, arms folded, nodded.

'His computer?'

'Nothing,' Karen said. 'But this morning, when he was going through some papers, the safe was open.'

'Okay.' Ray glanced across at where Karen was looking, the framed *Barber of Seville* poster on the wall. 'And you've checked, the safe's definitely locked again.'

Karen just looked at him.

'I'm only asking,' Ray said. 'There's no dupes in the bin?'

'Nothing.'

'So Frank's getting the money from Trust Direct. That changes nothing. We still have to find him and hit him when he gets the cash. Any ideas on where he might be?'

'He was *supposed* to be here.' Karen nodding at the .44 on Frank's desk, the plan being to stick the gun's snout in his face and sit him down until Ray arrived. 'Except the bastard never came back after lunch.'

'So we need to start looking at other options. What about the club?'

'I was thinking of starting at the house. With the mooch.'

'You think he'd be dumb enough, planning a skip-out, to bunker in at his own house?'

'I don't know. But I need to be doing *something*, Ray. Y'know? This sitting around, not knowing where Madge is, if she's okay ...'

'I hear you. Let's go.'

On the drive over to Frank's, dusk coming on, Ray said: 'You might want to start thinking about Anna, getting her out. In case we have to skip too.'

Karen fumbled on the dashboard for one of Frank's Marlboros, lit up. Ray, realising it was a touchy one, changed the subject. 'You really think he's doing a bunk?' he said.

'The way he was acting this morning, I got the feeling he knew something no one else knows. Too fucking smug, y'know? Especially with Madge gone missing a day early. Then, the insurance company rings, wanting Frank to ring back.' She looked across. 'You don't get anything from all that?'

'Sure. A migraine.'

Karen smoked on. Ray turned up the stereo, Springsteen singing about the New Jersey turnpike, rock 'n' roll stations, driving all night. Sounding echoey, ghostly, not really there. Ray, the way everything seemed to be slipping away, fading out, could sympathise.

Genevieve answered the door, recognised them straight off. 'Oh hi,' she giggled. 'Can I help you?'

'We're looking for Frank,' Ray said. 'Is he in?'

'Yeah.' She giggled again, a brittle sound. Smashed, Ray realised; in the bag at seven in the evening. She said: 'Not right now, though. I haven't seen him all day.'

'Maybe we could come in and wait? We need to talk with him.'

'I dunno. I kinda want to talk to him myself whenever he gets home.'

'We'll queue,' Karen said.

Genevieve, undecided, swung the door to and fro.

'Listen,' Ray said, 'I've got a killer migraine. You think I could get a couple of painkillers?'

She shrugged, held the door open, took them through to the kitchen; handed Ray a packet of painkillers, offered martinis all round, asked if anyone was carrying smokes. Ray lit her up. She chugged her martini and wiped her mouth with the back of her hand, smudging lipstick and almost burning the tip of her nose with the cigarette.

'Where do you think he's gone?' Ray said gently.

'Fucked if I know.'

'Wherever he's going,' Karen said, 'he isn't gone yet.'

'I wouldn't be so sure,' Genevieve said. 'I checked. They're gone.'

'What's gone?' Ray said.

'His Viagra. His corset. The David fucking Leadbetter video.'

'He take his computer?' Ray said.

'Computer?'

'Yeah. Or a laptop, something he uses from home.'

'I don't know. He usually keeps it locked in the desk.' She jerked a thumb over her shoulder and almost poked herself in the eye. 'In the study.'

'Mind if we have a look? Might help us all to track him down.'

'Be my guest.' She giggled. 'Guests.'

She wobbled getting up, then steadied herself and led them out across the hallway to Frank's study. She gestured at the bare desk. 'There's a laptop in there somewhere. But he only uses it, as far as I know, for downloading porn.'

Ray started with the bottom drawer of the three, jemmying it open with the ornamental poker from the set of brass andirons on the fake hearth. 'Bingo,' he said, hauling a laptop in black matte finish from the drawer. He set it down on the desk.

Genevieve, in a small, dull voice, said: 'You know about the money, right? I mean, the ransom.'

Karen nodded. Ray powered up. The laptop whirred to life, welcoming them all with a tinny little tune. Then it requested a password.

The doorbell rang, deep and resonant. Genevieve looked from Ray to Karen.

'You expecting anyone?' Karen said.

Genevieve shook her head.

'Then I guess you'd better answer that,' Karen said, 'and find out who it is.'

Genevieve stubbed her cigarette into Frank's blank blotter, then tottered out into the hallway. Ray heard the front door open, some low mumbling; the self-satisfied schlunk of the heavy door closing again. Genevieve reappeared in the doorway of the study, glancing back over her shoulder. Doyle followed on, carrying a brown leather briefcase.

'This,' Genevieve said, 'is Detective Doyle. She's looking for Frank too. I told her she'd have to, y'know, get in line.'

'Hey, Ray,' Doyle said.

Ray grinned. 'Stephanie.'

'You've already met?' Genevieve trilled. 'Cool.'

'Karen,' Ray said, 'meet Detective Doyle. Stephanie, Karen.'

'Any friend of Ray's,' Karen said. Ray wondered why Karen'd never smiled as sweetly at him as she did for Doyle. Doyle smiling too, polite as a nun's fart, holding up the brown briefcase now.

'Just thought I'd drop this off on my way home,' she said, 'see if I couldn't grab a quick word with Doctor Dolan. I know he's a busy man.' Saying all this, Ray couldn't help but notice, while looking past them to the desk. 'Is that his laptop?'

'Yep,' Ray said.

'I'm guessing here,' Doyle said, 'but what I'm guessing is that you're fooling around with that laptop without the good doctor's permission. Am I right?'

'Call this a guess-back,' Karen said, 'but I'm guessing you're not sup-posed to step inside the door without a warrant.'

'Not unless I'm invited,' Doyle said, moving to the desk.

'Cops and vampires,' Karen said.

'I'm invited,' Doyle said. She slung the briefcase onto the desk, turned the laptop around to face her, hunkered down. 'Anyone mind if I play some solitaire?'

Karen, staring at Ray over Doyle's head, said: 'We can't get in. We don't know the password.'

'And no one,' Doyle said, glancing up at Genevieve, 'has any idea of what it might be?'

'Nope,' said Genevieve. She hiccupped, placed the tips of her fingers against her lips. 'But if I had to guess, I'd probably start off trying "belly button".'

ROSSI

Sleeps was losing the plot. Bitching about the cold, how it was dark, he was starving, all this. Rossi could have coped, he'd been colder doing time and the moon outside was almost full. But then Margaret chimed in, backing up Sleeps; she was hungry too.

Another time Rossi might've started waving the .22 around, but with the half-mill in the post, a few Nervocaine down the hatch, Rossi was in the mood to be generous. So he sent Sleeps back into town to pick up cheeseburgers, shakes, some candles. Sleeping bags, if he could get them. Hot coffee.

Sleeps left. Rossi sat at the wooden table building a jay. Rolling by touch, he'd done it a thousand times before, skinning up in the dark. Now he kept his eyes on Margaret, on the other side of the table; her hands still bound, eyes glittering in the half-light. Waiting for something to happen, Rossi could tell. He roached the jay, sparked up, exhaled.

'I don't suppose,' she said, 'I could get a smoke off that?'

Rossi, surprised, handed the joint across. 'I wouldn't have thought you'd be the kind.'

'That's me. Full of surprises.'

Rossi watched her smoke. 'You must hate this guy—your husband.'

'Ex-husband.'

'Whatever. The guy's cutting you loose and you're what, fifty?'

'Forty-five.'

'Same fucking difference, am I right?' He took the joint back, had a quick toke. 'See, what I'm wondering is—'

The phone rang. Rossi picked up. 'Yeah? Go on.' He listened. 'No, I said *strawberry*. Bring me back a banana shake and I'll … Yeah, okay, sound.' He hung up. 'Where was I?'

'My name is Margaret. But people call me Madge.'

'So we're friends now? In cahoots and shit?'

'Could be.'

Rossi shrugged. 'Anyway, you were saying, you hate this guy Frank.'

'There isn't even enough to hate. He's just pathetic.'

'You like the dynamic type. A man who'll get things done.'

'Right now I don't have what you might call types.'

Rossi passed the joint across. 'See,' he said, 'what I'm wondering, with you getting divorced and all, is how long it's been since, y'know.'

'Not long enough.'

'Me, I'm just out. So I don't have what you might call types right now either.'

He caught the glitter in her eyes; Rossi warming up, feeling his balls start to crinkle. 'I can tell,' he said, 'you being the lady type and all—'

The phone rang again. Rossi swore, picked up.

'Look, Sleeps, it's fucking simple. You just—Oh, hey Karen.' He winked at Madge. 'Hold up, Karen. Hold *up*, Christ … Yeah, that's better. Now—did you get the money? No? Then why the fuck're you ringing?' He listened for a moment, then cut in again. 'Karen, the deal is that you get the money, then you get to hear her say she's okay. How hard is that to understand? No, you can't talk to her. No, you *can't*. Jesus … Also, Karen? I'll be wanting the Ducati too, and the .44. And the sixty grand, Karen, it's a matter of principle. Ethics.' He gave Madge the thumbs-up sign. 'So whenever you get the half-mill, call me. Otherwise, for every wasted call you make, I'll slice a toe off.' He listened, frowning. 'Karen— why the fuck would I want to cut off my own toes? Look, get the money and ring me back, we'll take it from there. Okay?'

He switched off, beckoned for the joint. Madge passed it over. Rossi dragged deep, tasted cardboard; grimaced and stubbed the jay. He got up, stretching, waiting for a jag of pain; Madge watching every move, breathing hard enough for Rossi to hear it. He moved around the table until he was standing behind her, began massaging her shoulders.

'Like I was saying,' he said, 'you're the high-class type. Am I right?'

Madge cleared her throat. Rossi went on kneading.

'I mean, you're used to the best. None of this wham-bam crap. You'll be expecting foreplay, all this.' He ran the tip of his forefinger down the line of her jaw, tilting her chin so she was looking back up at him. 'I'm making no promises,' he said. 'Like I told you, I'm only out. But I'll do my best to hold off for as long as I can.'

Madge squirmed under his hands. 'Are you,' she said thickly, 'going to, you know, *take* me?'

Rossi stopped kneading. 'Say again?'

Her voice was tremulous. 'Are you going to get rough?'

Rossi hawked venomously, spat to one side. 'You want it *rough?*' he demanded. 'Lady, I'll give you all the fucking rough you can stand.'

KAREN

'There's no such thing as a victimless crime,' Doyle said. 'It's a myth. Someone, somewhere, always gets hammered.' She sipped her vodka-tonic and looked around the booth, lowering her voice even though the only other customers were slumped on high stools at the bar. 'Take Frank's scam. Trust Direct pays out, sure, they take the hit up front. But next year it's you and me paying through the nose for higher premiums.'

'I hear you,' Ray said. 'But right now we're looking at an actual victim. If Frank doesn't get the money and we don't get it from Frank, Madge turns into your actual victim. The best she can hope for is to walk away without any toes. In a manner of speaking.' He glanced across at Karen. 'That's what he said, right? He'd start on her toes.'

Doyle considered that. 'What d'you think,' she said, 'is he armed?'

Karen shook her head. 'If he was he'd be shouting about it. How he's packing iron, all sorts of shit.' Karen thought it'd be best if she left out how she was packing Rossi's .44. 'And even if he is, it's no real biggie. He just likes guns. Waving them around, mostly.'

'The thing is,' Ray cut in, 'if it wasn't for Frank setting up Madge to be snatched, Rossi wouldn't be a problem right now.'

'Frang's a cund,' Genevieve slurred.

'Is she okay?' Doyle asked Karen.

Karen looked down to where Genevieve was stretched out on the seat of the booth, her head in Karen's lap. 'She'll make it,' she said.

'What I'm saying,' Ray went on, 'is that you have enough right now to put Frank away. Conspiracy to kidnap, unlawful detention, insurance fraud. Then there's the whole black market Nervocaine gig. I mean, the dopey prick kept e-mails on his laptop. So it's a gift, your score, you take him down. You personally.'

'Except,' Doyle said, 'you want me to hold off nailing Frank until you've handed the cash over to Rossi.'

'Not even that long. All you have to do is wait until we hit Frank for the cash. *Then* you nab him.'

'Meanwhile, you'll have disappeared. With half a million in cash.'

'So nothing happens to Madge,' Karen pointed out.

'Let me get this straight,' Doyle said. 'You're asking me to ring Trust

Direct and find out when Frank is picking up the cash so I can tip you off.'

Ray and Karen nodded simultaneously.

'And all this,' Doyle continued, 'is off the record. I mean, I'm telling Trust Direct I'm working undercover but I'm telling no one else. Like, for instance, my boss.'

'We appreciate you're taking a chance—' Karen began.

'A *chance?*'

'But by then you've already nailed Frank. And you have his records from the laptop, those e-mails he was sending his guy in Trust Direct, Doug Jennings.'

'A definite score,' Ray agreed. 'Cast-iron. Frank's going down.'

'Frang's a friggin' bastard,' Genevieve mumbled—dribbling, Karen couldn't help but notice, on Karen's thigh in the process.

'And what happens,' Doyle wanted to know, 'when Trust Direct start squawking about their half-million?'

'That's where you've shown initiative in the field,' Ray said. 'That's where, with a woman's life on the line, you've done what was necessary to secure her freedom, some bullshit like that. *And* nailed Frank, the guy running the show.'

'Trust Direct,' Karen added, 'aren't going to squawk too loud when it's a woman's life they're playing with. Christ, the PR they'll get, they couldn't *buy* that kind of coverage.'

Doyle sipped some more vodka-tonic. 'Okay,' she said. 'But what are you giving me? I mean, I'm going out on a pretty thin fucking limb here. What do *I* get?'

'What is it you're looking for?' Ray said.

'You,' Doyle said. 'What we already talked about. I'm going to need you to stand up and testify in court how Frank's this criminal mastermind pulling kidnaps all over. You tipped me off, got yourself a guilty conscience. That way I'm following up on Frank after the mugging, when he starts acting weird and pretending he doesn't own the briefcase. A briefcase, as it happens, that's covered in Rossi's paw prints. This is why I'm calling to

Frank's house, finding his laptop with the assistance,' she jerked a thumb at Genevieve, 'of Sleeping Beauty here. Because I'm building a file.'

'Pretend I'm a lawyer in court,' Karen said. 'How come Ray tipped *you* off?'

Doyle shrugged, winked at Ray. 'We'll call it pillow talk,' she said.

Karen looked across at Ray. Ray shrugged.

'I don't have a problem,' he said, 'with perjuring myself if it's in a good cause. I mean, if Madge walks away and Frank does time.'

'Fuggin' belly buttons,' Genevieve muttered.

Doyle drained the last of her vodka-tonic. 'One for the road?' she said, standing up.

'I don't think so,' Ray said. He nodded at Karen. 'We have to go see a man about a dog.'

TUESDAY

RAY

'Good news and bad news, Ray. Which d'you want first?'

Ray groaned and knuckled his eyes, switched the phone to his left ear. 'The good,' he said through a yawn.

'Okay,' Doyle said, 'but there isn't an awful lot of good.'

'Shit.' Ray rolled into a half-sitting position, pushing off the duvet as he reached for his smokes. 'What's up?'

'Trust Direct—as a result of negotiations that went on all fucking *night*, Ray—anyway, they've agreed to release the ransom.'

Ray lit up. 'That's good.'

'Except they're only releasing two hundred grand.'

'Fuck. How come?'

'Two big ones is what their expert actuary-types decided was the minimum a kidnapper would accept on the low side and the maximum their shareholders would accept going high. These being experts who were dragged out of bed to do their expertising.'

'So what you're really saying,' Ray said, struggling forward to perch on the edge of the couch, 'is they're playing games with a woman's life.'

'A woman, if you want to be precise about it, who isn't a shareholder.'

'Bastards.' Ray put his shoulders through a slow wriggle, straightening his back to iron out the wrinkles. Next time Karen wanted Anna to share her bedroom, he thought, she was investing in a bigger couch or waving adios to Ray. He could hear Anna now, even through the wall, the bass growl, the toenails clickering on the polished floorboards.

He tried to remember Karen's logic from the night before, why it had made sense for Ray to sleep on the couch and Anna on Karen's bed, but all he could recall was a chafing sense of injustice.

'Any more bad news?' he said.

'I'm riding shotgun on the money.'

'Shit.'

'They want their money back, Ray. Plus they've gone over my head.'

That much at least Ray'd been expecting. 'How far over?'

'Far enough. They'll be waiting for me to let them know where and when the pickup is happening.'

'And you'll be hearing about the pickup from …?'

'You and Karen, soon as you hear from Rossi.'

Ray grinned. 'That *is* bad news.'

'Isn't it, though?'

'So what's the ETA on Frank?'

'Ten o'clock, the city-centre Trust Direct building. You know it?'

'We'll find it. What're they using to hold the cash?'

'A khaki duffel.'

'Just the one?'

'You'd be surprised how little space half a million takes up.'

'Especially,' Ray said, picturing Rossi's face, the mean little boiling eyes, 'when it's only two hundred grand. You'll be there?'

'Yeah. But don't worry, you won't see me.'

'I think I'll do some worrying all the same. No offence.'

'None taken. And Ray?'

'What?'

'Make it hard for me. I mean, don't leave me looking a complete fucking blonde for losing you on a one-way street.'

FRANK

Frank believed he was having the best morning of his life. He'd gotten up early, showered and shaved, and was dining on a light breakfast of grilled kidneys, toast and orange juice when his shirt and suit arrived back from room service, so neatly pressed they looked almost new. He'd tipped heavily leaving the hotel, partly because he was high on a sense of adventure, the idea that he was living the first day of the rest of his life; mainly, though, because Frank didn't think he'd ever be tipping again. He wasn't entirely sure of the protocols, but found it hard to believe Haitians would be expecting too much by way of tips.

The morning was chilly but Frank didn't mind that; it'd be his last chilly morning for some time. Still feeling generous, he told the cabbie to keep the meter running when they arrived at the Trust Direct building, then strolled briskly inside.

By the time he reemerged, half an hour later, Frank's step wasn't anywhere near as spry. And that was before he heard the fat parp of the BMW's horn and realised the meter was still running. Still in a state of shock from hearing the words 'two hundred thousand', Frank shuffled towards the kerb, squeezing the handle of the khaki duffel and girding his loins for the battle of wits to come.

'Doctor Dolan?'

He'd turned before he realised he shouldn't have but by then it would have been too late anyway. She'd only said his name to distract him. Even as he glanced around, Frank felt something clamp down on his wrist, something cold and hard that clinked tight with a metallic clink.

He cleared his throat. 'Can I help you?' he said.

'You're a day late and three hundred thou short. Get in the van.'

KAREN

Ray only grunted. 'What she told me,' he said, 'was we wouldn't see her.'

'Maybe we should've blinked a little longer,' Karen said.

They watched as Doyle handcuffed Frank and relieved him of the khaki duffel.

'She's coming our way,' Ray observed.

'You don't miss a trick, boy scout,' Karen said as Doyle hustled Frank across the street towards the Transit. 'What d'you think she has planned?'

'You're the woman. You should know how she's thinking.'

'You're the criminal mastermind.'

'Retired.'

'I'm guessing,' Karen said as Ray leaned back to open the side-panel in the rear of the van, 'you're due an early comeback.'

Doyle pushed Frank into the van ahead of her, got him sitting on a large paint pot, slid the door closed behind her. Still standing, crouched, she nodded at Karen and Ray. 'Hey,' she said. 'There's been a slight change in plan.'

'We got that, yeah,' Karen said. 'Frank, Stephanie, meet Anna.'

Frank gaped in horror as Anna shoved her huge muzzled snout between his knees.

'How come the change in plan?' Ray said.

'Your guy Rossi?' Doyle said. 'He's already wanted for attempted rape.'

'Rossi?' Karen, shocked, shook her head. 'For rape?'

'Attempted. Although I don't know, that Marsha seemed flaky to me … You know the guy, right?'

'He's a prick,' Karen confirmed. 'I'm the first to say it. But not rape. Not Rossi.'

'Where to now?' Ray asked Doyle.

'Wherever you're meeting Rossi.'

'Actually,' Karen said, 'there's been a change in plan there too.'

'Tell me more.'

'You mind if I drive off?' Ray said. 'That cabbie's getting out of the Beamer.'

'Sure,' Doyle said. 'Find somewhere quiet, we need to talk anyway. And I haven't had a coffee since six this morning.'

Ray eased out into the traffic, swerving to avoid the irate cabbie, who pounded on the side of the Transit as they pulled away.

'What about La Ciabatta?' Karen said. 'The Italian place on the canal.'

'Great, yeah,' Doyle said. 'I've been meaning to go there, actually. I hear the coffee's drop-dead.'

Even over the roar of the engine, the clanking of paint pots, Karen could hear Anna's throaty growl, Frank whimpering.

ROSSI

Sleeps shuffled his feet as he gazed out across the lake.

'She looks a bit rough this morning, Rossi. I mean, raw.'

Rossi sniffed as he glanced back up at the cottage. 'Yeah, well, she had a tough fucking night.'

'I know, but—'

'She had it coming, Sleeps. She had it coming a long fucking time.'

'All I'm saying is what Pacino'd say. This shit's nothing personal, it's just business.'

'That was a movie, Sleeps. This is my fucking *life* we're talking about here. Although,' Rossi conceded, 'I'm not saying it wouldn't make a movie. With, I dunno, maybe Colin Farrell. What d'you think?'

'Maybe,' Sleeps said. 'It was me, I'd be thinking more along the lines of Johnny Depp. Good-looking guy, Rossi—he'd get the chicks queuing up.' He flicked his head in the direction of the cottage. 'Meanwhile, this is a bad time to get all emotional and shit.'

The chilly breeze coming off the lake, cold mud seeping into his trainers—nothing could distract Rossi from his sense of grievance.

'*Emotional* and shit? Look at me, Sleeps. I mean, will you take a fucking *look* at me? I'm a refugee from *Hello, Dolly!* in a suit I blagged from Oxfam. This because I'm just out, third fucking time, and I don't have the scoots to buy decent threads because Karen swiped my stash while I was banged up. And you're talking emotions and shit?'

'I hear you. But Rossi—'

'Then this bitch, she has it all, the big fucking house, the works—she wants me to get *rough* with her? Some fucked-up fantasy she's got going on?'

257

Rossi'd had a long night—Madge, spaced on pills and grass, explaining, like Rossi gave a fuck, why the idea of rough trade was her way of dealing with what had happened in the past, a fantasy in which she was the one who decided what happened, how far it went. Rossi sitting there pretending to listen, rolling the occasional joint to keep himself from sticking a fork in his heart.

'I told her,' he said, 'straight up, I said, "Lady, anyone who ever grew up in a home, did time, never had to fantasise about what it's like to be raped."'

Sleeps winced. 'And this is when she makes the jump. I mean, about you being this orphan.'

'All fucking *night* it went on. Telling me my real name's Rossini, how this Frank guy picked it after some opera maker.'

'Tough break.'

'Opera my skinny white ass. I *know* who my father is, Sleeps. Some pizza baker guy, got Shirley up the pole when she was fourteen then bolted back to Sicily soon as he heard.'

'Shirley?' Sleeps frowned. 'Shirley from down the canal?'

'Whoa, Sleeps. A little respect. That's my mother you're talking about.'

Sleeps digested that. 'So how come you're taking it so personal? If Madge has it so wrong about this orphan thing.'

'Because she thought she was right.'

'So?'

'So she asks me, "What would it take for you to shoot Frank?"'

'She was probably in shock. Being snatched and all.'

'She says, "If Frank dies, I get to take care of his estate for the girls. What'll it cost?" I mean, she's thought about this.'

'This is when she still thinks you're his son?'

'Wanting me,' Rossi nodding, 'for money, to shoot my own father.'

'What'd you say?'

'I told her, in Sicily, we don't shoot our own fathers.'

'Except,' Sleeps pointed out helpfully, 'he's *not* your father.'

Rossi flipped the butt of his joint into the lake. It fizzled, then bobbed gently on its own ripples. 'I want both of them, Sleeps, in the same room, answering questions. First one stutters gets a bullet in the knee. It's your basic Russian roulette with a Sicilian twist. What d'you think?'

'I got a better idea.'

'Like what?'

'This Frank being a doctor,' Sleeps said slowly, feeling his way into it, 'that estate she's talking about could be worth a bit. Like you say, she has the big house.'

'Go on.'

'Madge could be your golden goose, Rossi. Like, first you whack Frank, she pays up—what, twenty grand?'

'I'm whacking no one, Sleeps. Do time for *these* bastards?'

'Wait. First you get the money up front. Then you put a bullet in Frank for show, maybe the knee, like you said. What's she going to do, run to the cops because he isn't all the way dead? Then, Madge being the one who commissioned the hit, she's ripe for a little bounce. A couple of grand a month, say. One each, me and you.'

Rossi considered. 'You think?'

'Better'n capping him for nothing.'

'True. And then you have to consid—'

Rossi's phone rang. He picked up. 'Yeah?'

'Rossi?'

'Go ahead, Karen.'

Rossi found himself listening to the gentle splashing of waves, a sudden whicker from the reeds.

'Rossi?' Karen said. 'You okay?'

'Yeah, I'm just a little snowed under right now. You get the money?'

'We have it.'

'Okay, we're in business. One more thing.'

'What? Rossi, *don't* start—'

'This guy Frank. You know where I can find him?'

Rossi listened to a static-filled silence. Then Karen said: 'Right now he's in the back of the van, about to puke. You think we might be able to do some kind of deal?'

'Bring him along. We'll work something out.'

MADGE

'I think a little more blusher,' Mirror-Madge said. 'Up under the eyes.'

Madge peered into the vanity-case mirror. 'You think?'

'They're still going to look puffy and swollen. And there's nothing you can do about the bloodshot whites. But if you highlight the cheekbones, blend them in …'

Madge dabbed and brushed some more. 'How's that?'

'Not so bad,' Mirror-Madge said. 'I mean, there's this sick desperation in the way you're—'

Madge snapped shut the vanity case, zipped up her travel bag. Then, with rigid fingers, hands shaking, she rolled a cigarette from the debris Rossi had left on the table.

She took a deep drag, cupping the cigarette in her palm, the real reason for rolling it—Madge thought she'd never before been so cold and miserable. She switched the cigarette from hand to hand, warming each palm, smoking only to keep the tiny ember lit. She could have sipped the damp air through a straw.

'You've been colder than this,' Mirror-Madge said.

Madge, hugging herself tightly, just shook her head.

'That time you went skiing,' Mirror-Madge urged. 'Remember? In the French Alps? Where the ski instructor advised everyone, but women particularly, against peeing outside.'

Madge turned away from her reflection in the window and began walking around the table, rubbing her shoulders and upper arms. A long curved ash fell from the cigarette.

'And you were definitely more miserable,' Mirror-Madge went on, 'the night Frank, y'know, that time in the car. Or the time you gave up that little baby. Remember?'

But Madge didn't want to remember. In the last twelve hours Madge had done enough remembering to last her a lifetime—and no matter where she had looked, Rossi's eyes were iris-to-iris with her own: huge, round and dark with pain. She had always acknowledged the magnitude of her baby's loss; even in the worst times, the blackest nights, Madge had always been aware of how the child's hurt was immeasurably deeper than her own. But last night, unable to break away from the compelling gravity of his dark eyes, Madge had realised that Rossi's sense of loss was so vast as to encompass everything—the planets and stars, the entire universe. Because Madge now knew that, for Rossi, everything, from his inside out, sprang from loss.

'He's going to kill Frank,' Mirror-Madge mocked, 'isn't he?'

'I don't know.'

'But you *want* him to. And you want to watch. Otherwise you'd run away. I mean, Rossi's left you here alone, hands untied, and you haven't even thought of running off.'

'Where would I go?'

'The main road, maybe? To hitch a lift from there? It's only about a mile or so away.'

'I wouldn't make it,' Madge said, twitching an ankle. 'Not in these heels.'

'Perhaps not,' Mirror-Madge agreed. 'But then, you want to see Frank die. Don't shake your head. You *do*.'

Madge closed her eyes and shook her head so violently tiny lights danced in the darkness; it was as if the night sky had taken leave of its senses and was spinning according to no law of nature Madge had ever heard of. Not to be outdone, gravity took a little break for itself, and Madge felt herself tilt …

She came to when Sleeps crouched down to pat her cheek, although it seemed as if he was very far away. Beyond him, Rossi sat on a corner of the table, one leg swinging, the phone clamped to his ear.

'You alright, Madge?' Sleeps was saying. 'Can I get you a glass of water or something?'

'Hold on,' Rossi said. He hunkered down beside them, thrust the phone at her. 'Tell Karen you're doing great.'

Madge reached a long, long way to take her phone.

'Karen?'

'Madge? Are you okay?'

'Forget about me, Karen.' Madge heard her voice come weak and echoey. 'You have to think of Anna. Think of *Anna*, Karen.'

Rossi snatched the phone away. 'You get that?' he said.

Madge heard the distant twitterings of Karen's voice.

'Yeah, well,' Rossi said, 'at least you know she's still alive. Which she won't be in two hours' time if I'm not looking at the money and Frank.'

He hung up and switched off the phone, tucked it into the breast pocket of his suit. Madge thought he looked a bit blurry.

Sleeps came through from the kitchen. 'Sorry, Madge. I forgot there's no water. There's any amount of Nervocaine, though, if you have a headache.'

'That's okay, Sleeps,' Mirror-Madge said. Madge could hear her only faintly. 'I think, now, she's going to be just fine.'

The last thing she heard was Sleeps, from very far away, his voice a furious whisper: 'Jesus, Rossi—she's bleeding out her fucking *ear*.'

KAREN

'Think of *Anna*?' Ray sounding baffled. 'Why's she talking about Anna?' Ray with his head close to Karen's so they could both listen in on the call.

Karen stared down at the phone on her open palm as if trying to weigh the import of the message.

'What's up?' said Doyle from the rear.

'Madge didn't sound so good,' Ray said. 'Started rambling about the wolf.'

Anna growled. Frank whimpered.

'They're at the cottage,' Karen said.

'I don't get it,' Ray said.

'It's a woman thing, Ray.'

'Which we're calling what today—a hunch? Feminine intuition?'

'Neither. It's called lying to a man's face without him having a clue.' Karen half-turned in her seat to look back at Doyle. 'Okay, there's been another change in plan.'

'You know where they are?'

Karen nodded.

'And I'm guessing,' Doyle said, 'that where they are is nowhere near where the pickup is supposed to happen. I can't sanction that, Karen.'

'I know.' Karen poked the snout of the .44 into the rear of the van. Doyle looked at the gun, then Karen, one eyebrow raised.

'That's a hell of a change in plan,' she said.

Frank noticed the .44 and made a high-pitched noise in his throat, shied away, tugging Doyle off balance. Doyle, still staring at Karen, dragged him back.

'This way,' she said, 'afterwards, you didn't have a choice in the matter.'

'Is that thing even loaded?'

'Which would be better for you, loaded or not?'

'I'm not thinking of me, girl.'

Ray flashed a Renault out of an intersection. 'So we're heading for the cottage now, right?'

'Yep.' Karen still staring at Doyle. 'I'll need to take your phone away too,' she said.

Doyle hesitated. 'You're sure you want to do this?'

'I don't have any choice, Stephanie.'

Doyle passed her phone across.

'And you might want to think about unchaining yourself from Frank.'

'I would, but I don't have the key. They're not even my cuffs. I had to borrow a pair this morning.'

Ray groaned. 'Hey, why don't you just make a wish? That way, when the cuffs fall off, it'll be a woman's thing.'

Karen grinned. 'What's wrong, Ray? Worried I might be lying to *you*?'

'Men don't multitask, Karen. And right now I have to worry about you holding a gun on a cop.'

'You mean Stephanie.'

Ray rolled his eyes. 'What I'm saying is, how do we hand Frank up to Rossi if he's cuffed to a cop?'

'What's that?' Frank said.

Karen waggled the .44 in his general direction, then said to Doyle: 'I don't have to point this at you all the way there, right?'

'Is the safety on or off?'

'Off.'

'Then no. I don't get paid to take those kind of risks.'

Frank cleared his throat with a squeaky cough. 'Karen?'

Karen didn't look at him. She clicked her tongue to call Anna, unbuckled the muzzle, lifted it clear. Anna practically purred. Frank blanched.

'You want to step on it a little?' Karen said to Ray. 'I'd like to get there before it gets any worse for Madge.'

'You want us to get pulled over?'

'Oh Ray,' Karen sighed, patting her heart with the butt of the .44, 'you think of *everything*.'

ROSSI

'But how come it's *me*', Sleeps wanted to know, 'has to make the pickup?'

'Because the main guy always stays home with the troops,' Rossi said. 'It's good for morale.'

They were on the porch outside the cottage, Rossi straddling a chair,

Sleeps swamping a damp stump of log. 'Rossi—*I'm* your troops. Me. And my morale is already rock fucking bottom.'

'You ever hear of buckwheats, Sleeps? No? *Things to Do in Denver*, Andy Garcia. With buckwheats, you get a round up the hole. Horrible death. You see what I'm saying. About morale.'

Sleeps sighed. 'What if, when I get there, they won't come back with me? I mean, they'll be expecting to see Madge.'

'Tell 'em …' Rossi mulled it over. 'Okay, yeah—tell 'em Madge isn't fit to travel. If they want her, they have to come and get her.'

'So why not ring Karen and tell them to come here?'

'And what? *They'll* stop off for the cheeseburgers?'

'Okay, so why don't *we* go meet *them*, stop off for eats on the way?'

'Because this way,' Rossi said patiently, 'they don't know what they're getting into. They've no time to plan anything. And Sleeps—get sugar for the coffee this time. If I have to drink coffee with no sugar again, I swear I'll shoot some fucker in the eye.'

Sleeps stood up. 'Y'think,' he said, 'did Mussolini, Napoleon, all these guys—y'think did they threaten their troops all the time?'

'Fucked if I know. What d'you think, maybe they should've?'

Sleeps glanced through the doorway to where Madge lay prone on the floor, his jacket tucked up under her chin. 'What about her?'

'She'll do.'

'I don't know, Rossi. She looks pretty—'

'Tell you what I'll do, Sleeps. I'll sic five or six guys on her, for some reason they might want to bust her face in, maybe slip her one up the ass because there's nothing on TV. After that, if she hasn't improved any, I might get all worried and shit. How would that be?'

Sleeps slipped and slid across the muddy clearing. On the fringe of the forest he turned. 'Hey, Rossi—all this food and shit, that comes out of the expense account. I mean, I'll be getting expenses, right?'

Rossi took the lady-gun .22 out of his pocket, held it up. 'Buckwheats,' he said.

RAY

Ray jammed on the brakes when he saw the Merc top the small rise about eighty metres dead ahead, pulling the Transit in on a bend that curved down to the right and had space enough to tuck in to the side. The Transit pulling sluggishly with all the extra weight in the back. Ray didn't fancy trying the steep, narrow track with anyone looking down at him, not from some Merc and not in the middle of any forest.

He flashed his lights. The Merc flashed back.

'There's every chance,' he said, 'that this is Rossi.'

'Rossi's seen your van before,' Karen reminded him. 'And Rossi wouldn't have stopped, not for us.'

'So who is it?'

'How would I know? Flash it again.'

Ray obliged. The Merc moved forward a little, then reversed back towards the sheer drop behind.

'He's going to fall in,' Doyle said.

The Merc stopped on the brink, seemed to teeter, then edged forward towards the high bluff on the other side of the track.

'He's blocking the road,' Ray said.

The Merc began reversing again. 'Nope,' Karen said, 'he's going for a U-turn.'

'He's going to fall in,' Doyle insisted.

The Merc teetered again on the brink, seemed to shudder, then slid backwards off the track and out of sight into the gully.

Ray looked at Karen.

'Maybe,' she said, 'that *was* Rossi.'

'You think we'd get that lucky?'

He thought she said 'Never,' but he couldn't be sure because that was the moment Anna, pacing the van and sniffing the air, cut loose with a rib-shivering howl.

A gunshot cracked through the forest.

'Christ,' Karen said. 'He's *shot* her.'

MADGE

Madge sat up, stiff and cold, a little dizzy. Wondering what had woken her. Through the doorway she could see that Rossi had heard it too—he stood rigid on the porch, staring off into the forest, his pallor grey.

She threw back Sleeps' jacket and got to her feet, feeling woozy, a pounding at her left ear that might have been her brain pulsing out an SOS. She supposed she must have fainted and bumped her head on the way down; the last thing she could remember was saying to Karen about how she should look out for Anna …

Anna?

Now Madge knew what had woken her. She moved towards the doorway and stumbled out onto the porch, a treacherous heel catching on the rough boards. Rossi, hearing the scraping sound, whirled to face her.

There was, Madge noted as she pitched towards him, a gun in his hand …

Then he was catching her and staggering backwards. Her momentum carried them both off the porch onto the muddy incline of the clearing and they slipped and slithered downhill towards the lake, Rossi swearing up a blue streak.

The incline levelled out. Rossi dug in. They ground to a halt. Madge, breathless and still dizzy, laid her head on his shoulder and hugged him, grateful beyond words for his solidity, the way he didn't swoop and yaw like the rest of the world. And then, above the sounds of squelching mud, the blood roaring in her ears, Madge heard a sound she'd never heard before. A hoarse sound with a coarse timbre, a sound Madge heard deep inside, booming through a cavern she'd never even known existed.

'Haw,' he was saying. 'A-haw-haw-*haw*.'

The sound of her only son, laughing.

KAREN

Karen, squinting through the flickering trees, said: 'He's going to *drown* her now?'

The Transit crashed through the wooden-pole barrier and skidded on the thick mud, slewing to a stop, as Ray jammed on. Karen jerked forward, hearing paint pots rattle, Doyle and Frank shunt forward, Anna barking.

By now the cottage lay between the Transit and the struggle on the lakeshore; Karen scrabbled to release her safety belt, cursing it, aware that Ray was already out and vaulting the low wire fence, sprinting for the cottage, tugging something from his belt, the small of his back. She released the catch and jumped out of the van just as the rear door slid open. Anna bounded past her, howling. Then Doyle half-fell out of the van, dragging a bewildered Frank in her wake.

'He's *drown*ing her?' Doyle said.

But Karen was already stumbling after Ray, who was disappearing around the side of the cottage. Then she heard, even over Anna's howling, three flat cracks. A piercing screech. Ray appeared again, half-somersaulting to one side. He hit the ground hard and wriggled around in the mud, screaming.

Karen, it was like she'd been shot herself, felt a pang in her gut. Then, still struggling up the incline, she heard another flat crack.

Anna cut off in mid-howl.

ROSSI

Like, what was he supposed to do? Karen's guy comes charging around the side of the cottage, no warning, waving this fuck-off cannon—Rossi, his arm resting on Madge's shoulder, aimed for Ray's chest, the biggest target, and squeezed one off.

Except Madge shifted, causing his arm to dip. He snapped another couple off, Madge cringing away from the noise, Ray ducking away to one side but too late, going down hard, screaming.

Rossi had just enough time to admit it'd been a complete fluke, taking down a guy sprinting across rough ground, and then Stalin came hurtling around the cottage howling like a fire engine in flames. She skittered to a stop, slid another two or three yards of greasy turf on her haunches, the huge head turning as she sailed past Ray. Then she got her bearings and fixed that single amber eye on Rossi, howled again: a primitive, triumphant bellow that shivered Rossi to the core. In one fluid movement she got her back legs adjusted, tensed and shot forward.

But by then it was too late.

Rossi, still pumping on adrenaline, just twitched the barrel of the .22. He even had time to breathe out as Stalin loped towards them, slavering, her unearthly howl reverberating through the small clearing.

Rossi hugged Madge so close she couldn't move, rested his elbow on her shoulder. Stalin charged straight down the mouth of the gun, a one-wolf charge of the light brigade. Rossi sighting one-eyed along the .22's barrel, dead-centre on Stalin's forehead.

She leapt, jaws wide as a tunnel. So close Rossi could see the silvery drool strung between the massive teeth.

He *couldn't* miss.

He didn't.

FRANK

Stumbling along in Doyle's wake, Frank went down face-first to inhale a mouthful of cold, thick mud. Then he felt himself being dragged to his feet again, the metal cuff slicing into his wrist, and realised he was in a world gone dark.

He had enough presence of mind to realise he wasn't actually blind, that he must have gotten mud in his eyes. But the way things were going,

Frank would have taken blindness over his uncertain immediate future if anyone had offered the choice …

It was hard for him to believe that it was only two hours since he'd strolled into the Trust Direct building. In the intervening period, he'd seen his fortune halved, that half taken away, and got himself handcuffed to a cop who seemed to have him pegged for some kind of criminal mastermind. All of which was bad enough, but Frank was still trying to cope with the idea of Karen waving a gun around while a wolf tried to gnaw his testicles.

Worst of all, though, was the bowel-loosening realisation—one not helped by the intermittent spatter of what Frank believed to be gunfire—the realisation that he was to be handed over to some ruthless maverick called Rossi, and that his life had spun irretrievably out of control.

Frank, still blind, stumbled into Doyle, who had pulled up short. He heard a nasal voice say: 'That's Frank?'

He pawed at his face with his free hand, wiped the mud from his eyes. Then wished he hadn't.

KAREN

'Let her go, Rossi,' Karen ordered.

Rossi, not hearing her, said again: '*That's* Frank?'

Karen, palms up, arms outspread, advanced cautiously down the incline towards the lake. She was aware of Doyle and Frank behind her; to her left was Ray, squirming in the mud, all choked up behind clenched teeth. She moved past Anna, prone and lifeless, but Karen kept her eyes on Madge, the shuddering shoulders, hearing her sob.

'Don't do anything stupid, Rossi,' she said. 'Let her go.'

But then Karen realised, as Madge turned towards her, sniffling, that it was Madge releasing Rossi …

She turned all the way into Karen's arms. 'I'm okay, Karen. Really.'

'Now you are,' Karen said. Saying this while she patted Madge on the back, then on the hip. Then Madge's ribs, bringing her hand around the front so Madge was between Rossi and the blue-steel .44 in Karen's jacket pocket …

Rossi saying: 'You're telling me that skangy fuck is *Frank*?'

ROSSI

Rossi, waiting on Frank to show up, had been expecting something else. Not this sad sack of shit with shaky knees making a noise like a punctured frog.

'How come he's handcuffed?' he said.

'He's under arrest,' Doyle said. 'And my advice to you is, put the gun down and make things easy on yourself.'

'Make it easy on you, y'mean.'

'Rossi Callaghan, I am arresting you for aggravated assault, unlawful detention, intent to—'

A bullet sang out and struck the cottage about five feet from Doyle's head, showering cop and captive with tiny splinters. Frank squealed and shrank away. Doyle, Rossi was impressed, shuddered but then just wrinkled her nose and sniffed hard.

'Frank?' he said. 'How're you doing? I'm Rossi and we're going to play buckwheats. Ever heard of buckwheats?'

Frank, bewildered, shook his head.

'Well,' Rossi said, 'you take a gun …'

Except Frank keeled over long before Rossi hit the punch line, leaving Doyle tilted over at an angle, her arm pulled straight. Rossi said, to Karen: 'Where's the money?'

'In the van.'

'You want to, y'know, go get it? So we can all crack on?'

'If you want it, *you* go get it.'

Rossi thought that over and realised, hey, it wasn't such a bad idea. 'Okay,' he said.

Off to his right, still sprawled in the mud, Ray ground out one word from between clenched teeth: 'Six.'

Rossi glanced across, saw that Ray was still a long way from his Glock. He turned back to Karen. She was, he thought, a brand-new Karen—calm, poised, in control. Rossi was intrigued.

'So where's the Ducati?' he said. 'That in the van too?'

'There's no Ducati, Rossi. The Ducati's gone.'

'Six!' Ray screeched.

'Gone?'

'I traded it in. It was a gas-guzzling pile of flashy crap. Joyriders wouldn't be seen dead on it.'

Rossi digested that, then let it slide: half a million would buy him any amount of Ducatis. Karen said: 'And by the way—the money? There's only two hundred grand. But that's Frank's fault. He fucked up with the insurance company.'

'Bullshit.'

'It's true,' Doyle confirmed. 'You can ring them if you want.'

'You want me to—'

'Six!' Ray bawled, then lunged to his left, screaming in pain.

Rossi swivelled, pointed the .22. 'One more word and I'll blow your fucking—shit.'

Because Ray was past hearing, was scrabbling—and Rossi had to admire the guy's balls, if not his smarts—the guy crawling towards the Glock. If he was a gambling man, Rossi thought as he strode towards Ray, he'd have bet the Glock wouldn't fire anyway, not after falling in a mucky puddle. But he wasn't taking any chances. He booted Ray under the chin. Ray collapsed with a grunt.

Rossi tucked the Glock into his belt. All this crap, he fumed, when all he'd wanted all along was his stash, the Ducati. And he was pretty sure Karen wouldn't have the .44 either.

Except, as he turned back towards her, Rossi realised Karen did have his .44. Pointing it now from behind Madge—Christ, taking liberties—pointing his own rod at Rossi.

Rossi stared her in the eye.

'Six,' she said.

MADGE

Madge, still clinging to Karen, heard Rossi say: 'You're asking me to fire down on a woman?'

Madge felt herself being eased to one side by Karen. She stepped away and turned, wiping at her streaming eyes, and realised she was at home, asleep and deep in a nightmare in which Karen and Rossi were pointing guns at one another, Karen holding hers with both hands. Saying now, to Rossi: 'Even if you wanted to, you couldn't.'

'That's my .44, Karen. You traded in the Ducati, okay. But this is about principles. I mean, it's my fucking gun.'

'Take it.'

Rossi advanced up the slope, his small gun still angled at Karen.

'Six,' Karen said.

'What?' Rossi said, still moving, slipping sideways on the greasy turf.

'Three at Ray. One for Anna. One at the cottage.'

'That's five,' Rossi smirked.

'And one when Anna howled in the van. That's six.' Karen took one hand off the butt of the .44 to cock it. 'Get your hands out wide,' she said.

Rossi stopped, slid backwards a little. He looked down at his gun, shook his head. Saying, in a whisper Madge could barely hear: 'Piece-a-fucking-crap …'

He tucked the small gun away in his pocket, beckoned with his fingers. 'That's my .44, Karen.'

'So you keep saying.'

'You even *fired* a gun before?'

'Why would that matter?'

'Because holding a Magnum like that, you'd bust your wrist on the recoil. This is presuming it's even loaded. And I'm guessing it's not.'

'Is that a fact?'

Rossi nodded, began advancing again.

'I'll do it, Rossi,' Karen warned.

'In front of a cop? You'd fire down on a defenceless man in cold blood?' Rossi grinned, still inching forward. 'Not a chance. You care too much, Karen. Know what I mean?'

Karen smiled in return. Leaned back, braced her feet in the mud.

Madge closed her eyes.

RAY

Ray, his vision blurred, watched two .44s sail out over both of Rossi's heads in an arc so high the two Rossis had time to turn and watch the .44s plunk down into the lake.

The Rossis turned back to both Karens, saying: 'For that I take *all* the money.'

Ray's vision blurring up thickly, as if someone had rubbed Vaseline into his eyes, so he could see little more than shades of grey. Then it cleared, came back in less blurred. Or maybe, he thought, he was crying. The arm, Christ, busted again, this time above the elbow; worse, no exit wound meant the round had lodged in bone, and Ray'd know all about *that* once the adrenaline rush wore off …

Karen saying to Rossi: 'That wasn't the plan. You said if we brought Frank, we'd work something out.'

'Plan?' Rossi flicked his head in Ray's direction. 'What about Elvis there, waving his cannon around? Or the hound trying to rip my throat out? You see what I'm saying.'

Then he sauntered across to Ray, hunkered down. 'Where's the keys?'

Ray, his teeth clenched, just about managed a shrug. Rossi dug the Glock out of his belt, reversed it and hefted it by the barrel.

'We can do this clean, Ray. Your call.'

Ray weighed it up, looking past Rossi to where Madge had huddled in beside Karen, Karen on her knees beside the prone Anna. Hearing the squelching, the laboured breathing, of Doyle lugging Frank down the incline. He gritted his teeth. 'In the ignition,' he said.

Rossi frisked him, found Ray's phone, slipped it into his pocket. 'Tell you what,' Rossi said. 'You got balls. So I'll leave the van anywhere you want. What d'you say?'

Ray just stared. Rossi shrugged.

'Don't try to find me, Ray. No kidding. You won't even see me coming.'

He strolled across to Karen and Madge, doing the rounds, picking up their mobile phones, Doyle's too. Those he chucked into the lake. Then he stood over Frank. Ray watching it happen, helpless.

Doyle, who'd been speaking to Karen, saw it late, stood up to block Rossi off. Except Rossi tripped her up, sent her sprawling backwards into the mud, and then braced himself, taking aim at Frank's head.

Frank screaming now, hoarse …

Then Madge came in from one side to grab the Glock's barrel, tug it down.

Ray, relieved, closed his eyes and breathed out.

Then opened them again to see Madge pointing the Glock at Frank.

MADGE

'Don't do it, Madge,' Karen said.

'Put the gun down, Madge,' Doyle said.

'Don't jerk it,' Rossi said. 'Just squeeze.'

'No!' Frank screamed. 'Jesus Christ, no!'

'You're rotten to the core, Frank,' Madge said. 'To the fucking genes. Liz and Jeanie, Israel here—'

'Madge—how many fucking times? It's *Rossi*, and my mother's name is *Shirley*.'

'—but not me, Frank. There's nothing rotten about me. Not one damn thing. You tried to ruin me, pump your poison in and make me rotten too. It didn't work, Frank. And you'd want to hear the story I'm working on right now for when I see my first judge. One, you shot Ray because you were jealous, he was fucking me blind. Two—'

'If you're going to do it,' Rossi said, 'just do it.'

So she did it.

With the weight of the gun, the shock of the kick-back, the first round shattered Frank's shin. The second round, Madge's finger twitching instinctively, would have taken his head off if the Glock hadn't jammed.

Rossi took the Glock away. Madge let it go, felt a jag of pain in her wrist.

'That's your thing with the Glock,' Rossi said. 'They're temperamental bastards.' Then, to Karen, who was still hunched over Anna: 'All I wanted was the bike back, Karen. The .44. The stash. I mean, they were mine. You see what I'm saying.'

Madge thought she'd been electrocuted. Staring past the detective to where Frank lay passed out in the mud, Madge was palpitating. She met the cop's eye.

'Hi,' the cop said. 'I'm Detective Doyle. That story about you screwing Ray? It might need a little work.'

'By the way,' Rossi said to Karen. 'The truffles? You're welcome.'

Then he slip-slithered up the incline, around the side of the cottage, and was gone.

KAREN

Karen looped the tourniquet that had been Frank's shirt-sleeve around Ray's bicep. 'Y'know,' she said, 'it doesn't seem to be bleeding all that hard.'

'No,' Ray gasped.

'It's the same arm, isn't it? That's four-for-four now.'

Ray, thin-lipped, whispered: 'How's Anna doing?'

Karen swallowed hard as she fussed over the tourniquet, her eyes watering up and starting to sting. 'Bad,' she said. She pointed at her forehead. 'He got her right there. Point blank, it looks like.'

Ray reached for Karen's hand and gave it a squeeze. Karen let him, still shaky inside—Karen had never looked into a gun barrel before, never seen that big black O stare her straight in the face. Seeing it again now, Karen pointing, okay, the .44 at Rossi—except Karen'd never loaded the .44, was basically holding a busted flush …

'Why'd you do it, Ray?'

'Do what?'

'Stop a bullet for Madge.'

He tried to grin. 'That wasn't part of the plan.'

'No, but you knew going up there he was packing.' She waited. 'You didn't have to do it, Ray. Not for me.'

Ray closed his eyes. 'Can you keep a secret?'

'Sure.'

'From Madge?'

'Madge? Why Madge? Ray?' His eyelids were flickering now, the shock setting in. 'Can you hear me? Ray?'

'Call me,' he said so softly she wasn't sure she heard him, 'Israel.'

It took a moment or two before it sank it, but when it did Karen's mouth opened into a wide O that knocked the barrel of Rossi's gun into a cocked hat.

'Stay *with* me, Ray,' she urged, squeezing his hand fiercely. 'Don't go losing me now.'

His whisper was the faintest of breaths. 'Okay by me,' he said.

ANNA

In her dream Anna was chest-deep in soft snow. She struggled to free her hind legs, knowing she would die in the drift if she didn't, but that sent the pain searing through her skull. Unable to breathe, she panicked and tried to howl, all the while subsiding deeper into the drift that seemed, somehow, to be giving way beneath her.

She was cold, and she had never known cold before. It wasn't the snow, because her coat was too thick; but still it came, from somewhere inside her, marbling her lungs even as she tried to breathe. Spreading from there up through her throat into her head to mingle with the pain that swirled around behind the three-inch-thick plate of bone that was her forehead.

Then another strange sensation: the desire to sleep even though she couldn't breathe; the craving to relax, to settle down in the drift, even though that desire ran contrary to the faint impulse still ebbing through her veins. She was dimly aware of noises from beyond—the wind high in the pines, the sound of Karen's murmuring. She could feel, too, at some distance, the hands that reached through the drift to pat her ribs. But those things only had the effect of pushing Anna farther away, deeper into the drift, to somewhere she hoped would be warm and quiet and empty of pain.

Then she could hear no more.

Slipping away, Anna opened her nostrils to scent for one last time the sharp pine smell of her home from so long ago. Home? Yes—she was going home. Except there was something else on the breeze: a thick, sweet stench that stirred a memory deep in the darkness of Anna's dying. The thick, sweet stench that meant pain beyond endurance …

Her good eye flickered.

ROSSI

The first thing he needed to do when he made the main road, Rossi decided, was pull in and get rid of the clanking fucking paint pots. Every time the Transit slid sideways, or hit some muddy ruts, the pots rattled and banged, jangling his nerves. Rossi trundling along at four miles a fortnight.

He turned up the stereo, Springsteen, thinking how Ray'd want to freshen up his tunes. Like, seriously—Springsteen? With all the saxophone crap? One time the sax wailed *real* loud, giving Rossi the willies, sounding a lot like Stalin's howl. Rossi instinctively checked the rearview, then caught himself doing it, leaned in to wink at his reflection.

He flicked ash from the joint, luxuriating in the sweet aroma of good herb, the smell that always smelled like he was coming home …

He thought about the .44, sunk in the lake and lost forever; maybe it was the toke, but Rossi wasn't convinced that that was such a bad thing. If he'd caught Ray with the .44, in the arm or anywhere else, the guy'd be dead or dying right now, from shock or septicaemia, no one stops a .44 slug and goes dancing any waltzes after. It had hurt to do it, it was a good looking rod, but in the end Rossi'd chucked away the Glock too.

The .22, though, snug in his pocket—that was another matter. Sure, if you needed to be lethal it could do the business, put a man away for keeps. But if you were only looking to put someone down, the .22 was the thinking man's option. Plus it was an easy one to hide; just tuck it away, maybe down at the ankle, who's looking for a bulge down there?

Rossi was wondering about where he'd go looking for an ankle holster in Italian leather when he came over the brow of the hill and saw the Merc at the bottom of the gully. He pulled in and had a good look, but he couldn't be certain Sleeps was actually behind the wheel. He checked the rearview, the side mirrors, then wound down the window.

'Sleeps? Sleeps, man—you there?'

A voice wafted faintly up out of the gully. 'Rossi?'

'It's me, Sleeps. Hold on.'

Rossi was laying the joint in the ashtray when Stalin came crashing through the passenger window in a snarling, feral explosion of glass, the splinters raking Rossi's face. The engine was still running, so he jammed the Transit into first gear and floored it. Stalin's shoulders were too wide to get all the way in the passenger window, but when she surged again her weight caused the van to slide off the narrow track. It plunged into the gully, glancing off the bole of a fat pine to slam grille-first into another.

Rossi rocked back in his seat, stunned by the impact. Stalin surged forward again, slavering, her fur thick with matted blood. This time she got head and shoulders into the cab, her nails clickering on the metal door as she scrabbled for leverage. Rossi shied away, fumbling for his pocket, the .22—then remembered it was empty.

'Piece-a-fucking-crap,' he roared, turning to face her onslaught. No one'd ever say there were any reverse gears on Rossi Francis Assisi Callaghan …

She met him halfway, lunging for his throat, the huge fangs bared, the mouth a vast black hole that blotted out the whole world. Rossi, ducking under it, so the jaws clamped down either side of his head, actually heard the first ripping of flesh being torn from his skull.

ACKNOWLEDGMENTS

Heartfelt thanks, in no particular order, are due to my parents, Kathleen and Harry Burke; Marsha Swan; Oonagh and Andrew McCann; Gavin Burke; Michael Ross; and for their unflagging support, encouragement and advice, Ken Bruen and Jonathan Williams.